Flora's pulse roared in her ears as the blood pushed past the lump that had lodged itself somewhere near her heart. What the *hell* was going on here?

"Owen's dead," she bit out, feeling like she was being stabbed in the gut as the words tumbled from her mouth. She knew it to be true just as much as she believed it wasn't.

A perfectly contoured raven eyebrow rose. "Is he?"

"Yes." Flora didn't sound terribly convincing, not even to herself.

The smile became sly, the sharp cheekbones blooming as the woman approached her. It amazed Flora how gracefully she moved in her towering heels, how regal she appeared in her black suit, and the full fur coat loosely wrapped around her. Even the hat perched precariously on her head, a matching black feather skimming the air, oozed money and power.

"You and I both know that isn't the case, don't we Flora MacDonald?"

Flora's heart slammed into her breastbone. "How did you…?" she whispered, fear curling around her.

The woman slipped around her. "Would you do whatever it takes?" she murmured into Flora's ear.

"What are you talking about?"

"I'm talking about you saving Owen." Matter-of-fact. As if Flora had even an inkling of a clue what was going on.

"I barely know him," Flora told the woman.

"But is his life worth it to you? Would you save him if I told you, you could? Or would you give him up to the other side?"

Into the Otherworld

by

Kyra Whitton

Breaking the Veil Series

Into the Otherworld

Contact Information: info@thewildrosepress.com

Cover Art by *Kristian Norris*

The Wild Rose Press, Inc.
PO Box 708
Adams Basin, NY 14410-0708
Visit us at www.thewildrosepress.com

Publishing History
First Fantasy Rose Edition, 2018
Print ISBN 978-1-5092-2134-9
Digital ISBN 978-1-5092-2135-6

Breaking the Veil Series
Published in the United States of America

Dedication

For those I would cross the veil to retrieve;
may you always know who you are.

Chapter 1

Flora MacDonald found it rather ironic that getting divorced in America was a lot easier than setting up shop in America. Not that either were particularly difficult, but filing a non-contest divorce had given her less trouble than retrieving a lost computer password.

It had taken only a couple of months to get both of their signatures on the paperwork, something both of them were eager to do. More than anything, Robert had seemed embarrassed that he had to admit to his infidelity and gave into her every request, which, if she was perfectly honest, wasn't much. The condo had been his, as had most of the furniture. She didn't want it, anyway. But she asked for a large sum of money, instead, fully expecting him to barter with her, and when no counteroffer came, she was surprised to, instead, be unceremoniously offered a check for the full amount.

She mourned briefly for the friend she had lost, for the time she had spent living a lie she didn't even *know* was a lie, but mostly she realized how miserable she truly had been—not necessarily with her ridiculously short marriage, but with her entire life—and chose to look at the whole thing as a growing experience.

An expensive, stressful, anger-inducing experience.

At least it allowed her to completely rewrite her life. No longer were her days spent in contract negotiations, feet crammed into uncomfortable shoes, bum glued to a chair. Her alarm clock no longer chirped angrily hours before the sun rose, and she hadn't worn a hint of brown in months. Instead, she'd traded in her tailored suits for worn jeans and jumpers, her designer heals for fuzzy boots, and her carefully coifed knots for wild copper ponytails. She'd kicked her career to the side and welcomed her parents' disapproval to open up a shop in Middle America.

It was a drunken, spur-of-the-moment decision, and one that should have probably inspired more thought and foresight, but if Flora was one thing, it was stubborn. Following a self-pitying wallow at the local pub, McGregor's, after finding Robert in a compromising position with his personal trainer, she'd found herself inquiring about an empty space across the square and the equally empty apartment above it. She had taken possession of both on a month-to-month lease while she worked on the business permits, and then signed over the next year of her life to the owner a week before November rang in. Robert's money and betrayal had certainly paved her way to a new beginning.

She had never had so much fun in her life, something she realized wasn't really much of an accomplishment. She had always been so focused, fun had been something she kept on the back burner. "Fun" to Flora had consisted mostly of grabbing a pint after long hours of study. But finding supplies, ordering goods, planning the store, and opening boxes full of little bits of home filled her with an excitement she had never experienced before.

The Victorian building wasn't old by any means, at least not to the standards of her home country. But it had lovely hardwood floors, high ceilings, and a whole wall of exposed brick. The former occupant—a comic book guy, she'd been told—had left some old display cases, which she put to good use holding decidedly Scottish ornaments and jewelry made by Highland craftsmen. She filled the rest of the space with some large, imported antiques: a wardrobe to house tartan skirts and hand-knit cabled jumpers, a thick-legged and beautifully carved pub table upon which she could make her seasonal displays, glass-fronted barrister bookcases for, well, books. In the back, she had gone a little more modern, installing a refrigerated case for ales and grocers' shelves for the food items she would sell. She had been positively giddy when the first case of Cadbury Whole Nut bars had arrived. So giddy, she might have eaten three immediately. Or five.

Fine, it was five.

She had made it a habit to go to McGregor's for dinner every Tuesday evening. It was the slowest night for the middle-aged owner, which gave her a chance to dig for information about the town and clientele since she had been too nervous to actually venture out and meet any of her fellow shopkeepers. At first, the older man had been reluctant to talk, but once she asked about the pub and his background, he was more willing to open up. It turned out Mr. McGregor's parents had been Irish immigrants of Scottish background and had opened the pub upon retiring from their day jobs. He took it over when his father died at the age of eighty-four a few years back. His mother, he told her, could still be found in the kitchen some nights.

But when she wasn't cramming shepherd's pie into her mouth and washing it down with an ale, she kept to herself, setting up shop and making a home. Lucky for her, she had been so set on doing everything just right the first time, she had—past tense *had*—a nice little savings account set aside for a rainy day. She hadn't been able to think of a reason not to call finding her husband in bed with another man a rainy day, and nearly emptied the fund buying new clothes, getting her hair cut, and acquiring furniture for her little apartment—Roberts's money was all for the business, but she felt she owed it to herself to play with hers. She felt more like herself—though, to be honest, she was still trying to figure out who she was—than she ever had before, and that surely had to count for something. She thought maybe she would get a cat. Or a dog. Who knew? The possibilities were endless.

The town's preparations for the Christmas shopping season were in full swing; no sooner had the howling ghosts and round, orange pumpkins been retired than silver bells and holly popped up along the brick sidewalks. Friday night candlelight shopping was being advertised for every week up until Christmas, itself, and there would be carolers on the square, a giant tree would be erected, and Santa would arrive to listen to the wishes of local children. Flora's aim was to have the shop's Grand Opening on the Monday before the first candlelight shopping event so she could get a feel for everything before the rush.

Well, she hoped there was a rush. Or at least steady foot traffic.

And she only had three days to make sure all was perfect.

She was standing at the front of the shop, going through her inventory lists on her laptop when a series of bangs rattled the heavy metal back door. She jumped a little, nearly sloshing her tea over the side of her mug, and frowned. She'd never had anyone knock at the back before, and the delivery drivers always came to the front door, tapping lightly on the glass, which was covered on the inside with brown paper reading "Coming Soon: The Thistle and Rose."

Flora set her mug down and carefully slid her cell phone into a sweater pocket, just to be on the safe side. Still frowning, she made her way to the back, through the little store room, and into the landing that separated the shop from the stairs leading up to the apartment. Hesitantly, she opened the heavy metal door and peered out.

All she could see was a giant box. A pair of arms were wrapped around it, and two jean-clad legs were all that appeared from its bottom.

"Um, may I help you?" she asked, surprised to hear her usually throaty voice sound so squeaky.

"Sorry, this has been sitting out here all morning, and since it's starting to rain, I thought you might like it not to get all wet."

The voice belonged to a man. Which, upon further observation, she could have deduced from the size and breadth of the hands and the feet.

Flora looked up and around the box. Indeed, the sky was gray and low and steady rain fell. "Oh, all right. Um, here." She reached for it, but couldn't figure out how to take it from him without it falling on her feet.

"It's really heavy. How about you just tell me where you want it, and I'll bring it in for you."

She hesitated.

"I promise, as soon as I set it down, I'll leave. Scout's honor."

"I have no idea what that means, but fine. Could you bring it into the main shop?" She pulled the door all the way open and stood back.

The man pushed in, hefting the box up for a better grip. She followed behind him, letting the massive door clunk shut, and tried not to notice his rather impressive bum and broad shoulders. He squatted down in front of the display case, carefully lowering the box onto the ground rather than just dropping it, and stood back up.

Bloody hell, but he was gorgeous. His light hair, the color of fresh honey, was cut short. He looked back at her with gleaming green eyes. Even from a few feet away, she could see how green they really were, like spring moss. He had a straight nose and square chin with a slight cleft in it. Strong jaw. His shoulders were just as broad from the front as they were from the back, and there, he saw she was looking at him, and a dimple winked as he smiled at her.

She immediately regretted the too-big jeans slung around her hips and the overly large hooded sweater she had pulled on that morning, the low, loose ponytail of fuzzy coppery hair at the nape of her neck. She quickly averted her eyes and felt her pale cheeks flush red under her smattering of freckles.

"Um, uh, thank you," she finally stuttered out.

"No problem," he said settling his hands on his hips, relaxed. Then straightened abruptly as he realized he had promised he would go as soon as he offloaded the box. He pointed toward the back door. "I'll get out of your hair." He started toward the back, leaving Flora a little slack-jawed behind him.

"I'm Flora," she said almost desperately, suddenly wanting him to stay.

He gave her a dimpled smile again, and she thought she might melt into a puddle right there.

"Owen," he told her, his deep Southern drawl like melted chocolate.

"Nice to meet you." She held out her hand.

She had never thought of herself as petite. She was an average height, with an average build, but when he took her hand in his, she suddenly felt small, delicate, ladylike. She fumbled for something to say. To make him stay. "Are you, do you… Do you have a shop around here?"

He shook his head. "No. My sister owns the children's boutique next door. I'm just helping her out for a while."

"Oh." Oh? All she could think of was oh? "So, maybe I'll see you around?"

Lords above, what was wrong with her? She had never been this tongue-tied, thunderstruck, or flustered around any man, not even Robert when she'd first met him!

Perhaps that had been part of the problem…

He grinned at her, almost wickedly, and pushed out the door. "See you around, Flora," he called over his shoulder as he pulled the door shut behind him.

Flora dropped her face into her hands and groaned. What the hell was wrong with her? Not only had she acted like a complete idiot, she was just divorced! Shouldn't she be drowning her sorrows in a bottle of wine and swearing off men? Not acting like a sixteen-year-old girl and basically throwing herself at them!

She shook herself out, rolled her head across her shoulders, and turned back to the rather large box in front of her. She racked her brain for an idea of what might be in it, but she couldn't think of anything missing from the orders she'd made.

It was taped up rather well, so she had to go in search of a box cutter, but once the flaps were pulled back, she found herself staring at a rather odd assortment of Celtic items. Quite a few of the books looked to be antiques, a small metal bowl with some decorative pictures hammered into it, a rather lovely knife with etchings on its blade, and a carved wooden box filled with various silver jewelry items. She pulled everything out, one by one, turning them over in her hand and spreading them out across the glass countertop.

She honestly couldn't remember ordering any of these things, but she *had* placed bids on some lots being auctioned off from a few large estates in the Highlands and somewhere in Wales. Or maybe it was Cornwall? She searched through the packing material for a receipt, but there was nothing. She turned the box back over. Sure enough, her name was printed on the shipping label, but there was no return address. Odd.

Well, she supposed it really didn't matter. She would just have to catalog them and add them to the display somewhere.

She went back to work, carefully clicking through her spreadsheets, crosschecking, and cataloging. But her mind was still on the strange items in the box, and perhaps more importantly, the man who had brought it into her life. When she found herself staring off into space instead of working, she decided to take a break. She clicked over to her Internet browser and opened up the search engine. Reaching out, she pulled one of the old leather bound books to her and flipped open the cover. The pages were thin, delicate, and smelled musty. The ink was faded.

"*Mabinogion*." She sounded out the name—or what she thought the name might be. She flipped a few more pages and was greeted by a foreign language. She was certainly no expert, but it looked like Welsh. Or at least, the little bit of Welsh she'd come into contact with while on holiday in Cardiff and Tenby as a girl. The print was faded, the pages yellow and fraying on the edges, some pages torn and ripped, others missing completely.

Well, the title was enough to get started, somewhere, at least. She typed it into the search bar and hit enter. She clicked on the first link to come up and skimmed the opening paragraph. The *Mabinogion* appeared to be a collection of Welsh histories and folklore from the Dark Ages, which was translated and compiled by one Lady Charlotte Guest in 1877. This copy wasn't that old, the spine in impeccable shape, the cover unworn. But the leather was soft and supple, the gold brushed pages gleaming. She pushed it away and reached for the next.

Canu Taliesin. Now, Taliesin was a name she was more familiar with, although she couldn't think why off the top of her head. Another search revealed he was a sixth-century bard hailing from Wales or Cornwall or…somewhere in the southwestern regions of Britain.

The name likely came up in school, in days long forgotten as she set out on her university path.

The other tomes included journals, a sketchbook, a book about magic, and an herb encyclopedia. Clearly, she had been drunk when she made the bid on this particular box, because none of it was anything she would have had any interest in stocking, save maybe some of the jewelry. Perhaps that was it. Maybe she ended up with the rest of it as a way to get the silver pendants and amulets?

Deciding not to dwell on it any longer, Flora started adding the items to her inventory.

Chapter 2

The rattle of glass being tapped had Flora bolting upright. Her eyes were fuzzy, her mouth dry, her neck ached, and was that…yes, she had drool on her hand. She rubbed at it with the other, and used the opportunity to check the little silver watch on her wrist. It was just after seven. She must have fallen asleep sometime between the sketchbook and the weird bronze bowl. She had decided she was not fond of the hammered metal piece, the faces on it were haunting, eyes wide and searching, mouths oddly agog.

The rattle-taps came again, and she turned, wincing as pain shot through her neck. It was later than normal for a delivery, but she was waiting on a case of Dean's shortbread. She made her way to the front door, unlocked the deadbolt, and held the door open.

Agatha, the postal worker who normally delivered to her block, was not the one standing there. Instead, it was the man from earlier. Owen.

She blushed, and he smiled with a mixture of reassurance and amusement. "You, uh…" He pointed to the side of his mouth. She looked at him with confusion, and then frantically scrubbed at her cheek with the tips of her fingers.

"I fell asleep," she explained lamely.

The dimple winked at her. "I actually wanted to come by and ask if you have any dinner plans."

She crossed her arms over her midsection in suspicion.

"Or coffee," he suggested defensively. "A light snack? A chocolate bar?"

She couldn't help the smile that split open her face.

"I could probably find a bottle of cola if that's what you'd prefer."

She found she wanted to go, but felt like she needed to make an excuse. Wasn't there some sort of society-dictated waiting period before divorcées could mingle with attractive men? "I look dreadful," she said. She wasn't wearing any makeup and her copper hair was even fuzzier than it had been earlier, puffing out in a frizzy halo. The jeans were yesterday's, her hooded jumper had a coffee stain just above the right breast, and the slouchy boots had been bought for comfort, not looks.

"So, I'll take you to the pub down the street. It's dark and smoky, and no one will have to look at you."

Flora wasn't sure if she was embarrassed or delighted by his suggestion. She sucked her lips between her teeth and bit down, trying to work out how she should respond in her mind. Unfortunately, her mind was a jumbled mess and it allowed her to spit out, "All right, I'll meet you there in twenty minutes."

She waited to feel regret when she realized what she had said, but it didn't come. She started to shut the door so she could bound out of the shop and up the back stairs when—

"No."

"No?" She frowned, blinking in confusion. She hadn't expected a denial.

"No. If I allow you twenty minutes, you'll just use it to take a shower, put on makeup, go shopping for a new outfit, and you'll end up arriving two hours later."

She blinked at him. It was a fairly accurate description of what she planned, but she knew she could do it in well under two hours. "What if I promised it would actually be twenty minutes?"

"I would think you were lying. And depriving me of your company for purely vain reasons." He grinned lazily, the corners of his lips quirking slowly.

She quirked an eyebrow at the sarcasm and asked, "Did you just call me vain?"

"Aren't we all?"

She let out a sigh. "Ten minutes."

"Five."

"Eight."

He gave her a crooked smile, flashing his straight white teeth, and pushed his hands in his jeans, taking a step back. "I'll see you in eight minutes." He turned and began strolling down the tree-lined sidewalk.

Flora closed the door, locking it before hurrying up to the flat for her purse and keys. She wondered what the hell she was doing, but not enough to make her stand the guy up; she was too busy feeling giddy and excited and alive.

It was warm for November, at least it was warm for her. A breeze caught the last few brown, crisp leaves, sending them skittering across the drying sidewalk. It smelled a little like rain and the sky was heavy with clouds.

McGregor's was crowded, much more crowded than usual. She hadn't actually entered the pub on a Saturday night before, and she realized why avoiding it was a good idea. The pub looked to be standing room only and as she pushed into the smoky front room, skirting the band setting up in a corner. Mr. McGregor was nowhere to be seen, and in his place were three young bartenders; two women, one with an arm full of tattoos, and a young man who should have been gracing designer jeans advertisements.

She scanned the room again, and not seeing Owen, pushed through the throngs of people, to the back of the building. It did feel a bit like home; the clientele ranged from the early twenties crowd right up to some customers she would guess were well into their sixties. The back door stood open, leading onto a wooden deck and a fenced in courtyard. There was a large bonfire out there, chairs set around it. Only one was occupied, and she was relieved to see it was Owen.

He cradled a lowball glass in one hand, his legs stretched out in front of him, the top foot bouncing absently. Her heart picked up its pace as she came down the stairs and took the chair immediately to his right. It was surprisingly quiet, the sounds from inside very faint, the cracking of burning wood the only soundtrack to the evening.

"Seven minutes and forty-three seconds. I'm impressed."

"If that's all it takes to impress you, maybe I should…" she trailed off on a grin when her joke hit its mark and he chuckled softly. "I didn't realize this was back here." She changed the subject, indicating the fenced in area, the fire.

"Come here often?"

She blushed. "Every Tuesday night. I have a long-standing date with Mr. McGregor."

"If I had realized earlier you were involved with someone…" He looked at her from the corner of his eye.

"No, no, I just mean I come here for fish and chips and a chat. I guess I could say he was my first, well, my only friend, here."

"That does remind me. How does someone with such a nice accent like yours end up in a shitty place like this?"

"I believe I could ask you the same thing," she quipped.

A young woman with sloping shoulders and wide hips walked over, leaning down over Flora's shoulder. She caught a whiff of her perfume—it was a little overpowering—and the sour scent of old cigarette smoke. Flora recognized her as being the same waitress who had been there the first night she came to town. "Can I get you anything?" the woman asked.

"Scotch? Twelve year?"

The woman nodded.

"Neat."

"Add it to my tab." This came from Owen.

Flora waved him off and handed the woman her credit card after digging it out of her purse.

After the waitress had left, he scowled at her. "You're taking all of the fun out of the date."

Flora lifted a copper eyebrow. "I was not aware this was a date."

"I did ask you out for dinner and drinks."

She frowned playfully. "No, I do believe you asked me if I had plans."

He took a sip of his drink. "Touché. You never answered my question."

"And what question would that be?"

"Where are you from?"

"Inverness."

He nodded, and she could tell he had no idea where Inverness was. "And how was it growing up in Inverness?"

"Cold. And you?"

"I don't believe I had a particularly cold childhood, no. But that could be because I grew up in the South."

She found that she liked this bantering back and forth they had going. She liked his sense of humor and the fact that she had known him all of ten minutes, yet he was teasing her. But she also wanted to get to know more about him. She hadn't been this excited to get to know someone since…ever.

Robert had been a foreign exchange student when she met him. He'd come to Glasgow to do a year studying abroad, and happened to live in the same residence hall. They had become friends as a consequence of being the only two up and eating breakfast as soon as the dining hall opened; he because he was a morning person, and she out of necessity. There just weren't enough hours in the day for her to study as much as she *thought* she needed to.

University had been back in session for all of three days when she came to stand behind him at the breakfast queue. He had been looking queasy as he stared down at the trays of haggis, blood pudding, and kidneys behind the glass partition. The server just stood behind the trays, looking annoyed. As Flora had approached with her tray, the hairnet swung in her direction, and she passed her plate over for haggis, eggs, toast, and a tomato.

His gaze had followed the haggis as it was spooned onto the thick, plastic plate, and then as it was passed back into Flora's hands. She had thought he looked a little green.

She had been able to tell by his clothes and shoes he wasn't a native. Well, and the squeamish look on his face. She had coaxed him to try some of the haggis and they ate breakfast together for the rest of the year.

Once she was on the other side of the whole experience, she was able to pinpoint every instance in which she should have *known.* Like when she had been the one to initiate their first kiss, and it hadn't been passion filled. Her parents had been in the city and she had brought him along for luncheon. Both of her parents were pleased she had met such a pleasant young man, and her mother made noises indicating Flora should not drag her feet. It should have been obvious. Their first kiss had merely been sweet and shy and not even his idea. And he'd always had very few opinions about anything in their relationship. She took for granted the fact that he was understanding of her very busy schedule and the lack of time she had for him. Really, she should have been wondering why they weren't fighting to spend more time together. Now she knew it was because, in his mind, they really were just friends. She wondered how much it had taken for him to grit his teeth and have sex with her.

The bitter thought had her slamming back into the present.

"You're staying with your sister?" Flora asked the gorgeous, *interested* man sitting next to her.

"I just come to help out," he said, suddenly serious. "She's having a hard time of it right now."

"Oh. I'm sorry to hear that."

He waved it off. "It's fine. She'll be fine. And how did you end up so far away from… Where was it? Narnia?"

She answered around a laugh. "Inverness. Scotland."

"Oh, yeah, yeah, the one with the dragon."

"Nessie?"

"Something like that."

"Hmm." She chuckled. "Aye."

Not a moment later, the waitress arrived with her Scotch. She took it, holding it between her hands, not taking a sip.

"And?"

"I'm thinking," she told him.

And she was. She wasn't sure how much information to divulge. It was a difficult subject to work around, and she had never been one to lay her baggage out on the table. But perhaps her propensity to bottle things up was how she had ended up in the rather regrettable situation she had been in. Perhaps if she hadn't held her cards so close—and Robert his—they never would have ended up in such a tangled mess.

"I moved to Atlanta with my husband at the beginning of the year," she finally told him quietly.

"Oh. You're married."

She took a sip of her drink to calm the nervous feeling fluttering in her stomach. It was rich and smoky, biting as it slid down her throat, warming her stomach. "I was." She puckered her lips and looked at him through the corners of her eyes, from beneath her lashes. He was still lounging back, but his whole body tensed. His hand was gripping the glass with more ferocity than he had been but moments ago. His face had become an unreadable mask, the playfulness no longer there. As her words sank in, he relaxed a little, but still gave her a searching look.

"I don't know why I am admitting this to you," she said softly, shaking her head as if to clear it. A strand of copper hair fell into her eyes, and she pushed it back behind her ear. "It seems too personal a conversation for someone I just met." She took another sip. "I was married. For six months. I would like to place the blame all on the fact that I came home one afternoon to find him in bed with another man, and unfortunately, if I hadn't, I probably would be going along just as miserable as usual, but not even knowing it. It wouldn't have worked out in the end because it hadn't worked in the beginning. But I have no way of knowing how long the charade would have lasted."

He lifted an eyebrow. "So, you think the only reason why your marriage wouldn't work is because you *found* him in a compromising situation. The fact that he was—sorry, and I mean no offense—less than enamored with your particular brand of appeal had nothing to do with it?"

"Well, obviously," she said. "I just mean… I wasn't perfect, by any means. If his preferences hadn't been what they were, it still wouldn't have worked."

Owen cocked his head to the side. "And why is that?"

"Because everything was always about me and what I *thought* I wanted or should be doing or was told was the 'right' thing. I suffered from severe tunnel vision."

He drummed his fingers on the arm of the chair. "Well, this is the first time I've been on a first date and had the woman lay all of her flaws out on the table. Interesting approach."

"So, we answered that? This is a date?" She hoped she didn't sound too eager.

"Isn't it?"

She chose to drink rather than answer his question.

He was kind enough to change the subject again. "And the shop?"

She let out a laugh. "Well, after I found Robert and his...boyfriend, well, all I wanted was some good beer and a smoky bar and maybe a meat pie. I asked the taxicab driver if there were any Scottish pubs in the area, and so he brought me here."

"Here to McGregor's?"

She nodded. "I may have had a little too much and told poor Mr. McGregor I was going to start a shop where I could sell Scottish imports since there obviously were none around here, and he told me he knew where there was a vacant shop. So, I got divorced, quit my job, and started a business. I have never been happier."

"And no children?"

She laughed. "No. No, no, no. You?"

He shook his head in the negative, then got a faraway look. Flora realized the band inside had begun to play, and the music drifted out to them in the courtyard. Others were beginning to empty out into the space, perhaps to escape the Celtic-inspired band or maybe only so they could hear their conversations better.

Owen turned to her. "We should dance."

She blinked at him. “What?”

But he was on his feet and reaching for her hand. “Come on.”

Chapter 3

Flora drifted awake, feeling as if she hadn't slept at all. No dreams had drawn out the hours, and no alarms had pulled her from the dark depths of slumber. She was simply just not tired anymore and came awake.

It was an odd sensation. Pleasant, but odd.

Unfortunately, it didn't come without pain. Her feet still ached from the hours she had spent on them, her calf muscles begged to be massaged.

She had never had so much fun dancing in her life. She had never considered herself much of a dancer, and if she was perfectly honest, she had probably only gone out dancing a handful of times, at best. There had been no dancing at her wedding, and she had found no pleasure in going to the night clubs with her friends or classmates.

But last night had been magical. It was such a cliché way to describe what had transpired, but it was the best she had. They had been cramped together, their bodies having no other alternative but to brush up against one another as they were jostled by all of the other people *not* dancing at McGregor's. They had cheerfully been it. Owen had swayed with her through the ballads and bounced with her during reels. They had laughed at themselves, with each other, and at the absurdity of it all, and she found she liked him more and more. How could she not?

He walked her home under the heavy clouds, a hand at the small of her back. A hand she had been all too aware of. He brought her right to the door, held it open for her, and stayed there until it was soundly locked.

Other than being disappointed he hadn't tried to kiss her, she considered it a perfect night. And for the first time since her life had taken a drastic turn, she wished she could just stay in bed and bask in the excitement of it all rather than spend the day making last-minute preparations for the shop.

She took a little longer than usual in the shower, savoring the hot water and allowing herself more time than usual to shave her legs. And rather than donning her work uniform of late—jeans, a baggy tunic, and her comfortable boots—she put a little more effort into her appearance. Just in case.

Outfitted in a sheer blue, Swiss dotted blouse, a camisole under it, cropped black trousers, and delicate black, leather ballet flats, she skipped down the back stairs, unlocked the shop's rear door, and entered the storeroom. She flipped on the lights, gathered up her laptop and notepad, then settled in at the glass counter next to the cash register.

Streaming music through her phone, she got to work, catching up where she had left off the night before.

Unsure of what to do with the mystery artifacts, she ended up putting them on a bookshelf behind the counter, a space she had intended to use for items needing to be put on hold, restocked, or were returned. All except for the little silver pendant.

It was about the size of a fifty pence piece and looked like a wagon wheel. She wasn't sure what kind of metal it was, but it seemed old, worn. Well-loved, perhaps. It was laced through a slender piece of velvet ribbon, nothing special, but for some reason she was drawn to it. She slipped it on, figuring she would wear it for a while until she found something she preferred, and then she would add it to the collection behind the glass.

She hummed along with the music, sang the words when she knew them, but she became more and more preoccupied with the fact Owen hadn't shown his face. She didn't know why she thought he might or why she should expect him to, but the longer he stayed away, the more anxious she got.

Around four, she decided she was utterly useless to the shop, not that there was much else for her to do before the grand opening. So, she shut everything down, turned out the lights, and headed back upstairs. It was another gray, overcast day—something she didn't mind in the least—so the flat was dark and a little cold. It only served to remind her further how utterly alone she was.

Maybe she *needed* to get a cat.

Loneliness was something she had been struggling with. It was probably why she spent every Tuesday night at the pub, chatting up the bartender who was between two and three times her age. At times, she was just so excited to be discovering who she was, she didn't care if she didn't have any friends or family nearby. She didn't care about her lack of romantic relationship or social life. But then she remembered she didn't have a romantic relationship, a social life, friends, or family, and she wondered what she was doing.

This was one of those moments where she was caught in between. And she wondered if she truly liked Owen, or if she was just so excited to have spent some time with someone—anyone—that she was ignoring the big picture.

Finding herself even further in a funk, she decided she had no desire to cook. Just the thought of having to figure out *what* to make, and then make only enough for one made her want to crawl under the covers and never come out, so she opted instead to put on her coat and walk down to the pizza shop at the corner.

She had never tried it before, but it always had fairly steady foot traffic, and was downright bustling around the evening mealtime. She had been steadily making her way from one restaurant to the next, anyway, in an attempt to become part of the community, though it wasn't yet working. This would be one of her last stops before she would have to branch out a bit more and explore farther away from home.

The shop wasn't terribly big, and only half of the tables were full. She wondered if that was more a factor of the time or the day of the week. She walked up to the counter and ordered a whole pizza, partly because she didn't want to appear pathetic ordering the personal size and partly because any leftovers would contribute to her not having to cook later in the week.

The order was placed to-go, but she also ordered herself a Coke so she had something to do while she waited, and she sat hunched over one of the empty tables, lazily sipping at the cold drink.

When her order was called up, she took the hot cardboard, thanked the girl behind the counter, and left out of the shop. The square was all but dead, most of the other shops open on a Sunday closing early, the rest standing dark as they had all day.

She was about halfway back to her building when "Hello there, stranger," was murmured close to her ear.

She jumped, whirling around, her hand to her chest. She nearly dropped the pizza, but Owen reached out and took it from her.

"Sorry, didn't meant to scare you."

Flora let her heart rate even out before responding. "Just startled a little."

He grinned. "Didn't think that one out very well, did I?"

She laughed a little nervously and took the pizza box back from him. "Where did you come from?"

He waved a hand down the street. "I dropped something off for my sister and was on my way out of town when I saw you, so here I am."

"Oh."

"I did knock at your door, but there was no answer."

Her smile bloomed, and Flora tried to stamp it down. She had the worst poker face imaginable. "I was getting pizza."

"You don't say?" He flashed one of his crooked smiles, and his blue eyes twinkled.

"Join me?" she asked.

"Sure. We could go over to the park." He indicated the town square, the fountain at its center, carefully manicured hedgerows, and pavilions.

She peered at him under lowered brows. "Isn't it a little cold for that?"

He looked around, nonplussed. "I didn't notice."

She shrugged. "All right."

The square was the size of one of the city blocks bordered and bisected by brick sidewalks, dotted with delicate, old-fashioned gas lamps. They chose a bench overlooking the concrete and brick fountain, flanked on either side by large, round planters, the mums planted inside still in full bloom.

Flora curled herself onto the bench sideways, her legs crossed in front of her on the seat, her back against the armrest. She put the pizza box between them, not really wanting the distance, but thinking it was necessary, anyway. She opened the box, removed a piece of the cheese pizza and indicated he should do the same.

He didn't, though, instead regarded her. "Why a shop?" he finally asked as she finished chewing her first bite.

Either it was amazing or she was hungrier than she had originally thought. "Why not?" she countered, took another bit.

He shrugged, a very American gesture. "You just made it sound like it was a very rash decision the other night."

"Oh, it was," she said matter-of-factly around the pizza. "I was a barrister in Glasgow before I got married and came here."

"And after you moved here?"

"I worked in the international division of… Well, it doesn't matter. I called the morning after I left Robert and told them I'd had a family emergency and was going back to Scotland."

"Weren't you afraid to get caught in the lie? That one of your friends would let it slip you had just had a midlife crisis and jumped ship. Only made it twenty miles away? No references in the future?"

"No."

"No?"

"I didn't have any friends."

He looked mildly perplexed and embarrassed. "Afraid your boss would come across your shop while buying Christmas presents?"

"Hmm."

"Didn't think of that, did you?"

She grinned. "I did not."

He chuckled, and she realized she loved the sound, masculine and heavy, but still full of amusement.

"It isn't like I need the references, anyway," she told him.

"They might be angry with you Flora MacDonald. Very. Angry."

She threw up her hands. "Oh well!" She pulled another piece of pizza from the box. "And you? Surely you have some deep, dark secret. I've told you mine."

"Skipping out on a job is your deep, dark secret?" he responded, disbelief tingeing his words.

"Absolutely."

"That's *really* the worst you've done?"

"Well, other than being divorced less than a year after getting married in the first place."

"Hey, you made it longer than most people."

"Oh, really? How'd you figure?" She laughed.

"I read."

"What? The gossip rags?"

His lips twitched to the side. "What? I get bored waiting in lines at the grocery store."

She leaned back as she laughed, as much from the sheepish expression on his face as the mental image of him flipping through tabloids while he waited to buy milk.

"So, is that your darkest secret? You follow the lives of the rich and famous?"

"Absolutely. Doesn't get any darker, does it?"

"And here you were takin' the piss at me for leaving my job."

"Excuse me, but what?" he asked through laughter, a shocked expression on his face. "Taking the *what*?"

She couldn't say it with a straight face anymore. "Piss," she squeaked out between the giggles.

"What does that even mean?"

"Making fun," she explained. "Teasing?"

"Quite the slang you Scots have going for you."

She waved him off. "Piss isn't even the half of it."

They sobered a little when he reached over and brushed a strand of hair off her cheek, tucking it behind her ear.

She looked up into his eyes, sparkling in the lights propped on lamp posts.

She was drawn toward him just as he was drawn toward her, some greater force was pulling them together in slow motion. Her lips were a whisper away from his. His warmth cut through the cool autumn air, forcing her eyes to his lips, back to his eyes, and…

Her eyes were closed as their lips met, like a clap of cymbals, the crash of waves against rock, a crack of lightning. She leaned further into him, suddenly hungry for him, one hand bracing herself on the back of the bench, the other gripping his forearm. His hands cradled her cheeks, his touch light, caressing. He clearly had more self-control than she.

At the thought, she dipped her head away, suddenly feeling a little ridiculous, propped on a park bench, making out with a near-stranger over a pizza box. Embarrassed, she gave him a shy, fleeting smile that hurt her face. “I should be getting back to work,” she told him.

His expression smacked of disappointment, but he quickly hid it. “No problem. Let me walk you back.”

They were silent as she unfolded herself from the bench. He was already standing, pizza box in one hand, the other outstretched to her in offering. She took it, allowing him to pull her up. Her legs felt a little like jelly, perhaps from sitting in such an awkward position, or perhaps because he made her feel so out of her element.

She tried to take the box from him, but he held it out of reach, smiling in a teasing sort of way, his laugh lines becoming more prominent through the strawberry blond of his stubble. She took a deep breath and turned down the brick sidewalk leading her back to the shop, surprised when he slung his arm around her shoulders.

She was inwardly pleased with the little gesture. It was so intimate, yet…not. Familiar, perhaps. Yes, familiar. She leaned into him a little and he squeezed her shoulder. They walked in silence, just like that, his arm around her, her body pressed to him.

When they came to stand outside the front door of the shop, she wished she hadn’t cut their time short. She wished she could go back to their bench and stay there, chatting and laughing and kissing until the sun rose.

It wasn't until they had said their goodbyes that she realized she had allowed herself to fall back into her old patterns. No more, she vowed. No more.

Chapter 4

One more day. One more day and she would be open for business.

And all Flora could think about was Owen. She wondered where he was. What he was doing. When he would come by. She tried to focus on making sure she hadn't missed a detail in the shop, ensuring everything was just right, but instead she checked her appearance in the mirror approximately eighty-three times, wrote his name down sixteen, and drew hearts around it four.

By noon, she gave up. If the store wasn't ready, it was never going to be. She began pulling down the brown paper she'd used to cover the windows, the heavy material crinkling loudly, the sound reverberating off the tin tile ceiling and the exposed brick. She wadded it up in a giant ball as she pulled, and as the last corner detached, Owen stepped into view outside.

She couldn't help the pleased grin. Dropping the paper into the middle of the floor, she half skipped to the door, throwing the lock and holding it open for him.

"So, this is it, huh?" he asked, looking around. "Ready?"

"Yes. And no. I can't believe it's finally here." She turned from him to scan the shop for a moment, pride finally swelling. It looked good. It looked really good. "So, what's brought you 'round?" she asked him.

"You."

She gnawed on her lower lip as the beaming smile lit her face. "Oh."

"I thought you'd probably need some help doing the last-minute things."

"I wouldn't mind the company."

"Good. What can I do?"

"How are you at hoovering?"

He lifted an eyebrow and gave her a quizzical smile.

She grinned. "Vacuuming."

"Not any worse than the next guy."

"Perfect."

In the back room, she pulled out the vacuum and wheeled it into the shop. He took it while she rummaged around for her glass cleaner and paper towels. She wiped down the counters as he passed the vacuum over the wood floors, their eyes coming together over their work periodically, eliciting blushes on her part and knowing smiles on his.

The cleaning didn't take long, especially with the two of them working on it. And after the supplies were once again stored, she sank down in the middle of the floor. She sat there for a moment, looking around the shop before falling back onto the hardwood.

"Cheers," she said. "For the help."

He came to sit beside her. "So, tell me about…all of this. I've never seen half of it before in my life."

"Like what?" she asked.

"Well…that. The fur purse."

She laughed. "It's a sporran."

"And that is?"

"It's like a pocket. Kilts don't have pockets, so your wallet, mobile, keys, they could all go in there."

"So, it's a purse." He gave her an incredulous look.

She tried not to laugh. "No, it's a sporran!"

"Fine. Okay, then, what's that?"

The two-handled pewter bowl he pointed to was one of the items on the middle shelf of the glass case. "A quaich. It's for drinking. Mostly for special occasions or ceremonies, now."

He began scanning the shelves of her pantry section. "Is that really canned haggis?"

She nodded.

"What's it like?" he asked. She was surprised he didn't make the disgusted face most Americans did when they asked. The image of Robert's disgusted face rose in her mind, but she quickly squashed it.

"It's good. Well, I've always liked it. It's just a sausage, really. It has onions and garlic, seasoning. I've always preferred it with beef, so it's similar to seasoned ground beef."

"Really?" he said thoughtfully. "I'll have to try it sometime."

"Perhaps if I am feeling adventurous, I will make it fresh for you."

"You're a woman after my own heart, Flora MacDonald."

She grinned. They had just made plans—Plans!

"Are those really shrimp-flavored potato chips?"

"Prawn-flavored *crisps*," she corrected.

"Are they as terrible as they sound?"

"Absolutely." She laughed.

He continued to look around the room, his gaze falling on her display of tartan skirts. “Do you have a plaid?”

“Tartan.” She sat up, unfolded her legs, and stood. She had a sample book of tartan fabrics in one of the drawers of the wardrobe. She pulled it out and flipped through the swatches of fabric until she found her familial pattern. “There are a few depending on the occasion or branch of the clan,” she explained. “But this is the one my family wears for wedding, funerals…Christmas parties.” She pointed to a swatch of dark green, navy blue, black, and a bright red.

His gaze traveled over the shop, landing on self-explanatory things like books and chocolate bars, and then they rested on the gold lettering on the front window. “Why the Thistle and Rose?” he asked.

She shrugged. “I wanted to offer Scottish goods, but it’s hard to not also offer English products as well. The thistle is a symbol of Scotland, the rose a symbol of England. I believe it was originally used to describe Princess Margaret Tudor of England when she married King James of Scotland. Their marriage was supposed to mark peace between the two, but it didn’t last long.”

“The marriage or the peace?”

“Both. Ten years? Maybe?” She realized she had been fiddling with the tartan swatches and tucked them back into the drawer. “Well, I mean, he died. Was killed in battle or something. She didn’t find him in bed with another man and leave to go open a shop.” She paused. “I don’t think.”

When she turned back to him, he smiled at her like he found her fascinating and charming and perhaps a little funny.

She gave him a twisted, embarrassed smile back and came to sit down in front of him, crossing her legs so they sat knee to knee. He leaned forward, reaching out a hand to brush her hair behind her ear. His fingertip brushing against the top of her ear had her insides coming alive, her skin prickling. It was a gesture she found incredibly erotic, even in its most innocent form.

"Why didn't you go back?" he asked.

"I should have. It would have been… Well, that's what everyone would have expected." She gave a tight smile. "I guess I really didn't think of it as an option. This." She held up her hands to indicate the shop. "This was the first thing I thought of. And, I guess I didn't give myself the chance to rethink it. I just did it."

"Do you wish you had gone back?"

She took a deep breath and really thought about it. "Yes. And no. It will always be home, but." She swallowed. "But this—this is my big adventure."

"Your big adventure at, what? Twenty-four?"

"Twenty-five. Almost twenty-six," she informed him.

He tipped his head to her. "That's a long downhill slide."

"Well, fine, I haven't thought about it much. I told you, I just kind of…did it. I needed a chocolate bar," she said with feeling. "And the only way I was going to get it was to import it, myself."

He laughed and shook his head. "Couldn't have just called your mom and asked her to send you one?"

She shook her head. "Oh, no. She would have asked questions. This was a much safer approach," she joked.

"So, let me get this straight, it made more sense to open a store than it would have been to ask someone to send you a candy bar. Sounds legit." He nodded with mock agreement.

She laughed. "It is! You haven't met my family!"

"What are they like, then? What is Scotland…Inverness?" At her nod, he continued, "Inverness, what is it like?"

"Cold. Full of tourists."

****

"I'll walk you up," he murmured.

They had ended up talking until the sun had set and the moon had risen, the hands moving up the western side of the clock. Well, perhaps she had done most of the talking.

She was all too aware of the heat of him at her back, his breath close to her ear. She shivered, her mind on the kiss they had shared the night before. She wanted more, but was too shy to initiate herself, and too shy to ask.

She did a final scan of the shop before turning off the lights and pulling the back door to the storeroom shut.

He kept his hand on her back as they ascended the stairs, and she took them a little slower than she normally would so she could savor having him so close. There wasn't much room on the landing, and they were pressed close. She was all too aware of him there as she inserted her key into the lock. The pins fell into place and she turned, facing him. "Thank you for…" She trailed off as she searched for the words. "Walking me home?"

He grinned, slipped his hand into her hair so he could cradle the nape of her neck, and kissed her. It was sweet, a brushing of lips, a teasing. His lips were then gone, and he was striding down the stairs. “Good night, Red.”

Her eyes were still closed as he left her, and when she finally opened them, it was to see him disappearing down the shadowy stairwell. Her shoulders drooped in defeat and she turned into her flat. The door clicked quietly shut, and Flora turned, leaning her back against it.

She didn’t know why she was so anxious, why she was so determined for this to go as quickly as possible. She didn’t know why she wanted to rush, but damn it, she did. Frustrated with herself and with the situation, she shoved her hands through her hair and let out a heavy breath.

There was a knock on the door.

She whirled around, knowing it was him, and pulled the door open.

His mouth was on hers as soon as he was through the door, his hands in her hair. Her hands went to his wrists, steadying herself, and he kicked the door shut. Their mouths grappled as they pressed themselves against one another. He was all hard planes and warmth. She couldn’t seem to get close enough to him, wanting for press herself into him until there was no telling where she ended and he began.

He backed her right into the edge of her dining table, his hand reaching out to steady them both on the surface. Flora inched herself up, his other hand now under her thigh, helping her onto the wood.

Her hands were under his shirt, her fingers against his skin. It was smooth and warm, his muscles contracting beneath. She pulled his shirt over his head, and he tugged at the buttons of her shirtdress. The dress pooled around her hips, their stomachs came together, and she shivered. His hand squeezed the clasp of her brassier, and it loosened, falling down her arms. Their torsos parted long enough for the black fabric to be whisked away and thrown in the direction of the sofa.

And then his hands were on her and she could no longer think. She desperately pulled at the waistband of his jeans, but she couldn't get the button through the hole. He broke apart their lips, tipping his forehead into hers, and pulled her hands away. Once the button was through its loop, she dragged his mouth back to hers and pushed the denim past his narrow hips.

She sank back on the table, dragging him with her, lifting her hips up so her panties could be slid down, and then…

Oh. She was gone.

****

They were still on the table. She was laying half on him, her feet dangling over the edge. Absently, the strength of Ikea's dining furniture impressed her. And, perhaps, herself a wee bit for having put it together.

Flora fought to bring her breath under control, though Owen's had evened. His heart beat beneath her ear and it still thumped quickly.

She didn't know what to say or do. She knew what she would like to do, but she thought maybe it would give her a heart attack. "Um, can I get you anything? Tea?"

He chuckled, the sound like a rumble in her ear. "No, just stay with me."

She tucked herself more tightly into his side but found there was nothing comfortable about their current situation. Her head nestled on the crook of his shoulder was nice, but the feeling she was going to tumble to the floor if she flinched had her tensing up.

"That uncomfortable, mmm?" he murmured huskily.

She instantly felt bad. She readjusted, turning to lay across his chest, which she found she liked very much with its sprinkling of blond hair. She rested her chin on her hand, looking up at his face. His eyes were closed and his head rested atop one bent arm. His free hand had slipped up her back when she had moved, and his fingers circled the skin between her shoulder blades.

"I've never done this before," she whispered, unsure of why she was whispering.

"Could have fooled me." His expression didn't change.

She smiled, catching her lower lip between her teeth. "No, that isn't what I meant."

"I mean, I know you said your ex didn't enjoy your variety of—"

"No." She laughed, cutting him off. "I mean I've never slept with someone I just met."

"What are you talking about? We've known each other for positively ages."

She rolled her eyes, knowing he was joking. "I just don't want you to think that… I don't want you to think I do this kind of thing often. Or ever," she amended.

The hand that had been lazily circling her back was then around her waist, and she slid across the chest she had just been admiring. A kiss to the side of her neck, one to the corner of her mouth.

"It wouldn't matter if you did," he said against her mouth.

She closed her eyes and kissed him back, her lips opening to him. He was smoothing the hair away from her face, and she could feel him shift, freeing his arm so both hands would frame her face.

Her own hands were caught between her breasts and his chest, and she allowed herself to spread her fingers out, to feel his skin, the warmth, the beat of his heart.

The way he kissed her changed then, it became more primal. His lips pushed up toward hers as if he were drowning and she was his only hope for air. She met him with a fierceness she didn't know she possessed.

Owen's arm wrapped around her, ready to pull her beneath him, but she stopped him, instead, shifting herself to straddle him.

Only then did he open his eyes. The look he gave her was hungry and she reveled in it as she sank down upon him, feeling powerful and in control. Hands at her waist, he helped guide her into a quick rhythm, but she fought back, setting the pace slow. Almost painfully slow. But she wanted to feel every bit of him. And every bit of herself.

He let out a long breath, one she knew was a mix of accepting she was the driving force and of pleasure. She curled her lips between her teeth as she rolled her hips.

His hands skimmed over her flesh, palms smoothing over her rib cage and cupping her breasts.

His thumbs swept over her nipples, and she was afraid she would never be able to breathe again from the pleasure. She arched her back into his hands, urging him on, and then covered his hands with her own, begging for more.

Frenzied, she sought his mouth and their positions were reversed. He took control, cradling her to him as her legs wrapped around his waist. She clung to him as he stood, her ankles hooking just above his buttocks, keeping him within her.

She felt the cold of the door against her back just as he drove her into a white-hot oblivion.

Chapter 5

Flora was beginning to think she was the biggest fool in the world.

It had been more than a day since she had woken up in her bed completely sated, totally sore, and obviously alone. And alone she stayed.

That night, she had kept the oil burning late, as it were, but no one came knocking. She kept her mobile phone on her at all times, never mind they had never once exchanged numbers. Nothing. Just like she knew there would be.

The shop had seen a moderate amount of traffic, and she couldn't complain. Most were fellow expatriates looking for their favorite chocolate bar or salad cream, and a few were curious shoppers hoping to find a teacup featuring Princess Diana to go with their mother's collection. She found herself getting more and more anxious as time passed, her toes tapping, her feet wagging, but Owen didn't show his face. So, in a moment of desperation, she flipped her open sign to "Closed" and taped a note to the door stating she would be back in twenty minutes.

She didn't bother with her coat but wound a tartan scarf around her neck and skipped the five yards down the brick sidewalk to the next shop door. She pushed into the children's boutique.

A blond woman of indeterminate age was rearranging a display of festive hats and booties, head bent over the red-and-white accessories, but looked up when a charming little bell tinkled. She offered Flora a pleasant, tight-lipped smile. Flora recognized the eyes, though they looked tired and were rimmed with red, and the shape of the mouth, but that was where most of the resemblances ended. This woman was long and willowy, definitely a few inches taller than Flora, but she had an entirely feminine, delicate grace about her where her brother had been anything but.

"Good afternoon," she said with a warm Southern drawl. "Is there anything I can help you find?" Flora didn't miss the drop of her eyes, the way they landed on Flora's stomach.

Flora's gaze darted around the store. Yes, it was most definitely a boutique catering to expectant mothers.

"Oh, no, sorry, I'm not… I mean… I'm looking for Owen," she finally amended.

The woman's facial expression immediately changed. It became hard where it had been soft, her eyes becoming hooded when they had been open. "I'm sorry, but my brother is no longer with us."

Flora frowned and twisted her lips in an attempt not to cry. She balled her hands into fists as they began to shake, her fear becoming realized. He had left, no goodbye, no backward glance. She had just been a one-night stand.

She didn't want his sister to know that, though. She would salvage her pride. "Do you have a number where he can be reached? Or, um…you know what, never mind. If you talk to him, could you ask him to call me?

I mean Flora. My name is Flora." She waved awkwardly, then clasped her hands back together, realizing how stupid she looked. "I own the shop next door." She forced her lips to turn upward.

The woman crossed her arms around herself, her gaze dropping and her face looking even paler than it had a moment before. "I don't think you understand. My brother's dead."

Flora felt like she had been punched in the gut. "Wha—What? What happened? I just… I mean, he and I… What?" No, no, no, this couldn't be happening. Her world was shattering, falling apart around her, chest squeezing the air out of her lungs. Spots prickled her vision as she fought to drag in a breath, but she was drowning, every hope and dream she had for herself slipping away. When she had walked in on Robert, her world had merely changed. But Owen gone? Forever? She would never be whole again.

"It was a few days ago," his sister said, her voice cutting through the fog that had descended over Flora. "His helicopter went down in the Irish Sea. The army's still looking for his body, but there's really no hope at this point. We'll—we will be holding a memorial service on Saturday." Her voice started to shake, yet she held herself together.

"That's impossible," Flora told her, hope worming its way around the panic.

Cold, hurt eyes flashed at Flora. "I assure you, it's very much real."

"But I was with him two days ago," Flora burst out almost hysterically. "We were just together. He was with me…" The dizzy, blackening feeling dissipating. They were talking about someone else, clearly. She must have heard wrong, her Owen must belong to the owners of the Kiwi Bakery

"I don't know what game you're playing at." His sister moved to a pretty white French-style desk and pulled open a drawer. She removed a small, folded up newspaper and held it out to Flora.

Terrified of what she would read, but holding on to a small shred of hope, Flora carefully took the offered newspaper, unfolded it, and looked down. A picture of Owen—her Owen—stared back at her, a grainy red, white, and blue American flag waving behind him, the unmistakable lines of a military uniform, and the familiar lines of his face blurring as she recognized him.

Pentagon, Washington, DC—Major Gloria Cezar has confirmed that two United States Army aircrafts were involved in a training accident off the coast of the United Kingdom on October 31. The U.S. and United Kingdom were conducting a joint exercise when conditions worsened unexpectedly. An investigation to determine the events of the collision is still under way.

The bodies of Maj. Sean Keen, pilot; Cpt. Sarah Feldman, copilot; and Sfc Hector Alonzo, crew-chief; Cpt. Bryan Chen, copilot; and Sfc Joseph Cucinni were recovered. Cpt. Owen Drummond remains missing in action, however officials have ruled out the possibility of finding the Blackhawk pilot alive.

Memorial services for the fallen…

Flora couldn't read any more. She felt sick and dizzy and confused.

He couldn't be dead. They had spent the night together. She could still feel the soreness between her legs and the rawness on her skin where his stubble had scratched and scraped. She could conjure up the taste of him with her memory, the sound of his voice. She had spent hours with the man in the grainy picture.

And yet she was being told he was dead. To believe he had died before she had met him. She thrust the clippings back toward Owen's sister. "I'm, I'm sorry for your loss. I'm sorry. I need to go."

She pushed out the door, taking two steps into the cold and lifted her face into the wind. The tears on her cheeks shocked her with their coldness. She stood there for a moment, gathering her composure, and once she was sure those were the only tears she would cry, she dug her key out of her pocket, and unlocked the shop. She tore down her sign, balled it up, and walked toward the storeroom, only to come face-to-face with the most beautiful woman she had ever seen. Not sure what else to do, she stammered, "May I help you?"

The woman cocked her head to the side and smiled mirthlessly with bright red lips. Her bottle-green eyes flashed beneath thick, fanning dark lashes. "No, dear, but I may be able to help you."

Flora recognized the Southern accent. And not the South she now called home, but the one with the lilt of Cardiff or Cornwall. "And how is that?" Flora wondered aloud, fully expecting to hear a sales pitch.

"By helping you get Owen back, of course."

Flora's pulse roared in her ears as the blood pushed past the lump that had lodged itself somewhere near her heart. What the *hell* was going on here? "Owen's dead," she bit out, feeling like she was being stabbed in the gut as the words tumbled from her mouth. She knew it to be true just as much as she believed it wasn't.

A perfectly contoured raven eyebrow rose. "Is he?"

"Yes." Flora didn't sound terribly convincing, not even to herself.

The smile became sly, the sharp cheekbones blooming as the woman approached her. It amazed Flora how gracefully she moved in her towering heels, how regal she appeared in her black suit, and the full fur coat loosely wrapped around her. Even the hat perched precariously on her head, a matching black feather skimming the air, oozed money and power.

"You and I both know that isn't the case, don't we Flora MacDonald?"

Flora's heart slammed into her breastbone. "How did you…?" she whispered, fear curling around her.

The woman slipped around her. "Would you do whatever it takes?" she murmured into Flora's ear.

"What are you talking about?"

"I'm talking about you saving Owen." Matter-of-fact. As if Flora had even an inkling of a clue what was going on.

"I barely know him," Flora told the woman.

"But is his life worth it to you? Would you save him if I told you, you could? Or would you give him up to the other side?"

"I don't know. How? What is this? I don't understand what is going on." She couldn't seem to force her lungs to draw in a full breath, the warmth of the shop stuffy. Panic set in, her cheeks flushed, the spots returning to her prickle her vision.

The woman stood in front of her again, her perfume the scent of rain and earth and roses. Slender fingers reached up, wrapped around the pendant still hanging around Flora's neck. She rubbed the pads of her fingers over the spoked wheel before letting it fall onto Flora's sweater. "If you decide to save him from his fate, you will need to choose your weapons."

Flora's frown deepened. "Weapons?"

"Start with the *Mabinogion*, Flora." She turned her head to look at the shelf where Flora had left the items from the box. The box that had arrived mysteriously, the one with no return address. When Flora turned her attention back to the woman, she was farther away, a small brown leather satchel dangling from her slender fingers.

"You'll have to choose well, for you don't want—nor can you—overburden yourself." She laid the satchel down, keeping one hand on it. "Choose very well, Flora."

"What are you talking about? What the hell is going on?" Her confusion was finally making way for a new emotion, and she was getting angry. The anger built onto the fear, escalating to a point where she was reaching hysteria.

"He's a prisoner of another world, Flora. And you can rescue him. Only you." The smile was serene.

"And how am I supposed to get to this 'other world'?" Flora demanded. "And why me? Why can't you save him if you know so much about this?

The smile faltered. If Flora hadn't been watching so intently, she would have missed it.

The woman's gaze blinked away, fixing on a point over Flora's shoulder. "I am not of this place. Only one of his own can bring him back."

"But how?"

"Simply look for something out of place. Something that doesn't belong. It will help you across the veil." She threw this last bit over her shoulder, pushing out into the cold.

Flora pressed her fingertips to her eyes, hoping she could open them and her world would make sense again. "Who are you?" she yelled. But when she opened her eyes, the woman was gone. A crow bounced on the sidewalk twice in the place Flora was sure she had last seen her, and then it took off, flapping out of view.

****

Flora stared at the bag, then back to the items that had arrived in the box. She had spread them out over the counter. The *Mabinogion*; *Canu Taliesin*; the herb encyclopedia, most of which she had never heard of before, at least half of which were written in a language she couldn't identify; the journal, which she discovered upon further reading was about preparation for a battle and some woman named Elizabeth. A sketchbook filled with pictures of weaponry and armor from what appeared to be a century long past and the book of magic. None of the major players were people she had ever heard of before, nor were the locations familiar to her, though they had a distinct Gaelic feel to them, but she was no history expert.

The *Mabinogion* was the largest book, *Canu Taliesin* next. If she placed them in the satchel, there was room for nothing else but the jewelry. The woman had told her to start with the *Mabinogion*, but she had also told her to choose her weapons, and a book she couldn't even understand seemed like the last place to start. She pushed it and *Canu Taliesin* away, taking the small books, all of which would fit into the leather bag.

The other items were laid out as well. The weird bowl, all of the jewelry but the pendant she still wore, the carved box, the knives with their unique hilts.

If she put the jewelry in the bowl, she could fit them. The box was far too wide to go in the satchel, even if the bag were empty, so she placed it on top of the large books. She didn't even know what she was supposed to do with the knives. She'd probably end up stabbing herself, but because they just fit, she put them in, anyway, praying she didn't hurt herself.

And then she sat back and wondered what the hell she was doing. Had she completely lost her mind?

She was seeing ghosts. And strange women were breaking into her store, telling her she was the only hope of saving a man she had known days—a man who was *dead* according to his sister. And here she was, logical, organized, play-it-by-the-rules Flora MacDonald, acting like this was normal. If the weird lady says jump, apparently Flora jumps. Disgusted with herself, she pushed the satchel out of her view and dropped her forehead to the cold glass.

For three days, she had lived a beautiful lie. A perfect fairy tale. An exciting adventure. She had found someone worthy of the term soul mate, and she had been ready to see it all through. She had fallen in love with an idea, flirted with a vision. She had become so far removed from herself, she had felt alive for the very first time.

She would mourn for what she had lost. And then she would own up to the fact there was something wrong with her. Perhaps it was depression, or maybe she had a brain tumor. She must have eaten something dodgy or someone had slipped something into one of her drinks.

Drinks. Her mind snapped to attention. She had had drinks with Owen at Mr. McGregor's the other night. Surely the waitress would have remembered. It was Tuesday, after all, and she supposed she was getting a little hungry.

First thing in the morning, she would set up an appointment with a neurologist. This evening, she would close up shop, head down to the pub, and prove she wasn't crazy. Then she would come home and bore herself to sleep by reading the *Mabinogion.*

****

Flora always sat at the bar to eat her fish and chips so she could talk to Mr. McGregor. He always had a story about his parents and the "homeland," which she found rather comforting. She liked to think he enjoyed when she came in, though he tried to hide it behind his gruff exterior, thick graying beard, and sarcastic greetings.

But as she entered the pub, she didn't go straight to her seat in the corner of the old, scarred surface, but instead searched the many smaller rooms for the waitress who had brought her drink the other night. The girl was in the main dining room, wiping down a table. "Hello," Flora said nervously.

The girl turned around and smiled.

"I was here the other night…" Flora began.

The girl nodded. "I remember. You were the only one sitting outside for the longest time. It's why it took me so long to get to you—I didn't think anyone was back there."

Well, that answers that. It was official. She was insane. She wondered absently if she had been dancing by herself, as well. How embarrassing.

She smiled and made something up. “I was wondering… Did I leave my scarf out there?” She was pretty sure she hadn’t been wearing one, but she couldn’t ask about the man who obviously hadn’t been there for anyone else to see.

The waitress looked thoughtful for a moment. “No, but I don’t really remember. You could check behind the bar.”

“Cheers, I will,” Flora murmured as she turned away and slunk over to the bar. She slid into her usual seat, but with a groan, rested her forehead on the glossy wood, too defeated to even look Mr. McGregor in the eye as he ambled over.

“The usual?” he asked, somehow knowing his usual “You’re back,” or “Look what the cat dragged in” or “Don’t you have any real friends you can go bother?” weren’t what she needed.

Flora started to nod but stopped herself. “No. Whiskey,” she told him as she straightened, lifting her face to him, but letting her shoulders droop as she folded her arms on the glossy wood. “On the rocks,” she added.

“Whiskey? You? Really?” He pursed out his lips, thick eyebrows dancing up in surprise, and she realized she always had a beer or ale with her meal.

The lowball glass was plunked down in front of her with a thud, a clink of twin ice cubes and a splash of liquid. He then pushed it toward her, the signal she needed to emerge from the dark cocoon of the bar top.

Flora didn't bother asking what it was, instead she threw the whole thing back, letting it burn all the way down.

"Anything you want to talk about?"

She shook her head, pushing the glass back for a refill. He still held the bottle in his hand, lifting it into view, and more splashed into the glass. It lasted for only a moment. "More?"

He held back for a minute before refilling, eyeing her suspiciously. "That's it. After this, you're cut off."

She glared at him. "Am no' one o' yer Am-ay-rican birds," she growled, her accent thickening.

Mr. McGregor lifted an eyebrow. "All the same. You need to take it easy. Sure you don't want to talk about it?"

She finished the last drink and stood up. She hadn't been in the pub for five minutes, but she didn't want to stay any longer. "How much?" she asked.

"I'll put it on your tab."

Suddenly, her eyes felt watery. She looked up at Mr. McGregor. "Thank you," she said, her voice breaking. She offered the best smile she could, and turned out of the pub.

Outside, it was warmer than it had been the last few days. Her breath was still curling in a cloud in front of her, but her fingers weren't burning with the cold as she walked home. The world spun slightly around her, but she was able to stay steady. Scared, yes. But steady.

As she fitted her key into the door, she wished she had someone to talk to. Someone who knew her. She would have been comfortable talking to Owen. But she'd really just been talking to herself, right?

She grabbed up the *Mabinogion* on her way up the stairs, knowing the combination of whisky and epic poetry would put her right to sleep. She would figure out how to deal with all of this in the morning.

Outfitted in a large T-shirt and yoga pants, she climbed into bed, opening the book. But instead of seeing the text, a note had been slipped into the first pages. The paper had been folded across the middle, but it lay open. *Owen is a Prisoner of Annwn.*

The note hadn't been there before. Of that she was certain.

She took it out, holding it in her hand for a moment, and then folded it across the crease, laying it on her bedside table next to small ball of chartreuse yarn.

Yarn? That was odd. She had never knit anything in her life, and she certainly wouldn't have chosen such a shade if she had. She reached for it.

Chapter 6

Flora rolled over to her other side, desperate to get more comfortable and reluctant to leave the confines of her bed, even though it had become lumpy and hard. Her new position was no better than the last, so she flipped onto her stomach, yelping when something stabbed her hip.

She pushed herself into a sitting position and looked around her.

Her bed. Gone.

Her pillow. Gone.

Her sheets? Also gone.

She was lying on the ground, outside, her head atop the brown satchel, using it as a pillow. A small rock had been her tormentor.

She picked it up and tossed it away, fully intending to lay back down when it actually occurred to her she was outside, and this outside was unlike any one she had ever seen before.

Above her, a large tree loomed overhead. It was huge, bigger than any she had ever seen, even in photographs of the redwoods of California. Its branches were gnarled, twisting and curving toward a lightening sky, the leaves swaying in a gentle breeze that barely even ruffled her hair. She had been lying upon a thick layer of deep emerald-green moss spread beneath the tree, and over rocks and stones before dipping down into a small gorge made by a stream so clear, it could have been made of liquid glass.

Across the expanse of rolling moss-covered land, she could make out the lightening shadows of more trees nearly identical to hers, their fronds also green and large, large enough she could wrap one of the birch-shaped leaves around her like a blanket. She stood then turned, taking it all in, amazed and frightened, heart thudding in her chest. Was this part of the psychosis? Was she dreaming?

She pinched herself. Nothing changed. But did pinching oneself while asleep actually accomplish anything? She pinched again and again, noting her skin was becoming increasingly more irritated, the spot red and stinging. Would she even know the difference between dream pain, real pain, and psychotic breakdown pain? She doubted it.

Flora stooped down and grabbed the satchel, then slung the leather strap over her head and shoulder so it lay across her body, the leather pressing between her breasts. There was nothing keeping her in this particular spot, at least nothing she could see. Something urged her to follow the water, see where it took her. It wasn't a conscious thought, but more like a hook had sunk into her and gently pulled. Even if she had wanted to stop, she wasn't sure she could have.

Her feet were bare, which allowed her to appreciate just how soft the moss was. But with every few steps, the bottoms of her fragile soles came in contact with a small pebble or the sharp end of a stick. She curled her toes and tried to step with more care, only to misstep again. Shoes were an important part of her day, and she was rarely without them, even inside. She kept a pair of slippers at the ready, anticipating needing protection for her feet when she did take off her shoes. Bare feet were for beaches, baths, and bed, only. It really was too bad she hadn't packed the bag with a spare pair of thongs.

She was slightly chilled, her yoga pants and T-shirt not giving her much protection against the morning air. Her skin prickled into goose flesh, tingling and protesting the chill. But she kept walking, knowing the sun would rise eventually and she would be warmed.

She followed the stream, listening to early morning bird songs, and coming upon all manner of woodland creatures: pure white deer, toads the size of rugby balls, and something with a soft glow, but which was too small for her to make out. It flitted around, buzzing like a dragonfly, a high-pitched whine that whipped and whizzed through the branches. None of the creatures seemed particularly concerned with her presence, few even lifting their heads at the interloper. As the sun peeked over a far away hill, she came to a road—little more than a wide, rutted dirt path—with a wooden sign sticking out of bright green grasses like something out of a fairy tale, pointing her toward Caer Hafgan.

She decided to follow the path because where else would she go? Or maybe the invisible hook continued to pull at her. Still, she stuck to the moss, for the path was full of pebbles and rocks, and she wanted no more bruising.

It wasn't long before the trees became sparse, opening up to vast grasslands. The grasses waved in the breeze, great waves that rolled from green to gold and back again. The forest opened up atop a great hill, and she looked out into a valley. On the other side of the slopes, off in the distance, a tall, spired white castle reached for the sky. Green flags whipped from the tops of those towers, catching the light and streaming across the whitest of clouds she had ever seen. A sprawling town hugged the pearly walls of the palace, green-tiled roofs huddled together, sloping down the hill where they were built. A river skirted the nearest city wall, glittering in the golden sunlight.

It was a fairy tale. Clean and beautiful. Straight from a child's picture book. The scent of flowers, wet grass, and warm earth lingered in the air, becoming more pungent with each rise of the breeze. She thought of summer afternoon tea in the garden, her mother's blooms full and heavy, the tea light and sweet with fresh milk and sugar, the cakes delicate.

The path snaked down the hill, dodging large rocks and boulders. Birds soared above her, light streaming all around them. Her feet begun to hurt more and more with each passing minute, and she wished she had thought to pack shoes in the satchel. If this were a dream, her feet wouldn't hurt like this, right?

As she drew nearer to the castle, the village that rested at its feet grew around her. Wisps of smoke rose from white stone dwellings, rock walls divided up the grasslands, and green banners trimmed in gold swayed from their posts on the road.

She had no idea what else to do, so she just kept walking. She ambled over the gently arching stone bridge spanning the river, happy for the smooth, polished stones beneath her. She strolled through the village's stone gates, past a guardhouse, and into the general bustle of the morning. The people there were just...people. But different, somehow. Some had silvery blond hair, pale complexions, and long, willowy frames. They bore the most beautiful faces she had ever seen. They were interspersed with those less fair, their features unremarkable, of more average build like her. Those less fair were more human, more flawed. But they were all healthy looking, in good form. She saw neither the frail, nor the sick. No blemished skin, no uneven gait. Even the old had a youth and vitality about them, pushing carts, hauling baskets, and walking arm in arm.

If she hadn't been uneasy before, she was beginning to be. Something about this place was…odd. Even knowing it was some sort of weird dreamworld, it seemed a little too good to be true. Too perfect. She tried to imagine what kind of underbelly this city might have, where they might be keeping Owen. And what kind of tortures he must be facing.

No one noticed her, dressed oddly as she was. Both the women and the men wore a mixture of long tunics and leggings or some sort of dress robe. There were some ladies in long gowns, and some men in frocked finery. The fabrics were rich in color, bright pastels, whites, and creams. The gauzy fabrics whirled around them. She passed a man wearing bottle-green breeches, a wide-sleeved shirt tied into cuffs at the wrist, and an emerald vest. Several belts crossed his waist and his chest, an assortment of tools hanging from them. His mustache was dark, well trimmed, and thick. He looked to be a relatively young man, but the mustache looked like something that would adorn one much older than he.

A woman up ahead wore long mauve skirts and a bodice Flora would expect to see nowhere but a Renaissance festival. Or perhaps a Highland dance competition. She'd been dragged to plenty of those when she was a young girl, her mother having aspirations of her becoming an accomplished Highland dancer. Flora competed well amongst her peers, but when her academics began to shine, it was expected she give up sword dancing for studying. She had never complained, and now, years later, she wondered if perhaps she should have. She would have liked to be better on her feet.

Flora kept her gaze on the city's population, noticing how the fashion and dress mirrored and deviated from those of her own world. Hair was both long and short for both sexes, and one's gender did not dictate one's clothes. Nor did professions have a gender-specific role. She passed several soldiers who were women, their breastplates formed to adequately accommodate their chests, standing at their posts with the men.

She was nearing the edge of village where it butted against the castle gates. There, the pull she hadn't been able to resist lifted, disappearing like a snuffed flame, just a flicker of smoke that wafted into the air above. It left her alone and directionless.

What the hell was she supposed to do, now? Just waltz up and ask the guards where she was and if she was dreaming? Or perhaps if they knew where she could find—what was it—Annwn? And Owen Drummond? She didn't know much, but one thing she was pretty certain of was if she started talking like the village crazy lady, she would end up in a padded cell somewhere. Or worse. She had no plan, she had no information, she had no grasp of whether this was all real or imagined. Why was she even considering this?

Someone must have noticed her standing there, looking at the gate with a pondering expression, because a woman came to stand before her on the other side of the portcullis. Her hair was pulled back at the nape of her neck, tied into a funny little knot, odds and ends sticking out like feathers. She wore a simple green vest trimmed in silver over a tunic of mail, and she was about Flora's size in both height and build. A blade hung at her waist from a black belt matching her leather boots and a bow was strapped across her back, quiver full of green flighted arrows peeking over a shoulder.

"What's your business?" she asked gruffly, a look of perpetual boredom plastered on her face.

Flora stammered for a moment, not even knowing what her business was. "I, um, I'm looking…" But the guard's gaze wasn't trained at her face anymore, but instead on her chest. Well, that was an interesting turn of events. She wondered if she should cover herself, crossing her arms over her bust like she would if a man spent too much time on her bosom. She wasn't used to be ogled by other women, though, perhaps she should be flattered?

"Tarvis, open the gate," the woman called to someone behind her, almost desperately.

"Why?" was the whiny response.

"Just do it!" the woman yelled.

Flora frowned, not sure what to make of the urgency. As soon as the heavy iron barrier was lifted high enough, the woman wrapped a gloved hand around the upper part of Flora's arm and dragged her into the bailey.

"What's going on?" Flora asked, but it was more to herself than the guard. She was ushered across the dusty cobbled stones, through a matching stone tunnel and a beautiful courtyard with a glistening fountain. From there into what she imagined was the great hall. It was lined with light tables, their wood the color of gold, bowls filled with fruits and summer vegetables, golden plates, and goblets. At the end of the hall was a tall golden throne, an ageless man sitting upon it. He wore simple clothes, the colors matching those of the guard who ushered her, though they appeared rich in fabric. A green cape was clasped around his shoulders, a thin gold chain spanning across his chest, connecting the clasps holding the cape in place. An undecorated gold circlet sat atop his crown of black curls.

The guard stopped before him, pressed her fist over her heart, and bowed deeply. “Your Highness,” she murmured.

Flora wasn’t sure what she was supposed to do, so she offered an awkward, wobbly curtsy. It had been ages since her last etiquette class and she had been bored to tears through them all. Despite being a model student, of course.

“Approach,” the man, or king perhaps, commanded.

The guard immediately became more hospitable and swept her arm forward, indicating Flora should proceed. Flora shuffled forward, not sure what she was supposed to do next, when the woman spoke.

“Your Highness, Arianrhod has sent you her emissary, as promised.” Her voice rang high and clear, and for the first time, Flora realized she had a very American accent.

Flora wasn’t sure she had heard correctly. “Um, what?”

The king stood at once, then glided down the glimmering marble steps to stand before her. His hand reached out and grasped the pendant of Flora's necklace in his long, slender fingers. He ran his thumb over the pendant, his eyes growing wide and bright with excitement.

"By Don, she has finally sent you." He dropped to his knee, kneeling before Flora, taking her hand in his and placing a kiss upon the back of it. "Blessed ambassador."

Something told Flora not to say anything. What had the woman told her? To choose her weapons? Well, if her conscience served her right, the pendant was one of those so-called weapons, and it had just opened a door for her.

She stood as tall as she could. She wasn't terribly tall at five feet seven something, straightened her shoulders and pretended she didn't feel ridiculous standing before this man in her bare feet, yoga pants, and T-shirt. "I am here for Owen Drummond. You will release him to me." Damn, she hoped she sounded commanding enough.

The man before her stood up, his thick, dark eyebrows coming forward over his dark eyes. They clouded for a moment, his expression becoming an impenetrable mask. "I would gladly release him to you—to Highest Arianrhod. But there is no one here by that name."

"No? He's about six feet." She held her hand up, estimating his height. "Blond hair, blue eyes, nice face." She said this more to the guard, who was now standing to her right.

Both king and guard gave her puzzled looks, the woman gazing at her as if she had grown three heads and a forked tail.

"All I was told was to come rescue him from Annwn." She tripped over the name, not really knowing how it should be pronounced.

"Ahn—ooven?" the king murmured, politely.

"If that's how it's pronounced, then yes."

His demeanor immediately changed. The man turned his back on her, pacing silently back to his throne. It was flanked on either side by guards who held rather sharp-looking spears. They were dressed in shining mail and green silks with a coat of arms stitched into them.

The man threw himself onto the throne and lounged back into a corner, his legs splayed before him, one hand to his lips. "Is this some sort of test? Is she testing me?" He spoke with his hands as much as his voice, waving his fingers about, opening and closing them like yapping dogs.

"I can assure you, I don't know." At least that much was true. Was this Arianrhod the woman who had come to her at the shop? It made the most sense.

"Mmm." He pursed his lips.

And then, as if having a fine idea, he sat up straight and motioned to someone behind her. A young man soundlessly moved into her vision—perhaps her own age, she couldn't tell. A hood concealed most of his face, leaving all but his mouth and chin in shadow. What she could see of his visage was slightly shadowed in stubble, just under the full curve of his bottom lip and just over the pretty bow of the top. He did not wear the same green as the others, but was instead covered head-to-toe in black leather, two sinister-looking blades poking up from behind his back. He came to stand next to Flora and bowed.

"Iain," the king said, "see to it that my esteemed guest is given the finest of my rooms and whatever she wishes is provided. You will know better than any other what that means." His gaze swung back to Flora, whose stomach felt a little queasy at his words.

Would the man in black throw her in the dungeons? He appeared more torturer than butler.

"Ambassador, you would do me a great honor if you would join me at the high table this eve. It will give us a chance to discuss the matters at hand."

She gave her best impression of the Arianrhod smile she had received in her own little shop and dipped her head as regally as she could. No one laughed at her movements, thankfully.

Iain turned on his heel and soundlessly led her out of the main hall. He was taller than she had first thought, though perhaps not as lean as she had originally guessed. He was thickly corded with muscle, looking and moving like an Olympic swimmer. Just as they passed through a massive oak door, the king turned his attention to the guard.

"Your time has come," he murmured lowly. His tenor faded as Iain led her away, but she caught his last words, "Protect Highest Arianrhod's emissary."

Whatever that was.

****

Iain showed Flora to a big room with large, colorful tapestries hanging from three of the four walls. They were all spring and summer scenes of water nymphs sunning themselves upon rocks, unicorns frolicking in fields, and maidens dancing with long, brightly colored streamers. The tapestries were bright and cheery, perfect for the warm, scented air and cool breezes wafting through the open corridors and through the door of the chamber.

The rest of the fabrics were the same emerald-green color piped in gold. They covered the canopied bed, an armchair next to the single arched window, and the bench at the end of the bed. Gold tassels and ropes trimmed every available edge. The decor was understated, if a little heavy on the green and gold.

Iain stood in the doorway as she walked in, dropping her satchel onto the bed. “Is there anything I can bring you, Your Excellency?” he asked. He had a warm Welsh accent that reminded her of fresh toffee.

She wasn’t quite sure what to think of her new title. It made her feel uncomfortable. Like some sort of shifty spy or con artist. She looked down at her clothes and her dirty feet. She had been walking most of the morning, maybe even into the afternoon, and she was certain she needed a shower. An excellency she was not.

“I hate to be an imposition, but perhaps you could point me in the direction of the washroom?” Due to the silence that followed she imagined if she could see his face, he would be giving her a quizzical look. “I could use a shower. Or bath,” she added quickly.

He gave her a curt nod. “A bath will be brought to you.” He turned to leave.

“Wait!” she called, perhaps too loudly. Her voice echoed off the light stone walls.

He turned back to her.

"Do you think anyone would have some clothes I could borrow? So, I don't stand out so much? I realize I was sent without proper attire for the king's court." Her stomach growled. "And something to eat?"

His thin, straight line of a mouth never changed position, but he bobbed his head once in acquiescence.

She smiled her thanks as he left her, and then fell back upon the bed. It was soft and fluffy, as though it was filled with nothing but the down of a thousand geese. The room should have been dark and shadowy, but between the white stones and the large open window, it was light and airy. And it smelled of fresh flowers and spring dew.

She was beginning to rethink her dream hypothesis. She had always been a dreamer, but never had she had a dream to include so much detail, one in which she could see so many colors, smell so many things, or *feel* the ground beneath her. She had also never known a dream to be so coherent. Usually, her dreams jumped from one odd improbability to the next. The last dream she could recall, she had been having dinner with a friend who was long deceased, and they watched from his bedroom window as adults played with giant toy train tracks on the street below.

She wasn't sure what exactly this was, but this was different.

As Flora muddled through her dream perceptions, there was a knock on the door, and seconds later, a bevy of people entered, hauling a tub and buckets of water. No sooner had the steaming buckets been poured into the golden bath than those people were gone and new ones were arriving, laden with clothes, and yet more with a tray of food and what she assumed were wine carafes.

The bath was nice for a few moments, soothing the aches in her feet and legs. She dunked her head, wetting her wild, bushy curls before coming back up for air, and then scrubbed her hands down her face. The water was lightly scented with lavender oil. She lazily scrubbed at her dirty feet and massaged her aching muscles, but she soon grew bored and curious about the mountains of clothes laid across the bed.

Wrapping herself in a rich, fluffy green towel folded along the back of the tub, she began picking through the clothes. She had no idea what would be appropriate for a meal with…whatever he was… And she wasn't even sure she knew how to get into half of what was there. Most of it appeared to be just simple lengths of fabrics, no seams or sleeves, or even a place for her head to poke through.

Remembering she had been given a personal guard—whether she was there to stop her from leaving or protect her from some outside force, Flora didn't know—she poked her head out the door.

The guard who had first recognized the pendant stood outside, back ramrod stiff, arms at her side, looking straight ahead. Flora studied her profile for a moment, taking in her straight nose, pointed chin, prominence of her brow. She wasn't terribly old, perhaps younger than even Flora.

"Um, hello," Flora began. The guard didn't acknowledge her, didn't even blink. "I was hoping you could help me."

Still nothing.

"Do you have a name?"

"Eve." Well, it was a start, even if the name didn't seem to fit. It lacked the soft innocence of her features, even if the harsh syllable complimented her demeanor.

"All right, Eve. Look, I am sure you can keep an eye on me in here just as well as you can out there. Would you mind helping me?" She hoped she sounded sincere and appealed to the other woman's sense of duty.

Eve hesitated for a moment, but then gave a single nod and followed Flora back into the room.

"First things first… What does one wear to dine at the high table?" she asked. Flora had spent many hours learning proper comportment, but none of them had prepared her for sitting at a high table with a king who was neither British nor of her own world.

"Whatever pleases you, Your Excellency," the other woman murmured as if by rote.

"Oh, please don't call me that," Flora pleaded before she even realized the words were out of her mouth. "I mean, my name is Flora. Please just call me Flora."

Eve nodded but didn't say anything. Flora wasn't entirely sure she would honor her wish, but at least she had tried.

"I don't want to offend anyone, and clearly the customs here are much different than I am used to," Flora told her, hoping she sounded important and convincing. "What would you wear?"

Flora watched as Eve's gaze went from her to the giant pile of silks and satins piled on the bed, and then, with a sigh, she moved toward the brightly colored assortment and began holding things up. "This for the dinner."

Flora smiled her thanks and took the length of fabric, the towel tucked under her arms. “And…how exactly do I put it on?”

She could tell by Eve’s body language the other woman was exasperated with her, but she helped, anyway. The flowing green chiffon-like fabric was draped and wrapped around her, a large gold sash-like object wound around her waist and tied at the side. The sleeves were long and full and billowy, like something out of a painting depicting Arthurian legend, and the skirt ended up being a nice A-line. She felt a little like she was playing dress-up in her mother’s housecoat, but smiled her thanks all the same. She knew she would never be able to figure out how to get out or back into this thing again.

A few pairs of very delicate-looking slippers had been placed on the floor, and with Eve’s help she chose a pair with gold embroidery. She was surprised to find they fit.

As she twisted her hair up into a makeshift bun, wrapping a gold ribbon around it in hopes it would act as a hair elastic and hold everything in place, Flora asked, “What do I need to know before going to dinner?”

“I don’t understand, Your Excell—Flora,” Eve amended when Flora stared her down.

“I know I am asking a lot of you, but can you, perhaps, act as my guide? I know nothing about this place or people or customs… Or anything! All I know is that I was sent here with instructions… Well, not even really instructions, more like vague suggestions. I don’t even know how to fulfill them.”

Eve continued to regard her with skepticism. “I will do my best, so long as it does not compromise my duty.”

Flora wasn’t sure what that meant, but she let out a little sigh of relief, anyway. “Thank you.”

Chapter 7

Flora was led to a high-backed chair next to the king's own seat. The light wood—a gold color, in fact—was intricately carved into thousands of little leaves, all overlapping one another, in a most beautiful filigree. The velvet seat covers were pristine, jaunty green in color, and she felt a little like a fairy princess as she sat there in her finery in a castle of sunshine and greenery.

The king looked much the same as he had earlier in the day, his dark hair curling around his face and the nape of his neck, his mustache perfectly styled. It turned up a little at the ends, like lips lifting into a smile. He wore the same emerald green she'd noted throughout the castle, gold at his cuffs and collar. Bright green jewels, likely emeralds, were showcased in gold settings, winking on his fingers. They appeared overly large and heavy, but the weight didn't keep him from tapping his fingers steadily to some inward symphony.

She had thought perhaps close up, she would be able to gauge his age, but he appeared just as ageless up close as he had from a few yards away. He could have been as young as she or well into his sixties—a perfect specimen of a man who could have graced movie screens the world round. If he were old, he had been blessed with the incredible appearance of youth, yet if he were young, he held an air of experience.

She had learned from Eve that he was, himself, Hafgan, and though he was king, he had to fight for his sovereignty every equinox at the "Battle of the Ford." The unspoken understanding was that Hafgan would conquer his opposition, King Arawn's forces, as winter turned to spring, and he, himself, would yield summer to fall. It was a show of mutual respect if not friendship, a tradition indicating both houses were of equal importance. They were perfectly matched, two sides of a coin. And yet, at the last battle, he had been tricked somehow, had lost his right to the win on the battlefield, and was forced to pledge his fealty to the other king.

The way he regarded her, Flora had a sinking feeling he thought she was the key to ensuring things once again turned in his favor.

King Hafgan made quite a fuss over her, plying her with sweet honey wine and fresh produce. The feast had fresh fruits and vegetables, cheeses, and breads, and abundant seafood. Fish, crab, snails, lobster, prawns, oysters, clams, and…well, she wasn't entirely sure what some of it was. It was spread across the tables on wide butter lettuce leaves, garnished with thick citrus wedges. Golden plates were set before them, golden flatware laid out across bright green cloth napkins. She almost didn't want to place hers in her lap, afraid she would sully it somehow.

She was quite pleased with her meal of berries, apples, plums, and cheese, feeling it perfectly reflected the nice, summery weather. Which was odd, if she thought about it, seeing as how it was November.

Or was it here? Just thinking about it gave her a headache.

She eyed the seafood speculatively, wanting nothing more than to try a bit of everything, but not used to the cuisine or the cooking habits of this place, she was a little loath to try anything that might make her horribly ill. One ill-fated meal of prawns at the seashore when she was a child was enough to make her wary when it came to some items.

The others ate and drank with great merriment, and she couldn't help but notice all of those in attendance were draped in flowing, billowy fabrics in bright colors. The women had their hair pulled up off their necks, coiled and draped in intricate braids and twists. Their dresses pulled away to expose their limbs to the warm air. The men were similarly underdressed, their sleeves rolled up to the elbows and their tunics left to hang open at the throat.

The king called over the bards and the minstrels to entertain her, weaving stories about her benefactress, Arianrhod. It was a sad tale, chronicling the woman's refusal to acknowledge her son, and then forcing him to win his own name, his arms, and then a bride to prove himself a man. At least that was her takeaway, her ears not used to the singsongy storytelling style. Yes, she did sound like a truly repugnant woman, forcing her son to endure such humiliation. Flora really didn't think she wanted to be claimed by the woman at all, but she hadn't exactly been the one making the claims in the first place, now had she?

It was actually becoming quite academic as she fought to decipher the meanings from one song to the next. She had to hang onto every word, playing it over in her head, not allowing her mind to wander as it was wont to do, so she could keep up. She nearly wept for joy when the young woman gave her final bow and took her leave. Flora thought she would finally be able to sit back and relax, but she was, sadly, mistaken.

"Ambassador," King Hafgan began with a murmur.

His voice was higher than she would have expected, like that of a young man who had only recently come into his man's voice. He could have been young, but she didn't think he was *that* young.

"Flora, please," she begged. She was fairly certain if she were working as someone's emissary, she would have been told, and she wasn't excited about claiming a title she hadn't earned. In fact, she had always rejected titles altogether. Not that she had an *actual* title, but she had always found it particularly uncomfortable when Robert introduced her as anyone—or anything—but "Flora." He had always been quick to tell others of her accomplishments—or even her nationality—before even mentioning her name. More people likely knew she was Scottish and a barrister than they knew she had been given an actual name.

"Ambassador Flora," the king compromised. "I have waited quite some time for this meeting. I was beginning to think your benefactress had changed her mind, keeping you cloistered in the Archives."

Flora schooled her features into a serene countenance, knowing she couldn't let her face betray her complete lack of understanding about, well, everything he had just said. "She works in her own time," she murmured when she realized he was looking for some sort of reply.

He guffawed. “That she does! That she does.” She knew she had made a wise decision with her reply and slowly let her breath out through only slightly parted lips. His hand went to his mustache, and he smoothed it between his fingertips. “I’m sure you know of my…plight,” he murmured.

Flora assumed he spoke of the Battle at the Ford, the unprecedented loss. The pledging of his fealty to another. She gave a curt nod, hoping she correctly calculated.

“Good, good, then she hasn’t been as cantankerous as I feared. When I received word she would be aiding me, I admit I was skeptical. She did send the two warriors as a show of good faith, as well, but what are they other than well-trained lapdogs? And though Eve strives to serve me well, we both know where her true allegiances lie, and that isn’t with me.” He let out a delicate shudder, in a foppish sort of way.

But she supposed he got his point across.

“Now, one of you…you are worthy of the task at hand. One of you commands respect.”

Flora didn’t know what else to do, so she cleared her throat lightly, as politely as she could. “I fear—I fear I was given very little instruction other than to seek out and free Owen Drummond from Annwn.”

“And that you shall, that you shall. It is something we both want, is it not?” His eyes were twinkling, yet a viciousness lay buried underneath his mask of jovial goodness. “I have yet to determine why your benefactress finds this arrangement mutually beneficial, but I can only hope the others agree Arawn’s behavior cannot go unchecked. It is unseemly and goes against our very way of life. Such as it were.” He gave a little chuckle at whatever joke he had just made. "But for my cooperation in aiding you with the release of, what was his name again?" He waved his hand absently. "It doesn't matter. If I am to aid you in acquiring this person you seek, I need you to dispose of this new general of my enemy quickly. Before the next battle. I can't have any loose ends."

"Dispose?" She nearly choked on the word.

"Mmm." His eyes grew hard. "See to it he has passed through the gates out of Annwn before the new battle and I will help you extract your target, as well. I will even offer him amnesty within the Spring Kingdom if it pleases Her Holiness. It's unconventional, but desperate times call for desperate measures. Just ensure this general's timely disappearance isn't tied to me in any way. I can't have Arawn getting it into his head that I am a willing participant in espionage and politics. It's dull and base."

"How? How do you expect me to 'dispose' of someone?" The word was like spoiled milk in her mouth. It tasted just as bad as it sounded and made her stomach curdle. She was fairly certain she knew exactly what he meant, but she could hope she had misunderstood, right? That he was really not asking something evil of her?

She could believe it, though. This man may appear jovial and good-natured, but the air of selfishness and greed wrapped around him like a cloak.

He gave her an indolent smile before drawing his finger lazily across his neck. "And if my help is not incentive enough," he murmured, eyes hooded, "those warriors who will be accompanying you will not hesitate to impart the same fate upon you, emissary of

Arianrhod or no. I will make sure of it." The amusement that had tugged at his lips slipped away. Blackmail.

She knew extortion was exactly what he meant, what he was playing at. He was blackmailing her into doing his dirty work, and he was blackmailing them into ensuring they followed his order.

"My livelihood depends on you fulfilling this task, just as your benefactress said you would. And, so does *your* livelihood it would seem." The words were murmured, a warning only she could hear. "I'm sure she wouldn't greatly miss one of you. There are more where you came from."

A shudder went up Flora's spine, but then the anger set in. At whom, she wasn't entirely sure, this man who had absolutely no qualms in threatening her or the woman who was using her as some sort of pawn in a game of chess about which Flora was completely ignorant.

He sat back lazily. "We both want the same thing, Ambassador. I assure you. I am sending them to help you. But with some insurance for myself and some motivation for you."

"And I assure you, I was plenty motivated before the threat on my life." She was pleased with the acrid hostility that dripped from her words. She felt it deep in her bones, a sharp biting anger.

Hafgan gave her a quizzical look. "I admit I am ignorant of how things work in the North and in the Archives, but to be released from this life by my hand—so to speak—would be a great honor to most." He regarded her curiously, his head tilted ever so slightly to the side, as if she were a puzzle he hadn't quite pieced together.

Flora swallowed, becoming more and more uneasy with this place. It was a beautiful illusion, and one that covered up some truly ugly machinations. She gave him a tight-lipped smile and turned her attention back to the center of the hall and the performers who were taking their places. He did not turn from her, however, instead watching her through those unnerving eyes. She couldn't help but keep him in her periphery, looking her over in a possessive manner. She wondered if he thought he owned a bit of her, that she was just a plaything for him to toy with. The silence bloomed between them, though she became more and more uncomfortable with it and the way he regarded her as the acrobats began their routine.

"You know exactly who I seek, don't you?" The words stumbled out of her mouth, bursting forth, the idea only just entering her mind and then spilling out, unable to be contained.

And though the king still had his gaze on her, and though his lips curled upward, he did not answer her, leaving her, yet again, with more questions than she had answers.

Chapter 8

Eve woke her before the sun rose. The light of the moon streamed through the windows, illuminating the stone so it glowed softly around them. Flora had been curled up on her side, her head resting upon the crook of her arm when Eve softly shook her awake. "Ambassador, we must leave soon if we are to make the best use of the daylight."

Bleary-eyed, Flora frowned at her. "But there isn't any daylight."

"There will be soon enough."

Flora grumbled a bit, definitely not a morning person, and absolutely not an it-isn't-even-light-out person. How she managed to rise so early to study four years out of her life, she would never know. Whatever motivations she had been able to work up then had left her long ago.

She yawned as she sat up, slumping into herself. The feather-stuffed mattress had been awkward at first, but as she was being forced to leave it, she wanted nothing more than to sink back into it and never leave. Eve was busily rolling things and stuffing them into a pack that looked like a larger version of Flora's satchel, which lay atop a washstand across the room.

The night before, Eve had helped her pick through the clothes she had been given, eliminating anything that would tie her to Hafgan, but also shedding anything that wouldn't be useful in some way. She was left with a couple of pairs of leggings, some tunics, a quilted bodice, a leather jacket Eve had referred to as "armor," and a silver gown that looked like something out of a King Arthur movie.

Flora dressed as quickly as she could under Eve's direction: leather leggings, boots that reached to just below her knees, tunic, bodice, jacket. She slung the strap of the satchel across her center, ready to go.

Eve shouldered the larger pack, which wasn't really terribly large considering, and motioned for Flora to follow her. They were to meet Iain in the inner bailey outside the great hall.

Iain, who said even less than Eve, just nodded when they arrived. A brown hood was pulled up over his head, half of it hanging down over his face, shrouding him in mystery. He offered a small pack to Flora, and she hefted it over her shoulders like a backpack. It was light, and if she had to guess, she would say it held little more than some blankets. He, too, had one, but he also carried a sinister pair of swords at his back and wore a full metal breastplate.

It was then she noticed Eve, too, wore metal armor, her sword at her side.

Flora suddenly felt a little underdressed. "Are you expecting to run into some highwaymen? Lions? Bears? A dragon?" she asked in a teasing tone.

But both looked at her with marked gravity.

Flora's face fell almost instantly. "Should I go change?" she asked, a slight tremble to her voice.

"You'll be fine. We'll be here to protect you," Eve told her.

"That does not inspire much confidence."

Eve shrugged and started walking away. Iain followed her.

"Where are you going?" Flora called after them.

"To Annwn," Eve called back, not even turning.

Flora frowned, then jogged to catch up. "On foot? Aren't there horses? Or unicorns or something?"

She thought she heard Iain snicker from underneath his hood.

"What?" she demanded.

Eve didn't even bother shaking her head. "It's just better to go on foot."

"Why?"

"Difficult terrain."

The explanation seemed like reason enough, Flora supposed. The three of them trudged out of a small castle gate and into the darkness.

Flora concentrated on the setting around her. The moon lit their path well, and she realized she had never truly realized how powerful its glow could be without the artificial lights of cities. But what was most amazing were the sounds. The rustle of grass, the faint call of birds as they awoke, the distant clink of water running over rock were all around her, uninterrupted by motors or engines or generators. She strained her ears, hoping to take in every sound from the pebbles and sand crunching beneath their boots to the bellowing of livestock in the fields.

She almost wanted to say something, at least make small talk with her companions, but she didn't want to spoil the symphony around her. She was lost in it, completely in awe. She devoured it, and the sun had brought morning over the horizon.

It was Iain who halted them. They were in the open grasslands, hills rolling around them, the odd tree or shrub sticking out, the grains dancing around them. Iain dropped his pack onto a large rock overhanging the stream along which they had been traveling, and hopped down to the water, cupping some in his hand and splashing it on his face.

Eve knelt down to unload her own things, then looked up at Flora, who remained rooted to the ground. "Rest. We'll be leaving soon," she said in an almost friendly tone.

But not too friendly; friendliness would have been very uncharacteristic, if Flora wasn't mistaken.

Flora smiled sheepishly. She didn't feel particularly overburdened, so she left her own light pack on her back as she hopped down to the bank of the stream. She extracted the bowl from her satchel, dipping it into the water and bringing it to her lips to drink. She hadn't realized how thirsty she was until the water touched her lips. She gulped deeply, emptying the vessel before dipping it back into the water to refill.

"What are you doing?" demanded Iain. His tone was a mix of disbelief and chastisement. She jumped, the water sloshing on her face and dribbling down her chin.

"What?" she asked, confused.

"Where did you get that?" he asked with both suspicion and wonder as he knelt before her.

It took Flora a moment to realize he was talking about the bowl. "What do you mean? It's just...mine." She shrugged.

He was shaking his head slowly, very slowly, back and forth. "Did she give it to you?" he asked with reverence and suspicion.

"She?" Flora asked, raising her eyebrow.

"Your benefactress."

Flora shrugged. "I suppose. In a roundabout sort of way."

Iain reached out, as if he wanted to touch it, but drew his hand away. "But how did she get it?" he asked, more to himself than to anyone.

"Who? Me? Or her?"

But he wasn't paying attention to her, his gaze was too busy assessing the symbols.

"And you drank from it?" he asked.

Flora felt the urge to look around for a hidden camera. "Um…yes?" Was this some sort of trick question?

"Do you feel any different?" he queried.

"You're beginning to frighten me. What are you getting on about?"

"You really mean you don't know?" scoffed Eve, who was standing over her. For the first time, she had taken her helmet off.

Eve's hair, a deep shade of brown, stood out starkly against her pale skin. It was sheared short in an uneven pixie cut, as if she had cut it herself. Maybe with a dull knife. Flora pursed her lips. "I really have no idea what is so special about drinking out of an old bowl, no."

"I think that's… I think that's the Cauldron of Knowledge," Iain muttered.

Flora waited for him—either of them, really—to elaborate. They didn't. "And?" she finally asked.

"And if you drank from it, you received the knowledge held within."

"Well, then it must be broken, because I have no idea what you are talking about," she told him. She drank the rest of the water, then shook the bowl out, dislodging the few droplets clinging to the sides, and shoved it back into her pack.

"It is said to belong to Cerridwen." Iain frowned.

Flora looked at him blankly.

"Are you sure Arianrhod sent you?" Iain's reverence had turned to skepticism.

Flora smiled mirthlessly. "Iain, to be honest, I am not sure of anything."

****

They approached a small village as dusk settled in. Flora had been able to see the little hamlet from the top of one of the mighty hills over which they traveled. Four or five small stone houses, a larger building that might be a central meeting hall, an open square, and stone wall surrounding it all.

As they drew closer, she was able to see moss covered the stone of the walls, and just outside of them was a camp, covered wagons pulled into a circle, the beginnings of a giant fire at their center. Upon seeing the bright colors of the wagons and hearing the soft rhythm of a drum paired with a stringed instrument, she immediately wondered if they were gypsies.

Iain and Eve ducked their heads together, murmuring softly just out of earshot, probably discussing the presence of the other travelers. Flora, however, allowed her curiosity to get the best of her. While her companions waved their hands around in argument, she crept closer to the camp.

Small pockets of people were sitting around the campfire, some talking, some playing music. There was a group of women who looked to be kneading dough, and some men—hunters, perhaps?—cleaning weapons.

"You're not from our world, are you?"

Flora bit back a scream as she jumped back, then turned to see who had come up behind her.

The woman was small, perhaps only five feet tall. She was lissome with a long face, and small, slender ears pointed out of her hair. The golden tresses swung around her waist, curling only slightly at the ends. Her complexion was flawless, and she had a mysterious serenity about her.

"I'm sorry, I didn't mean to frighten you," she apologized in a singsong voice, the notes ringing like the tinkling accent of western Ireland.

"It's all right," Flora told her, her voice wavering. "What did you mean?"

The woman offered a small smile but didn't elaborate. "You may call me Delyth," she murmured, as if granting Flora permission to speak with her. Her voice lowered, and she leaned in toward Flora. "Do they know?"

Flora's frown deepened. She felt as if she wasn't even a part of this conversation; she was merely eavesdropping and only hearing one side.

"Do they know where you come from? That you come from beyond the veil?"

The veil. The other woman had told her the same thing. That she would have to pass through the veil to save Owen. "What do you know? How?"

Delyth continued to give her ethereal smile. "I can help you, you know."

"Ambassador!" Eve rounded the stone wall, panic in her voice. She visibly relaxed when she saw Flora. For a moment. Then, her attentions turned to the camp. "We can still make it a few more miles," she told Flora.

Flora frowned at her. "Why not stop, now? We'll have company. And it's already getting dark."

The sun had sunk below the horizon, and the land was left with the awkward blue that comes between daylight and darkness.

Eve stood her ground. "No. We need to keep moving."

"Why?"

"I'll tell you later," she ground through her teeth.

Flora let out a sigh and turned to apologize to Delyth. But the woman was gone.

Flora frowned as she considered the woman's odd disappearance. She hadn't even heard her walk away.

Flora followed Eve back to Iain, who waited impatiently by the road. He held in one hand a small brown sack, and in the other the limp body of a goose. She tried to ignore it, but she couldn't take her gaze off the poor creature. As they approached, he turned and continued down the road, leaving the two women to follow.

They didn't walk much farther, just long enough to put the village and the Gypsy camp at a distance. She could no longer pick out the smoke from the fire, nor hear the sounds of the music.

Iain steered them toward a lone tree at the bottom of a great hill, dropped the small sack to the ground and unloaded the pack he carried on his back. He squatted down to the ground and began plucking the goose.

Eve immediately went to work gathering kindling, leaving Flora standing around feeling rather useless.

She unburdened herself of her pack and satchel. "Why did you want to leave the village?" she asked Eve as the other woman tented the wood over the kindling.

"It wasn't the village that had us nervous," Eve bit out, a defensive ring to her voice.

"You mean the Gypsies?"

Eve was confused. "Is that what they are called in the North?"

"I thought that's what they were called everywhere," Flora answered, just as puzzled.

Eve shook her head. "No. Here, we call them the Ellyllon. The elves."

"Elves?" Flora echoed, surprised. Elves? Was such a thing possible? They had looked just like people. Perhaps they were a bit smaller in stature than most, but otherwise…they were just people. Weren't they?

She thought about Delyth and the strange exchange they had shared. Of her mysterious appearance and just as mysterious disappearance.

Eve lifted an eyebrow. "You know, Fae half-breeds from the other side of the veil. More magic than us humans, but less than the Fae. But tricky with it. They're not good for much, and they just tend to stick their noses where they aren't wanted."

"Why do they make you nervous?" Flora wanted to know, truly curious. Delyth had been kind, sweet even.

"Why *don't* they make you nervous?" was Eve's retort.

Flora didn't answer. She supposed there was nothing she had seen to make her nervous. There had been no waving of weapons or chanting of strange incantations. Delyth had seemed like anyone else. What threat could such a slender, petite woman make?

"The Ellyllon are known for their trickery. They can be valuable allies when the time is right, for they have many connections and knowledge of the way of things, but they can be even worse foes. It is best to just steer clear of them and not get on their bad side, otherwise the power that might have helped you is suddenly aimed *at* you."

"If you have nothing to do with them, then how are you to become friends? Or at least allies? Perhaps they could help—would want to help—but you aren't giving them a chance?" Flora asked.

"It's better to err on the side of caution." This came from Iain. He had finished his plucking of the fowl and was fashioning a rotisserie. One edge of a sturdy yet slender stick had been fashioned into a sharp point. He slid it through the bird. "What do you mean by trickery?" Flora asked.

"Let's just say it happens."

"Not a good enough answer. I don't follow prejudice blindly," she snapped, suddenly wanting to defend the other woman, for all of her kind.

Iain twisted his mouth to one side as he considered her from beneath the hood. She couldn't see past his nose in the darkness, but she knew his gaze was on her.

"Just don't take anything they say at face value. Always expect betrayal."

****

Flora was exhausted, but found she couldn't sleep. She stared at the waning fire, thinking of Owen's face. The face of a man she hadn't known a week, the face of a man she hadn't really known at all. She had somehow traded her life—a life that was, admittedly, in a state of extreme upheaval but showing some great promise and direction—for a chance at giving him his life back.

She didn't really know what that meant. She knew he had a dazzling smile, she knew he made her heart skip, and he set her skin on fire. But she didn't know what he did, or what he liked. She didn't know his mannerisms or his quirks. She didn't know whether he preferred mornings or late nights, coffee or tea, scones or croissant, being single or in a relationship or…or anything. All she knew was that she wanted the opportunity to find out.

As the grass rustled, she turned over on her back and looked out over the valley. A few yards away stood a dark figure. Flora started to call out to wake Iain and Eve, their sleeping forms like dense shadows on the other side of the dwindling fire, but something stopped her, and she sat up, instead.

The figure moved toward her until the small fire illuminated the face.

"Delyth? It is Delyth, right?" Flora asked softly.

The waifish smile brightened. "You remembered. Good." She moved closer, lowering herself to sit on Flora's blankets, sitting close as if they were close. The best of friends. Sisters. "I want to help you," Delyth murmured. Even at a whisper, her voice was high and singsongy.

"Help me?"

Delyth nodded emphatically.

"We both know you aren't from this side of the veil. Your kind coming here is rare. Very rare. And those who come here are brought by the gods to do big things, big important things that change not just this world, but others. I don't know why they brought you here, but I want to be a part of whatever it is." Her gaze was on the two sleeping forms as if she were waiting for them to awaken and see her there. "We should move away," she murmured. "So as not to waken them."

She stood, then, with fluid gracefulness, and Flora quickly followed, all limbs and butt in the air. They linked arms and stepped out into the darkness, into the waving grasses and cool wind.

"I'm not sure I understand what you meant at all. What are you talking about? And what is this 'veil' that everyone keeps talking about?"

Delyth rolled her eyes, the whites of her eyes catching the glow of the moon and giving the movement away. "The *veil.* It's what separates your world from ours."

"Why does everyone seem to know about it here? I've never even heard of it. Or…here. Whatever it's called."

Delyth stretched out her arms. "This is the Sídh, the land given to all of us by the Fae. It was created for the good people, the Ellyllon, the true believers, and the dead. When the Romans brought their new, single god to the old lands, the people stopped believing. And so, the gods returned here to the Sídh, what you call the Otherworld, taking the last true believers with them. They then locked the old world out behind the veil. There are a few who still believe on your side, just enough so the gods can continue to pass through the veil. And the dead can still slip in and out through the thinned barriers. But the gods, they rarely answer the call of your people, anymore. Your people's voices have grown quiet. They have forgotten or they simply no longer care. Their tie to the gift of the gods is fraying."

"Then why cross at all?"

Delyth shrugged. "Boredom. Necessity. Habit. Time is different, here, so perhaps they go to see the changing of time in their old lands. Perhaps they hope, someday, to win you back."

"And you're…Ellyllon?"

"Ellyll. When there's just one of us," she explained. "Most of your kind call us elves."

"And fairies? They exist here, too?"

She nodded. "And dragons. Griffons. All manner of beasts that the gods brought with them."

"How do you know I am from the other side and no one else does?"

Delyth shrugged. "We, the Ellyllon, are much more connected to the old ways than the others. We still talk of the crossing, of the old world. We tell the tales around the campfire every night and every morning as we break camp. We sing the songs of the old world, and we live it. The Fae are the chosen. They were the gods' people before the rest of us, and they care little for the goings on of the rest of the world. And the humans…" she made a clicking noise with her tongue and bobbed her head from side to side. "And the rest? Dead. Living this life until they can pass on to the next. But to answer your question, one of *you* is rare. So rare, you're not even talked about. They probably think you're what? A servant of a god?"

"King Hafgan called me an ambassador of Arianrhod."

The other woman regarded her for a moment before responding. "It's your accent," Delyth explained.

Flora frowned. "My accent?"

"It's from the North. The land of the Pict barbarians."

"And here I thought it had something to do with my necklace." Flora absently ran her fingers over the smooth metal.

Delyth's brows hooded over her eyes, and she leaned closer to inspect the pendant. "Where did you get that?" she asked slowly, as if asking herself more than Flora.

"It's a long story, I—"

"Ambassador?" Eve called.

"We should return to the camp," Flora murmured to Delyth.

Delyth bowed her head in agreement, and they picked their way back to the sleeping pallets and warm embers.

"Sorry, I didn't want to wake you," Flora told Eve.

Eve looked bleary-eyed from Flora to Delyth. "What is she doing here?" she asked accusingly.

"She wants to help."

"Help?" Eve snorted, indignant.

"Look, you're tired, I'm tired, and there is no use arguing about it. I would like Delyth to come and help *me.* Her being here doesn't keep you from doing your job."

"Doesn't she?" she demanded.

"Only if you allow it."

Flora leaned down and grasped one of her blankets and handed it to Delyth, who started to protest. "It's warm. I'll be fine."

The small elven woman took it, wrapping it around her, and then went to lean against the trunk of the tree.

"Until morning," she murmured in much the same way a mother says good night to her children.

"Until morning," Flora murmured.

Eve grumbled, pulling her own blankets over herself, but was soon snoring softly.

Chapter 9

Flora was beginning to wonder if Delyth was right and time really was different on the other side of the veil. She wasn't sure how long they had traveled, but it felt like it could be months. Or perhaps it was only days. Hours? No, that didn't seem right. Try as she might, she couldn't remember how many nights she had spent sleeping under the stars, wrapped in blankets and furs, stones digging into her back.

She had never been one for the outdoors. Her father was a sportsman, stalking in his free time with the other members of his club. She had never found any particular draw to it, though, and refused to join him on the misty moors, a rifle in hand. Her mother preferred nature from a distance, and so they had never gone camping when she was a child, either. After her time sleeping in the wilderness, she was glad of it. She could find few redeeming features, though the ceiling of stars as far as her eye could see did have its draw.

The farther they traveled, the more golden the plains became, the greens less vibrant. Their grasses continued to wave, but with a brittle bend that had their long, slender stalks close to snapping. They had grown heavier, the mass pulled closer to the horizons, warmth trickling away as its color went from fresh honey to saturated tangerine. Fewer flowers dotted the hillsides;

they were replaced by thick, heavily ripened fruits and thick seed pods. The air felt still and warm and heavy.

As they crossed the landscape, she and Delyth picked various leaves and what was left of the flowers, carefully packing them away to be dried. She had begun noticing certain plants as they walked by, and just couldn't shake the feeling she should be taking samples. She would only take a leaf or two here, a single flower there, and would press them into the encyclopedia of plants. One evening, she realized she had been collecting the vegetation she had found in the book, and the scribbling she had once thought was odd gibberish in another language she could then understand.

Delyth had seen what she was doing and started doing the same, claiming the plants would help her magic. And then one afternoon—Flora supposed it was afternoon, anyway—they came upon a wide, shallow river with sandy banks and long sandbars running through it. Eve and Iain stopped and marveled at it.

"Here it is," Eve whispered reverently.

Iain's exposed lips, the rest of his face still in shadow, remained in a straight line. "Yes."

"The Ford."

Flora remembered Hafgan had mentioned something about a "Battle at the Ford," but she didn't know much more.

"Is this where the battle was?"

Iain didn't turn to Flora, but he answered, "Yes." He squatted down, picking up a smooth rock, squeezing it in his hand. "King Hafgan and the King of Annwn have battled many times here at the Ford. Just before the hunt and harvests and again as the flowers and new fawns arrive. And every battle, King Arawn takes the first day and King Hafgan the second. The next goes to Hafgan and then Arawn. It's just the way of things. The turning of the coin. Warmth to cold. Cold to warmth. Until the last battle. Arawn used trickery and deceit, and he altered the rules of the game to force His Majesty, King Hafgan, to pledge his fealty to Annwn." Iain stood, running his thumb over the rock, back and forth, back and forth.

"What do you mean 'trickery and deceit'? How do you fake a battle?"

Iain threw the rock forcefully. It hit the water near the opposite bank, splashed, and sank. "Arawn didn't fight the battle. He sent a proxy in his stead."

"I don't understand. Why even fight this battle?"

Eve and Iain both turned, giving her a look that said they didn't even know why it was fought themselves. She would have to ask Delyth later. Now didn't seem like the time to consult her, and she picked her way along the banks, anyway, far from earshot. She was small, like a child, bending down to examine a rock or to look at a fish. Flora wouldn't be surprised if she came away with a handful of samples, little keepsakes to remind herself of the Ford. The others had made their feelings about her presence rather obvious, so she often kept to herself, falling behind, her eyes on the sky or a distant mountain. Flora often felt like she needed to shield Delyth from any of their outbursts. But, avoidance seemed to serve her well.

"Right. Well. Onward?" Flora asked.

They waded into the water, and it was much colder than Flora would have guessed, splashing their way into the shallow depths. Water seeped its way into Flora's boots, and she instantly regretted not taking them off and rolling up the leggings she wore. But it didn't seem to bother the others, so she refused to let them know it bothered her.

The other side of the bank felt markedly cooler. There, the breeze picked up, brisk and cool, and some of the humidity that clung to the air had dissipated. As they found a merchant's path, Flora noticed the leaves were more gold than green and the grasses seemed even more brittle than they had on the opposite banks.

If she wasn't mistaken, they had crossed right from summer into autumn.

****

The screeches were unlike anything she had ever heard, like the high-pitched call of an eagle coupled with the growl of a big cat. They echoed against the mountain sides and were followed by an even more unfamiliar sound. The piercing calls split through her ears, slicing into her mind, making thought almost impossible.

Flora looked to the others through watering eyes. The sun was just beginning to lighten the sky to a royal blue, the first fingers of morning appearing at the edges of the horizon. It was just enough light for Flora to see Delyth pull her cowl over her head, lower her eyelashes, and hunch her shoulders as if she were trying to appear as small and insignificant as possible.

Eve's hand went to the hilt of her sword, gripping it tightly, the leather of her glove groaning as the shriek paused. Iain drew his blades from his back, one in each hand, at the ready. Again, Flora realized just how vulnerable she was.

Not sure what else to do, she edged her hand under the flap of the satchel and rested her hand on top of the handle of the small knife. It wasn't much, its blade only a few inches long, and she knew she was probably more likely to stab herself with the thing than any attacker, but it offered her some sort of comfort, nonetheless.

"What was that?" she asked no one in particular.

Eve and Iain exchanged a look, and neither of them said a word. She looked to Delyth, but she, too, remained silent, her pale skin appearing even more ashen. Her flaxen hair fell down her shoulders in two ropes, making her appear even younger and more vulnerable than she had before.

The screeches came again, followed by the sound of wind hitting sails, over and over again. Flora's coppery hair brushed into her eyes and clung to her eyelashes. She beat it away, shaking her head as she did so to keep it clear of her vision.

And then they heard the screams of men. Of women. They echoed out over the rock, bouncing across the mountains, ricocheting so the wails were all around them. The sounds filled her with dread, her blood pounding in and out of her heart like the hooves of a racing horse.

Heart in her throat, mind not registering the decision even as she made it, Flora ran toward the screams and the unknown, the alarmed calls of her companions unheeded.

As she crested the ridge, she found images out of her wildest dreams. Great serpents covered with shimmering scales, circled a valley lit in flame. One was on the ground, its tail whipping behind it like an angry feline, its wings spread out wide, jaws snapping at its victims. The other hovered in the air, smoke billowing ominously from its nostrils. Across the landscape were hundreds of soldiers, but few were armed, and even fewer still looked able. Fires blazed. Tents and bodies lay littered along the rocky terrain, illuminated by the orange flames that grew ever larger and more violent.

One of the drakes, was easily a hundred feet long, cornered a small group just below her. The soldiers appeared to be unarmed but for one, and he held up his sword painfully, his opposite hand covering a wound, blood oozing between his fingers. The red seeped between the digits and over his knuckles.

All of Flora's senses dimmed, and she moved without thought or emotion. She slid down the rocky hill her left hand scraping against the ground, her flesh becoming bruised and scratched. Her other hand was still on the handle of the small knife. Her fingers tightened around it. As she slid nearer, she pulled the knife out.

She was only a few yards above the soldiers, now. The drake's hot breath curled around her like heat escaping an oven. The drake lunged at the soldiers. Her skin crawled. The man holding the sword lunged forward with a practiced grace, tip poised to sink into drake flesh, but the beast's large head knocked the weapon from his grasp, sending him reeling.

The drake reared back to lunge again, and with all her might, Flora threw the small blade. It whistled through the air, but only bounced off its mark, the handle smacking the drake's gaunt cheek before clanging on the rocks below.

The large head swung in her direction, its golden eyes fixing on her. The drake let out a quick breath of hot, acrid air before breathing in her scent. Barely even recognizing what she was doing, Flora reached back into the satchel, grabbed a handful of the small yellow leaves she'd collected from some low-lying shrubs on the mountains, and tossed it into the drake's face.

It reared back, making a choking sound, giving her just enough time to clamber over to the discarded sword and swing it over her head just as the teeth-lined jaws snapped at her. With all her might, she drove the sword upward as if she were pointing it to the heavens, and it crunched through hard, scaly flesh before sliding into the soft meat beneath.

The drake screamed, the volume and pitch so terrible Flora dropped to her knees, covering her ears with her hands, her eyes squeezing closed against the pain. It continued to scream and thrash, losing footing on the side of the ridge and stumbling down into the blazing camp.

The ground shook as the giant body crashed into the valley, and she opened her eyes to watch the scene below. The soldiers who were capable attacked immediately, silencing the great beast. The other drake, seeing its partner fall, took flight, fanning the fires and sending dust whirling around them. Arrows pelted against it, and with one final cry, it left the valley behind, heading to the snowcapped mountains.

A hand at her shoulder startled her, and she lowered her palms from over her ears. The sounds of roaring fires and calling soldiers flooded the glowing, the smell of smoke mingling with the falling ash.

"Are you all right?"

She turned, expecting to see Iain, but instead, she looked up into the green eyes of Owen Drummond.

Chapter 10

He looked different.

He was the same, but not. Her Owen—if she could even call him hers—had been, perfect. His skin had been unmarked, his face without blemish. His eyes had been dancing and light with amusement and happiness. He had a mouth that enjoyed a perpetual smile.

This man, however, had a much harder face. A faint white scar ran from the corner of his mouth down to his right cheek. His eyes were hard, guarded, and she saw no evidence of recognition.

She wasn't sure what she had expected, but it wasn't this. Perhaps surprise to find her on this side of the veil with him, perhaps excitement or relief when he realized she had come for him. Definitely not the gaze of a stranger.

"General!" someone called, and he turned to acknowledge them.

His attention was back to her. "Are you all right?" he asked again.

"Y-yes," she stuttered, her mind still not comprehending what was going on around her.

He still clutched his left arm with his right hand, the blood there fresh and bright in the glow of the fires. The blood had seeped onto his dark tunic, an even darker wet splotch against otherwise rich cloth.

"But you're not," she said more to herself than to him. She righted herself, reaching for the wound and brushing his fingers away.

The gash was deep and looked painful. Blood seeped from it, but to her very untrained eye, it appeared to be slowing down, which was a good thing, right? He seemed surprised by her actions for a moment, and then replaced his hand, reapplying pressure, staunching what little flow there was.

"Let me help," she murmured.

"It's a scratch. It can wait." Owen frowned, as if he were angry at himself for speaking at all. He turned away from her before she could protest. "Captain, see to her."

The poor soul who had been put in charge of her probably wasn't much younger than his commanding officer, if Flora guessed correctly. She put him somewhere in his mid-twenties, his skin unblemished and supple, but the beginnings of crow's feet branching from the corners of his eyes. He was completely disheveled, wearing nothing but an askew metal breastplate and leather pants, the codpiece ties one strong gust of wind away from falling open. The captain was a very large man, though not one who was particularly tall. His bulk came in the form of thick muscle and broad bulk, his arms bulging. She was afraid of being caught staring, so she shot her gaze back up to his head, noticing it was completely shaved above his thick eyebrows.

She nodded to him, not entirely sure what "seeing to" she needed. But, she knew two things were true—Owen was her final destination, despite whatever it was Hafgan had planned for her, and though she was on relatively friendly terms with her travel companions, they were, first and foremost, there to keep her in line.

The captain looked around nervously, clearly not sure what he was supposed to do with her, either. They stared at each other for a moment.

"I can help," she finally told him, hoping to ease some of the tension.

He looked taken aback and then relieved, his shoulders sagging. "Good. Come on."

He led her down the rocks and then they were in the middle of the fray.

People rushed about in various states of undress, hauling buckets of water and moving the wounded as far away from the fires as possible. Flora motioned to the captain to help her, and together, they balanced an injured soldier between them, moving her closer to the stream running through the valley with the other wounded. Together, they helped at least a dozen, the captain calling out orders to his soldiers as they did so.

"Check the tents for soldiers, and then let them burn," he called.

Not that there was much left burning, anyway. Everything was becoming black, charred ash. Smoking, but no longer blazing. The water the able had fetched to put out the fires was instead given to those who were wounded.

Flora helped as best she could, but without supplies, there was little anyone could do. Water was set to boiling and whatever cloth was available was used for bandages, but many had been severely burned, and even more hadn't made it to dawn alive.

When she finally reached her limit, Flora removed herself from the ruckus, inching her way to the bank of the stream, and turning her back on the scene behind her. She gazed at the dark, low clouds spreading out over the rolling countryside, threatening rain. They reminded her of shores of Loch Lomond, the way the mountains reached up to the sky, covered in dark green, the sky seeming to stretch into forever.

She had never seen death before. When she was young and the family cat had died, she had been at school. She had returned to the news, but none of the aftermath. She had never seen Martha, only the small tin box her mother had brought home after her passing, the one in which her ashes had been placed. Death, to her, had always been tidy, something that happened somewhere else, and she was only aware of it from the periphery.

She'd never seen so much suffering, either. Never heard the moans of someone who was in so much pain they wished they *were* dead. Or felt the desperation of someone as he struggled to overcome the fear of what was happening.

She stayed within earshot of the captain but tried not to eavesdrop as he coordinated with his lieutenants and gave orders to the sergeants. Flora decided he must have forgotten about her, or at the very least, had decided she wasn't going anywhere. She appreciated how calm he was under pressure, how nothing from the scene was keeping him from being helpful and effective. She envied him his ability to see exactly what needed to be done and do it despite whatever his own limitations may be.

Someone sat beside her. She didn't move to see who it was, but the warmth seeped into her own body, pleasant and comforting despite her mentally exhausted and numb state.

"Why did you do that?" The voice was Delyth's, light, just a whisper more mature than a young girl.

Flora turned, rested her head on her bent knees, and wrapped her arms around her legs, hugging herself. "Where did you come from?" she asked instead of answering the question.

"I've been here. Helping with the wounded."

"Eve and Iain?"

Delyth shrugged. "I don't know. Perhaps they are helping, as well."

Flora nodded, knowing they wouldn't have abandoned her. Eve was definitely the type to always follow orders, even if she did huff and complain when they were given to her. She wasn't sure what Iain's type was, but she knew his allegiance was to Hafgan.

"Does this kind of thing happen often?" Flora asked in a hushed voice.

"What? The dragons?" Delyth shook her head. "No. Attacks are rare. The stuff of legend. And killing one?" She gave Flora a look, one of both awe and warning. "There will be stories of you that will reach all across the Sídh. Maybe even to Tír Na Nog."

More words she didn't know. More things that made no sense. She chose to ignore what Delyth said. It had been more complicated before the dragons had set in.

She sighed. "We should get back."

"There you are."

Flora turned to find the captain standing over her. He had found some more clothes, but the naked vulnerability on his face was clear. He was relieved to have found her. She didn't know why—she had never been far away.

She stood, brushed off her leggings and pulled her tunic down. Both were stained with blood and damp with sweat and water.

"The commander wishes to speak with you," he said.

Flora turned her gaze to Delyth, then back. She remained silent, but nodded.

She followed the captain through the remains of the camp, staying close. They picked their way through wounded and the dead. She tried desperately to fill her mind with anything but the tableau of blood, and charred flesh.

At the far side of the camp, they came to a huddle of large tents that still remained intact and erect, their canvas sides swaying gently as the wind rushed into them. Flora and the captain slipped behind some soldiers in full armor and behind the tents.

The captain put out an arm to stop her. Before them were a few others, backs to them, poring over what appeared to be a map and some documents. At the other side was the blond man she would have recognized in her sleep, his two hands propped on the table, nodding his head at this, waving his hand at that. Then his gaze met hers.

He had had a chance to dress himself in more than the tunic. He looked as if he were caught between two worlds, but not hers and this one. His garb hinted at both the Roman Empire and the Middle Ages. His shining breastplate, with a hound etched into it, splayed across his chest, a deep red cape lined with gray fur was slung over his shoulders. The rest of his armor was an odd mixture of artfully crafted leather and shining metal, and the crossing his hips were utilitarian, not decorative in style. The long sword she had taken possession of now hung to one side, a smaller dagger at the other. And something looking curiously similar to a sporran hung between them.

The three men and two women, seeing him stand, took the cue as theirs to leave and shuffled past her. None of them made eye contact. Owen looked to the captain who still stood at her side, gave him a nod. The captain shifted, and Flora turned, looking around, only to see they were alone together.

She waited, expecting him to come to her, to kiss her and tell her he had been waiting for her. The recognition and relief would grow in his eyes as he thanked her for releasing him from his prison.

"Who are you?"

"I'm sorry?" She didn't know what else to say.

He lowered his head and seemed to mentally take a step back. "I apologize. I asked you here so I might thank you. The attack on our camp was, well, it was unexpected. And if it weren't for you, I'm afraid we would all be dead right now."

Again, she didn't know what to say. She allowed her manners to take over. "I—You're welcome."

He frowned at her. "How?"

"How?"

"Yes. How were you able to take down the dragon? Those who encounter dragons are almost always slaughtered, and yet more than half of my army is walking away, though some are a little worse for wear. You did that. How?"

"I don't know, I—"

"Who are you?" he repeated, again. She knew she was being interrogated, but she wasn't exactly sure why.

"My name is Flora, I'm—"

"My lady!"

Flora wasn't sure if she was relieved or annoyed by Eve's interruption. A guard had a hand on Eve's arm, trying to pull her away.

"We've been looking for you."

She turned back to Owen. "Please, she's with me."

He nodded to the guard, who stepped away, allowing Eve to stand by Flora's right elbow. The other woman fairly vibrated with nervous energy, but Flora was also sure, if she leaned back just a bit, she would feel the tip of a knife pointing in the direction of one of her kidneys.

Her smile had faltered, and under his hard, almost-angry gaze, she forced it to reappear. "I'm actually here for you," she started, but he interrupted her this time.

"Me?" His frown deepened. The vee that formed between his blond eyebrows looked as if it belonged there more than any laugh lines. "Yes, I'm here—"

"At the behest of Her Holiness, Arianrhod." Flora turned to Eve, eyes narrowed and lips pursed in annoyance.

Eve ignored her, pushing forward so Flora was staring at her armored back. Her one consolation was that Owen looked just as annoyed by Eve's intrusion as she was.

Eve gave an overexaggerated bow. "Sir, may I introduce Flora the Pecht, witch to the House of Arianrhod, and ambassador from the North."

Witch?! Flora wanted to cry. She was physically holding herself from kicking Eve in the backs of her knees and beating her over the head with her own helmet. What was Eve trying to do? Get her hanged? Beheaded? Burned at the stake? It may have been a few years since she had studied history, but she was fairly certain no one ever took very kindly to witches. She closed her eyes and waited for the next shoe to drop.

Nothing. She opened her eyes.

Owen still gazed at her with an odd, angry, quizzical expression. "I suppose this is an honor, then." He didn't sound honored. He sounded skeptical.

She didn't blame him.

He crossed his arms over his chest. She had appreciated his form—oh, how she had appreciated it—but she didn't remember him being quite as bulky. Yes, he had definitely had a leaner build. Less bulgy and overstuffed. She wasn't sure how she felt about his changed physique.

"There are several matters to which I must attend," he told her. "Perhaps we can speak later?"

She struggled between smiling and remaining tight-lipped, and ended up giving him only a half shrug. "Of course, I'll be… Trying my best to help," she said. She clasped her hands in front of her and gave him a kind of bow-curtsy—and swung around to leave, nearly knocking into Eve. She gave the other woman a murderous glare, and marched into the most devastating scene she had ever been a part of.

Eve was nipping at her heels, and once they were out of earshot, Flora whirled on Hafgan's guard. "What the bloody hell, Eve?" she demanded. She would have preferred to scream it, but instead, she ground out the words between her teeth.

Eve didn't say anything.

"A witch? You're telling people I am a witch, now? Are you *trying* to get me killed?"

Eve's expression changed to one of confusion.

"Why would you say that?" Flora demanded.

"Because you are one." The answer was matter-of-fact.

Flora sputtered, threw up her hands, then put them on her hips, not sure what to do with herself. She turned away from Eve, but then rounded on her again. "Why do you think that?"

"The herbs. The flowers. The plants. You gather them, using them to help you sleep or to cure a headache. And the other day, I heard you mutter something about the rain, and it stopped. Immediately."

"Fine, but why tell him?"

Eve looked annoyed. She crossed her own arms over her chest and shifted her weight to one foot. "Because we—*you*—need to be in his good graces. This will not only do that but also get you into Arawn's court. You'll be able to get whatever information you need about your man."

Flora wanted to scream. "But I *found* Owen. I don't want to go sit in anyone's court, I just want to get him and get the hell out of here."

Eve looked surprised. "You found him? Here?" She looked around as if he would be standing behind her.

"Yes!"

"Where?" Eve turned, looking around as if a giant arrow would pop out of the sky and indicate one of the soldiers as the so-called prisoner.

"The general, Eve! Owen is the general!"

Eve's face drained of all color. Flora let out a breath and made to storm past her and back into the camp, but Eve grabbed her by the arm and swung her around. Flora could feel the point of the knife Eve held to her back. "We're going to find Iain."

He sat atop a large rock overlooking the stream, an apple in one hand, a small knife in the other. He lazily peeled the red skin from the fruit, letting it dangle in long curls.

"We have a problem," Eve told him. She still held Flora's upper arm and pulled the taller woman between them.

Iain didn't bother looking up, he just kept peeling his apple.

"The prisoner isn't a prisoner at all," Eve told him.

Flora stood obediently in front of Eve, even though the stronger woman had removed her hand from Flora's arm.

"He's the general of Arawn's army. The imposter!"

Iain still didn't look up. The curl of peel fell to the ground. It looked like a ribbon laying upon the moss. "Annwn's army is decidedly smaller, now," was all he said.

"It wouldn't exist anymore at all if it weren't for her," Eve spit out.

Flora frowned; she couldn't believe Eve would prefer all those people to die.

Iain shook his head. "This is better."

"How is this better? We could have marched right up to Caer Annwn and taken the kingdom without a fight!"

Iain was very, very interested in the apple. He turned it over in his hand, and finding what he was looking for, brought it to his mouth and took a bite. The bite he took crunched loudly, the fruit perfectly ripe and crisp. "That's not why we're here, Eve," he chided after swallowing, as if he were speaking to a small child.

"So? We could have decimated all of the Annwn forces and the king would easily retake the Ford!" Eve was waving her hands around, clearly frustrated with Iain's nonchalant attitude.

"He was going to retake the Ford, anyway, Eve. Just be a good girl, and do as you were told. Help the ambassador take this Owen back to Arianrhod."

"But what if she doesn't?"

Iain chuckled and swung his gaze to meet Flora's. "You really don't know anything, do you?" He hopped down from his perch and strode up to Flora.

She thought he would walk right by her, but he leaned in before passing, his lips right next to her ear so Eve couldn't hear. "You have a lot of work to do, don't you?"

****

Dark settled in, and the army fell eerily quiet. The only sounds were coming from those who were too delirious to keep quiet. Their moans and cries rang out against the mountainside, embedding themselves in Flora's mind.

She worked quietly with the other healers, Delyth not too far away from her. They mixed medicines and packed poultices, using the army's stores of herbs.

Since that afternoon, she had kept to herself, stopping only long enough to quench her own thirst. And every time she drank from the small metal bowl in her satchel, the more confident she felt in her mixtures, the words she spoke as she mixed and applied them rolling off her tongue before she could even think them.

As the moon rose, the wounded were loaded into wagons. The draft animals were laden down with the equipment that had been in the wagons, and the army looked, for all intents and purposes, to be moving out.

She held the hand of a nearly unconscious boy who couldn't have been more than eighteen. His long black hair had escaped from a simple braid at the nape of his neck, clinging to his sallow cheeks. More tired young men came to load him onto a simple canvas stretcher, and he clung to her, mumbling something incoherent. Not knowing what else to do, she gently patted his hand before lightly disengaging his fingers so he could be lifted away. She stood, exhausted, and pressed the back of her hand to her head.

Her head ached with the long hours she had spent with no food. Her morning meal had been little more than berries and some small eggs Iain had produced from one of his early excursions for food. The days did seem to be getting shorter, but she also wasn't used to the long hours she was putting in, and the headaches were probably more a warning she should eat more than anything else.

"My lady?"

She swiveled to the left to find the captain staring at her.

The movement was enough to make her a little lightheaded, and she smiled wanly at him. "Captain," she said warmly. "What is your name? If we're going to keep running into each other, I do think we should at least pretend at the pleasantries, don't you?" She didn't think she sounded much like herself. That was happening more and more.

He took a step closer and gave a bow. "Evan Griffith, but everyone just calls me Griffith, my lady."

She gave a silly little curtsy. "A pleasure."

"The general wishes your presence."

"Hmm, well, he is in luck, then, isn't he? Because I wish to give it to him."

She slid her arm around the captain's, allowing him to escort her to the same place he had shown her that morning. The tents had been broken down, and a bevy of soldiers were busily packing things into small trunks. Owen stood in the middle of it all, hands on hips, head thrown back, looking at the stars. Well, she assumed that's what he was doing. Not many stars could likely be seen with the clouds slowly rolling in.

She released the captain and went to stand at the general's side.

"Owen?"

She immediately recognized her mistake. His head snapped toward her and his whole body went rigid. "How did you…?" His voice was barely above a whisper.

She pretended to laugh it off. "Oh, you know…witch."

Something about his expression told her he wasn't entirely sure the title was true, but he relaxed a little.

"You wished to see me?"

"Yes. We're moving out. It's not ideal, but…" He trailed off.

"You don't want to wait around in case the other one comes back?"

"Right. I would also like to thank you, again. Not only for saving us, but for"—he held out his hand to indicate the camp—"helping with the wounded."

"You don't need to—"

"And I would like to extend the protection of our army to you on your travels. As far as Caer Annwn, anyway."

She gave him a tight-lipped smile. "I very much appreciate that. In fact, Annwn was my destination."

He frowned. "It *was*?"

She nodded, and then looked around. When she saw no sign of Iain or Eve lurking in the shadows, she leaned into him. "My destination was actually *you*," she murmured .

"Me?" He guffawed. "What could an ambassador from the North and a *witch* possibly want with me?"

She swallowed. He wasn't anything like the Owen she had known for those few days. He might sound like him, might look like him, but he had an angry edge, a brutality about him, she wasn't sure she liked.

"I was told you were imprisoned in Annwn," she finally said. "I was coming to rescue you."

He stared at her for a long moment. "Right. Well, as you can see, you were misinformed."

"I suppose I was," she murmured, more for her own benefit than for his. It was then it all sank in; again, she was an unwanted player in a game she thought she was meant to play. Taking a risk—even one she hadn't exactly meant to take—didn't change her fate. "I would still like to accompany you back to Annwn. If you don't mind."

He held up his hands. “The offer still stands. I hope you don’t mind walking. The horses are needed for the supplies.”

He turned from her, dismissing her, and her cheeks grew hot with embarrassment. She wasn’t sure what she had expected, but it wasn’t for him to think she was crazy or to laugh at her. A part of her had honestly thought he would be grateful she had come, that they would leave this place, together. As she tended to the wounded, more than once she had imagined they would escape together into the night, and he would know how to get them home, back to reality. What she thought was reality, anyway. She wasn’t really sure what was real and what wasn’t, anymore.

Anger finally bubbled to the surface. Anger that she had no control—had she *ever* really had control? From the moment the mystery woman had walked into her shop, the control over her life she had finally wrested had become nonexistent. She was done with it.

She strode after him. He was just beyond the light of the nearest torch, locking the last of a group of small chests that would be loaded for the journey.

“Owen.”

He turned just as she pressed herself to him, standing on her toes so her mouth could meet his as she pulled his head down to her. He didn’t seem as tall as she remembered.

He opened his mouth to protest, and she kissed him with all of the passion she could conjure up. She thought of the night they had spent together, wrapped around each other, panting and sweating and wild. Just the thought of his hands—those hands had made her skin crackle with electricity—so close to her had her pushing herself more tightly against him.

His breastplate pressed into her chest, her silk tunic and suede jerkin little protection against the cold metal. Her hands were in his hair and it felt shorter. Softer. There wasn't enough there for her to really push her fingers through. And his face was badly in need of a shave. The faint stubble there was not old enough to be soft—perhaps only a day's growth. Had he missed his morning shave due to the events of earlier in the day? It didn't matter, the rasping against her cheek made him feel all the more real to her.

And he tasted the same. So much of his was different, but this…this was the same.

She kissed him for only a handful of seconds, but all of those feelings and thoughts rushed through her mind, and then she pulled away. She looked into his eyes just long enough to see something other than the anger and the hardness she had seen there before. She wasn't sure what it was she saw there, confusion, yes, but there was something else, and it was enough.

Flora turned and slowly walked back to what was left of the camp, forcing herself not to run, knowing he stared after her. She searched out Delyth, and vowed from that moment forward, the game would belong to her.

Chapter 11

"You keep the company of an elf?"

"Mm?" Flora looked up at Captain Griffith. She had heard him ask a question, but her mind was so fuzzy from lack of sleep, she hadn't really comprehended it.

"Your servant."

"Servant? I don't have a servant."

"The elven girl who travels with you?" he explained.

"She's just a friend," Flora said around a yawn.

"You can be friends with an elf?"

"She says she is Ellyll," she said this off-handedly.

"Isn't it the same thing?"

"I don't know. I suppose?" Flora made a mental note to ask Delyth if it really was.

"Aren't you afraid she'll curse you?" The last was said in a whisper.

Flora turned to look up at the captain. She and Delyth had been walking with him and his troops, most of whom were piled into wagons, moaning with every bump and rut in the road. She knew he would have sought her out at his commander's insistence, anyway. It just seemed easier to seek him out herself.

"Didn't you know I'm a witch?" She was really beginning to enjoy the title. She waited to see his reaction, but the lack of one left her disappointed.

"Witches heal. They help. Usually. Elves…they can't be trusted. They're tricksters."

"Delyth has been nothing but helpful to me."

"Are you sure?"

She sighed. There really was no point in arguing. She decided to change the subject, instead. "May I ask you a question?"

He looked down at her. "I suppose."

"What were you doing in the valley? Why was a massive army just camped out, ready to be destroyed by a pair of dragons?" It was something she couldn't quite figure out—what they had been doing there in the first place.

"It was only for the night. It takes a lot of time to move an army of this size across the mountains." He shifted his gaze down to her, clearly feeling as if he was explaining troop movements and logistics to a primary school student.

"I don't understand. Why were you 'out' in the first place?"

"The battle."

"The battle?"

"Aye. The Battle of the Ford." A matter-of-fact answer. As if she should have known.

She frowned. "How long ago was the battle?"

She was met with another of those peculiar looks everyone kept giving her. "Right," she muttered, wondering if these people even had a standard of time. "It's just that, well… We came down the river, you see—" She was supposed to be from the North, right? "And we saw no sign of the battle having been fought."

He nodded sagely. "Yes, well, our retreat is not what it is for the other side." There was a sense of pride in his words, as though being large and slow and clumsy were causes for admiration.

She wondered what the bloody hell he meant by that and added it to the giant list of things to which she needed answers.

****

Caer Annwn clung to the side of a mountain, shrouded in mist and shadow. It was a low keep, a dark, sprawling fortress that was nothing like the white spires of the Summer and Spring Kingdom's court. It looked cold and dark and damp, its backdrop a watery tableau of the coming winter.

Guards stood atop the walls, looking out at the long line of the army behind their dark metal helmets. Arrow slits decorated the square towers erected on either side of the drawbridge, a worn and ancient portcullis closing off the entrance. As they approached, it was lifted, chains clanking and rust grinding against stone.

The walls of the castle had to be twenty feet thick, the stones that pieced it together almost as wide as she was tall. They marched through a shadowed tunnel and were led into the outer bailey, their boots becoming heavy with caked, wet mud. It sucked at her heels and toes. The majority continued around to the barracks and hospital. Flora intended to follow, melting into the mass with the excuse of helping the wounded, but Captain Griffith—Evan—was right at her heels, steering her toward the inner bailey and the keep within its walls.

Other officers followed their commander farther into the fortress, his deep red cloak the only splash of color in an otherwise gloomy environment. She couldn't keep her gaze from his golden head. As they marched up the stone steps into the main hall, Iain and

Eve appeared beside her. It was the first she had seen of them since they had left the charred camp, and she wasn't particularly happy to see the pair.

The main hall was just as dark as she expected it to be, the only light coming from torches mounted on the dark walls. It was decorated much like the hunting lodges of the highlands, antlers on nearly every inch of available wall space. Carved into the stone were the likenesses of large hounds with long, thin bodies, slender, yet powerful legs, and pointed ears. A small throne sat at the far end, flanked by thick candles dripping wax onto the stone beneath them. As she approached, the officers fanned out, standing to the sides of the great room, their backs to the walls, legs apart, and hands clenched tightly at their sides. Even Griffith abandoned her side to take his place.

She halted a few feet back from Owen, uncomfortable and unsure of what to do with herself, but damned if she would let anyone see it. She squared her shoulders, tilted her chin up, and wished she had been given a chance to change into something that wasn't splattered with mud, dusted with dirt, and smelled like she had been wearing it for over a week. Which she couldn't tell was an understatement or an overstatement—how long *had* they been traveling? She wasn't sure.

Everyone stood quietly, like statues. And stood. And stood. She was strongly considering just laying down on the cold floor and taking a nap when an elderly man shuffled in to stand before the commander.

"General, I am afraid you have arrived at a most unfortunate time," he half croaked. "His Worship, Highest Arawn is hunting with the hounds."

Flora was surprised—she thought the old man was the lord of the castle. She could see by the set of his shoulders Owen was displeased.

"I cannot ask the men to wait," he told the old man. "We have been traveling through the nights to make it here with the wounded and dead. I am releasing them to the barracks."

The old man gave a nod, though his disapproval was as obvious as Owen's, who raised his right hand, index finger straight up, and turned the hand in a circle. The officers relaxed somewhat and filed out of the hall.

Even more unsure of herself, Flora stood rooted, staring Owen down in hopes of receiving some direction. Hopefully to a chair. Or a bed.

"Come with me," he told her.

She followed him back out of the great hall, Iain and Eve at her heels. She hadn't seen Delyth enter with them, and so she hoped the woman had gone with the healers. It was what she would expect of her, anyway.

They walked through a narrow corridor, down an even narrower stairway, the only sound that of their footsteps. The staircase led outside, and she found the sun was beginning to set. They passed through the bailey and back inside, up some more stairs. Owen opened a large door, holding it wide for her. As soon as she saw it was merely a room, she closed the door in Eve's face. She knew the other woman and Iain would be listening on the other side, but she preferred to pretend they weren't.

With one eyebrow quirked, Owen looked at her She stared back. He blinked, and then pulled off his gloves and bracers, tossing them on what she assumed was his bed.

The room was sparsely decorated. The bed had a red coverlet, but the foot of the bed was covered with at least three furs. A small table stood next to the bed, a book lying next to a lit candle. She figured someone must have readied the room for him when they arrived, but nothing else seemed terribly in need of readying. No food waited, no bottle of wine or fresh bathwater. It was odd, but she decided not to question it.

Yet.

He tossed the red, fur-lined cloak on the bed, but flinched with the movement. Only then did she remember his injury. He had hidden it well. She wasn't sure for whose benefit, but she had certainly forgotten.

"Here, let me…" she murmured, taking his arm. She pushed up the sleeve of his tunic, creased from being under his leather bracer, and looked at the hastily wrapped bandage.

"It's fine," he said, pulling his arm away and turning from her.

She dug out the herb book from her satchel, took a few of the leaves she had pressed into it. "Well, if it's bothering you, crush these up into a little boiling water. Just enough to make a paste. Then spread it over the wound." She laid the leaves on top of the book.

He gave her another look as if he were trying to figure out where she had left her mind, and then fell into a chair next to a wide wooden desk opposite the bed.

She indicated the room with her hand. "Why did you bring me here?" she inquired.

"Until made otherwise, you are *my* guest. I have nowhere else to bring you while we wait, and so I brought you here."

"Rather forward of you, don't you think?" She lifted her shoulder and fluttered her lashes coyly.

He blushed. Actually blushed. And then stammered, "No, that's not…" He stood. "I'll have your guards come in."

"No, no, I was just…" She bowed her head, then looked back up. "I'm sorry, I made it awkward. Perhaps we can start again?"

He frowned at her.

She decided to take his silence as a yes and held out her hand. "I'm Flora."

He looked at her hand, then back up at her face. "Yes, you've said."

She let her hand drop and sighed. She didn't really know what to do. He was right; he didn't exactly need rescuing. And she wasn't really sure how she was supposed to get him to leave with her. Or, for that matter, how she was supposed to get home.

"So…" she said, wanting to fill the silence with anything but her own thoughts.

He raised his eyebrows.

Ugh, could the man be any less vocal? "How did you become bait for a pair of dragons?" she asked.

He frowned, which she was starting to think was his natural state. "Why does it interest you?"

"Why wouldn't it interest me? There were two dragons!"

"Yes, well…" He trailed off, looking at some inconspicuous spot on the stone floor. "We *had* been baiting them. To use for training the new recruits. Someone didn't do his job and brought some of the leftover bait into camp. The dragons came to retrieve the bait, some overzealous fool thought he could fell them himself, and there you have it. Half an army decimated."

She sank down onto his bed. It wasn't very soft. "What happened to him?"

"Who?"

"The 'overzealous fool.'"

"Early morning meal."

Flora swallowed. "How… How many did you lose?"

He looked up at her, as if he wasn't sure he wanted to answer, as if he questioned her reason for asking. "Three hundred last count."

"And the wounded?"

"At least twice that." A few heartbeats of silence passed between them. "It would have been more if it hadn't been for you."

She smiled, not knowing what to say.

"You could very easily have been part of their early morning meal. Don't do that again," he admonished.

"Aye, aye, sir," she muttered sarcastically.

Silence passed between them for some time, he staring at her, she pretending she didn't see. When the knock on the door came, Flora jumped, startled at the sound since there had been so little.

Owen stood, taking three long strides to the door and pulled it open. Some words were exchanged between him and whomever was on the other side, and when he turned back to her, all he said was, "He's returned."

****

Arawn was not what she had expected.

He was young, at least in appearance. She would put him around her own age. His skin was unmarked and he had bright blue eyes and black hair. He had a twinkle in his eye that seemed almost insincere, and a mouth predisposed to smile. His beard was trimmed, his hair curled around his ears and collar and the crown on his head was a circle of small antlers. Yards of red fabric trimmed in gold swirled around him as he lounged on his throne. He held a golden goblet in one hand, twirling the short stem between two fingers.

Flora entered the throne room behind Owen, dressed in the silver gown she had been given at Caer Hafgan. It was an oddly versatile gown she had found as she attempted to dress herself. Eve had slipped into the commander's quarters after he had left Flora to change, but rather than coming to Flora's assistance, she had shuffled through the paperwork on his desk, annoyed grunts and sighs coming from her throat as she found nothing of substance.

Flora was left to conquer the odd arrangement of clasps and laces and belts on her own. It was only after angrily stomping her feet, ripping the bloody thing off, and throwing it on the floor did the other woman bother to help.

The silver dress was wrapped around her, and then the bodice was brought up to clasp at her shoulders. Eve then quickly wove the royal-blue sash around her midsection, did some fiddling behind her back, and then turned her to the old, dusty mirror positioned in the corner.

She had never felt so divine as she did in the dress. The skirt fell perfectly to the floor, a small train pooling behind her. The blue sash was wide, pulling in her waist and falling from the small of her back to add to the train. The sleeves, which had given her so much trouble, could be clasped at the front with delicate silver broaches to create the beautiful bell sleeves she imagined Guinevere might have worn, or they could be opened to fasten at her back into a cape. She wore them closed because of the cold, but she was particularly intrigued by the versatility.

The shoes Eve had packed for her were the same deep blue, but little more than satin slippers with a light leather sole that reminded her of ballet shoes. She wouldn't be going far in them, and probably not too quickly, either.

When she emerged, it was to a freshly dressed and shaved commander. He still wore the same fur-lined mantle he had worn before, but the breastplate had been discarded. A rich red tunic lay against his chest in its place, rich with gold embroidery. His trousers were a dark leather, not black, but not brown, either, perhaps made of buckskin. An ornamental sword was at his side, held by a thick leather belt etched with an odd array of symbols that looked somewhat like dancing deer.

He looked her up and down before turning on his booted heel and stomping back up to the great hall, leaving Flora to scurry behind him in the ridiculously delicate shoes.

The great hall was awash with firelight. The two large fireplaces were blazing, and torches decorated the stone walls. She recognized the officers who stood at attention, along the edges of the room. Others were there, too, curious onlookers who wore all manner of finery. As she discreetly studied their faces, she saw most were ageless, their youth or lack thereof a mystery to the naked eye.

Owen bowed before the youthful ruler.

"Llewellyn tells me you came back with only half an army, Commander," Arawn called down from the dais in a singsong voice, almost as though he didn't take the whole matter very seriously.

Owen straightened. "You would have no army, Excellency, if it had not been for this woman."

He took a step to the left and held out his right hand to indicate Flora move forward. She took a step forward and executed her best curtsy, which, she had to admit, was still pretty awful.

"Llewellyn did mention my new general returned with a guest. A witch, are you?" He looked her eagerly up and down.

"That's what I've been told." She was surprised at the fake assurance that rang through her voice. It reminded her of her old self, the one who knew exactly what was expected and what she had to do to carry it out. Since leaving Robert, she had tried so hard to discover herself rather than the person she had been playing at all those years. But standing there before someone she didn't know, someone who, presumably, was very powerful, she realized she would be smart to give them exactly what they expected. Eve, Iain, all of them. She gave Arawn the bored smile she had perfected well before she sat for her A-Levels.

He grinned. "I always wanted a witch," he said, like a child who had been given a toy he had been coveting.

She shrugged. "And I always wanted a pet kelpie," she said not without sarcasm.

He pursed his lips, seriously considering her statement, not taking it as the joke she had meant it to be. "I'm afraid those are extremely rare and not native to this stretch of the Otherworld," he said. "Would a griffon suffice?"

It took her a moment to realize he was *actually* haggling with her. "I am open to negotiations."

He clapped his hands together. "Aha! Tonight, we celebrate. Tomorrow, we negotiate!" He gave a wide grin that said he was pleased with his little rhyme. He stood, arms outstretched. "Come, let us feast on the stags my hounds felled and drink to the new harvest!"

The doors flew open. Large wooden tables and benches were carried into the great hall.

Arawn beckoned her closer, and she stood next to him as another large wooden table was placed where his throne had been on the dais. A chair was brought for her, and she sat, suddenly feeling her nerves catch up to her. She stamped them back down and told herself this was her job, at least for now. She had always been good at her jobs, and this would be no different.

Goblets, golden pitchers, and large loaves of bread were placed before them. Someone to her right filled her goblet, and when she turned, saw it was Owen next to her. She smiled her thanks but kept her hands in her lap, waiting to see what the others did.

After Arawn had sipped from his own vessel, the others did the same, and she followed suit. The drink was odd, unlike anything she had tasted before. It was like an ale, but mixed with mead and spices. She couldn't decide what she thought of it. She must have made a face, for Owen leaned over and whispered, "Bragawd," close to her ear.

“Pardon me?”

“Bragawd.” He nodded to her goblet. “It’s a…favorite in these parts.”

“Oh.”

He suddenly looked uncomfortable, as if he regretted having said anything. He turned his attention to his own goblet, his right hand wrapped around its thick, short stem.

Chapter 12

She was given her own chambers inside the castle, and the two large rooms were to house her and her "servants." The smaller of the two was actually her bedchamber, which was dominated by a large, square canopied bed with crimson bed curtains and gold damask bedclothes. A large stone basin that looked remarkably like a tub was in one corner, and a wardrobe stood in the other. It was about the same size as the room she had been given in Hafgan's palace, yet this one felt cozier, less light and airy. The other room was twice a big with cabinets and tables lining the walls. The seneschal told her to make a list of any supplies she would need, and they would be provided. She had nodded while she mentally started a list of all the things she thought a "witch" might need.

Delyth had been sent for, but Iain and Eve stood at the entrance to her chambers, Eve looking uncomfortable. Iain just stood emotionless as he usually did, hood pulled halfway down his face. She wondered why he hid his features; for whose benefit?

Delyth arrived, and the two women cloistered together in Flora's bedchamber, door closed between them and the two guards.

"Why doesn't he remember me?" she asked the Ellyll woman.

"He must have been given the Drink of Oblivion." She says this matter-of-factly.

"And what is that?" Flora demanded on a loud whisper.

"Just that. A drink that removes one's memories."

The pit that had been growing in Flora's stomach widened, threatening to swallow her whole. The odd, fluttering feeling that came with anxiety washed over her and she suddenly had the urge to pace.

"Can it be reversed?" she demanded, desperation tingeing her words

"Not that I am aware," Delyth said with no small amount of remorse.

Flora fell onto the bed and let out a heavy sigh. "Well, what else can you tell me of this place? What of Arawn? Why does he seem uninterested in the fact that half of his army is dead?"

"Because he knows there are more soldiers." She shrugged, clearly unconcerned with the prospect of half an army being decimated by flying lizard demons.

"He has a limitless supply of men?" Flora scoffed.

"Yes." Her voice was clipped. She clearly felt she was talking to a moron.

Flora frowned. "How is that even possible?"

"You really have no idea where we are, do you?" Delyth regarded her with something akin to resignation. Clearly, she had not known she was taking on such a hopeless case.

"That's what I've been saying!" Flora was beyond frustrated, feeling her own ignorance was drowning her. It pulled at her, its hands sweeping over her head, forcing her to flail about irrationally, looking for any sort of purchase that would allow her to pull herself up.

"This side of the veil, what we call the Otherworld, it is more than just the land of the gods. Nestled here, between the rounded mountain ranges, are the lands where your dead settle. Where they know peace and prosperity and protection for a time before they choose to cross over for another chance at life. Some of us, like the Fae, the Ellyll and True Believers, have and will always live on this side of the veil, never to cross over to the other side. But others cross over in death."

"You mean I'm dead? Owen is *dead*?" The panic attack that had been rumbling underneath threatened to awaken and consume her. Her eyes grew wide and wild, and her hands were in her hair, fingers pressing down on her scalp, soothing the ache even as it was building.

"No, you were allowed to cross through the veil. You came through willingly, using a key, I assume?" She looked at Flora expectantly, but went on when she was met with only a blank stare. "Though rare, no, I do not think you are dead. And I believe the same is true of the general even if his energy feels…different. But the others? The soldiers? They cross the veil to Hafgan's kingdom. They drink of his honeyed wines, they dance, they enjoy their time… And then they fight the darker days. They struggle to keep the warmth and the light, but eventually give way to Annwn's long nights. Arawn takes them, then. Welcomes them with the great feast, asks that they fight to bring the next group through, and then send them back to your world."

"Send them back? Like what? Reincarnation?"

"Exactly."

"But what about Owen? And me? How do we get back?"

"That I don't know."

Flora rubbed her hands over her face. She was exhausted, and she knew her mind was pretty much overwhelmed as it was. "In the morning, the farce continues. Do I have your help?"

"Of course," Delyth said simply, offering her a pleasant smile.

Flora didn't move from her spot, after Delyth left her. Flora simply hugged herself, her eyes seeing only the lavish tableau of her imagination, of death and blood. Feeling the weight of all the information bearing down, she fell back onto the bed, and curled up to one side, making herself as small as possible. She still wore her silver-and-blue gown, its folds enveloping her like a blanket. She knew she should take it off, but she just didn't have the energy for it anymore.

****

Despite her exhaustion, Flora awoke before the sun rose. She didn't know how long she had lain there, staring at the shadows on the wall before drifting off to sleep, but it had seemed like hours. She had not changed position once in the night, and despite the ache that had set into her shoulder, she lay there for what could have been hours, could have been minutes, finally sitting upright when the sound of voices drifted up from below her window.

She stretched, relieving the uncomfortable twinges, swung her feet down to the floor, and padded across the cold stone to a small, diamond-paned oriel window, and pushed it open. The crisp autumn air slapped her in the face, waking her up fully. Below, the soldiers and officers trickled into the courtyard, milling about in loose formations. They all wore identical uniforms.

Their training clothes, she thought to herself, tight pants, boots, and black tunics. She folded her arms on the sill, resting her chin atop them, and watched the scene below.

They were too far below her for her to make out any of the conversation, but she was fascinated by the goings-on. The archers clumped together at one end, the soldiers in possession of large broadswords surveyed the rest almost regally. Flora wondered how many more there would be if the other day hadn't happened.

Suddenly, the chatter stopped and the soldiers quickly moved into lines, their backs to her, an officer at their front. Her eyes swept the scene below her until she saw Owen striding toward them. He looked…stony. Emotionless. He looked fearsome.

He came to stand in the center, his hand on the sword hanging at his side. And then his gaze met hers

She shuddered, but she told herself it was a shiver from the cold. He looked away, as if dismissing her, and barked out a series of orders.

Flora backed away from the window and closed it. She had plenty to do herself, and admiring the commander was not one of them.

She opened the door separating her bedchamber from the other anterior room. It was thick and heavy, its hinges protesting when she pulled it too far open. Eve stirred at the sound but didn't move. Delyth was nowhere to be seen. Iain was already up, sitting in a corner, head bent as he cleaned one of his blades. Flora wondered if she had ever seen his entire face in the light. She wasn't sure she would recognize him, but then wondered if the attempt at anonymity was on purpose. And whose benefit it was for.

"Could you have some water for a bath brought up?" she asked him quietly.

He gave a curt nod, stood, and slipped almost silently from the room. She supposed it was rather presumptuous of her to use him as her personal lady's maid. His skills were obviously not in the realm of domestic services, though he gave no protest. Come to think of it, he really said very little at all.

Flora waited in her chamber, perched on the side of the bed, half wanting to curl back under the covers, half wanting to return to the window and the scene below, but refusing to do either. When Iain returned with a pair of servants carrying steaming water kettles, she hastily stood.

It was only then she realized she was still wearing the silver gown, and heat flooded her face. She hoped none of the servants thought she had been doing anything untoward.

The water was poured into the stone bath, and she thanked the two women before they left the room. Iain pulled the door closed, murmuring, "I'll wake Eve." He made no mention of Delyth, and Flora wondered if he knew where she was. Or if he even cared.

Flora struggled out of the gown as quickly as she could, a task much easier than getting into the bloody thing, and then stepped into the hot water. She shivered, the water prickling her skin almost painfully, but she sank down in the tub anyway, closing her eyes and leaning back. It was so wonderful having warm, clean water. Bathing oneself in a stream had not been nearly as effective as a warm bath.

She washed quickly, a combination of having few bathing accessories and the desire to just *get on with it*.

By the time she had emerged from the still-warm water and dressed, Eve was up, and Delyth had returned to the room. Eve looked bored and Delyth had pulled out some vellum, ink, and a quill. Flora lifted her satchel onto the wide table in the middle of the room, and spread its contents out. The wheel pendant rested atop her tunic, and she had lost one of the knives, but the bowl, the other jewelry, the encyclopedia, the book of magic, the journal, and the sketchbook were there.

She hadn't really looked through any of them save the encyclopedia. Eve was watching, and she was still loath to let Delyth know exactly how much she didn't know or understand, though she figured her ignorance was becoming more glaringly obvious with each passing day.

Even closed, the encyclopedia fanned out, refusing to lay flat. Between its pages, she had stuffed dozens of samples, flowers, leaves, a piece of bark here, a scraggly root there. "I need something to store all of these in," she said to Delyth.

The other woman dipped the end of a quill in dark ink and made a note.

"A mortar and pestle. A slab of marble. Candles, not tapers, small ones. Where's the hearth?" She looked around the room.

"There." Delyth pointed to a darkened corner. The hearth was little more than a dip in the stone floor, a stone hood over it.

"A cauldron. And a decent supply of wood. Matches." She noticed she was ticking off the items on her fingers, keeping mental track of what she would need.

"Matches?"

“Yes, to start a fire.”

“Flint,” Delyth supplied.

“Fine, whatever.” She waved the suggestion off before she lost her place in the growing mental list.

They continued like that, Flora making notes aloud, Delyth writing them down. Eve lazily sharpened her sword in the corner. The sound of steel on whetstone became a rhythm, like a beating heart, and it began to grate on Flora’s nerves.

“Why don’t you go train with the other soldiers?” she asked.

“Why would I do that?” Eve didn’t even bother looking at her.

“Because you’re clearly bored and that sound is annoying me.”

Eve didn’t reply.

“Fine. Be bored.” Flora looked desperately for something—anything—to occupy her mind over the metallic ring of Eve’s sword.

She picked up the journal. She hadn’t spent much time with it, mostly due to the fact that all of the daylight hours had been spent wandering across a vast landscape. The encyclopedia had been easier to skim through and had at least allowed her to exercise her mind in a sort of game. Match the plant to the drawing or description.

But the journal was more a mystery. She had flipped through it before, then tossing it aside because the light was too poor or her mind was running in a thousand different directions. It hadn’t appeared particularly interesting, anyway, and she likened it to the journal she had kept in her early teen years. Surely the mystery woman—whom she now suspected was

Arianrhod—had given it to her for a reason. "Choose your weapons," she had said.

There was something in there she needed. It would help. Of that she was sure.

And so, she began to read.

I was supposed to die on that sixteenth day of April, on that damned muir. I had taken one musket ball to the leg, and the pain is something I will never forget. It burned hotter than a hand to the fire, and it felt like death. I was in far too much pain to notice the suffering of my soldiers or our allies who lay writhing on the ground. I was in so much pain I was unaware that Cumberland's men were picking through the wounded and finishing them off rather than allowing us a chance to return home to our wives and children and mothers to recover. To fight another day.

It was a tactical move. One I don't blame them for. We are fiercest when we have something to fight for, but men are not in unlimited supply.

They would have been on me in a matter of moments, putting me out of my misery if it hadn't been for her. There was so much blood and it was pouring out faster than wine from the bottle. They may have been a mercy. A far greater mercy than she.

She came to me, through the pain, the most beautiful creature I had ever seen, with her raven hair and alabaster skin. She told me she could make it all disappear: the pain, the coming death, the agony of defeat. She told me all I had to do was take a drink and I would see my beloved once more. It was all the encouragement I needed. To see my Ailsa, one more time. To feel the brush of her hand, see the smile of her lips. If I could but tell her of my love and my regret.

I will never know if she bewitched me in those moments or if I was in too much pain to truly understand what I was agreeing to, and so I pledged myself then and there. I gave her my oath, and she took me from that blood-soaked field into the Otherworld.

I had heard the tales, mostly from the servants and the village children, when I came to Carlisle. They are superstitious folk, the Scots. Fables of mystical creatures and fairy folk who would creep from the cairns and across the moors abound. But I was raised by a Godly parent, taught to confess and repent. This Otherworld is something I never could have imagined in my first life. I was awed by it all, and proud that I had been the chosen of a goddess, not knowing I was simply one of many, cherished not for myself but for some minor skill I possessed.

I gave myself to her fully at first, forgetting everything that had sent me to Drumossie Moor and everything that should have kept me away from her. She took as gladly as I gave. The only thing I received in return was a clean mind and a second chance at life.

I have no recollection of the time that has passed since she saved me from the executioner's shot on that sixteenth day of April. Only that I was a fool, and I will find a way to escape this prison in which I have placed myself.

Flora felt her skin prickle. Every Scottish child, especially those around Inverness, knew what happened on April 16. They knew Drumossie Moor was now called Culloden. And they knew Lord Cumberland had massacred some of their ancestors on those fields, among the tall grasses and the heather, under a sky stretched out into forever. They knew—she knew—

1746 was a death sentence to many Highlanders and their way of life, whether it came at the end of a musket barrel or through the laws punishing them for the uprising.

Carlisle was a name she recognized, but history had never been her favorite subject. She knew there was something of significance there, and she pressed her fingertip to the name, hoping it would come to her. It tickled the edge of her mind, but when she moved to capture it, it flittered away like a butterfly.

She sighed inwardly. It sounded like the author of this journal had been given a second chance. He was supposed to be dead. He should have been dead. But a mysterious woman with black hair had saved him.

Delyth had called mortal walkers of the Otherworld rare. So, others had come before her. But how many? And did they ever cross back? How? Flora wondered if the same mysterious woman showed up in small shops beckoning divorcées to go on grand adventures. She was pretty sure she knew the answer to that. The questions swirled, twirled, toyed with her. Something of significance was in this journal. She just needed to dig it up.

I find that by writing down my thoughts, I am better able to remember them. If I document the days, I know how long I have been here. I still do not truly believe that time works the same way here as it does on the other side. The days seem longer, as if they will never end sometimes. But marking every sunrise has helped to ground me.

It never helps to count my own sleep. At first, this was my strategy. I would lay myself down to a darkened sky, but wake up to one after a restful sleep. I would be unable to keep myself from my bed when the sun was still high. The movements of the tides and the changing of the seasons make little sense. I have watched. I have tried to understand, and yet that understanding never comes.

Instead, events are the timekeepers of this world I have learned to converse with others here in their own way, never speaking of fortnights or days, but of things that have happened: Meals, storms, battles of the Ford.

And so, the sun is the only teller of time in the way I understand it. I track it across the horizon, marking each instance it peaks in the sky. And yet, I find it difficult to fully comprehend a day or a night.

She seems to be able to slip through the veil whenever it pleases her. I have been watching. She will be there one moment and gone the next, like a flame blown out by the wind. I can still catch a whiff of her scent after she had gone, proof that she was there at all. Her fragrance is faint, but distinctive, like wood smoke and the dampness of autumn. Most ladies bask in the perfume of flowers, but she smells of battle.

I know that she goes back to the other side, for each time she leaves, she returns with another of us, men who have been forced to take up the sword of the musket, to fight. I don't know why she is drawn to us, or why she collects us as she does, but the very thought of myself acting like the others, like a lovesick puppy, causes me to lose my appetite. They trail after her, begging to please her, to earn her respect, or worse, her attention. I loved... I love my wife, but ours was a rare partnership. Our marriage was built on respect. My Ailsa made me see her as a person, not unlike me. But that respect is not something shared here.

The more disenchanted I become with her, the more I remember the life I left. Memories of Elizabeth, my Ailsa, haunt me. I know that I would have lost that life whether I had pledged myself or not. Cumberland's men would have seen my breath snuffed and my body in a cold hole, if not worse. But the memories have me mourning what I have lost.

I think, nay, I know that if I can make it across the veil, I can beg for Elizabeth's forgiveness. And I know, without pause, that she will grant it.

Flora skimmed through his description of Elizabeth, his wife. Sometimes he referred to her by her Christian name, Elizabeth, but more often than not, "my Ailsa," as if he were whispering her name reverently. Was it a pet name? The way he droned on and on about her every virtue was enough to make Flora roll her eyes. The woman was as beautiful as she was clever, as witty as she was modest. Her hair was as silk, her skin the color of milk. It was almost worse than a romance novel, and not one of the good ones where something actually happens, but the predictable ones about the men who fall instantly in love with the next door neighbor but couldn't have her because he had just been widowed and left with quadruplet infants.

She yawned through it, flipping through page after page of his remorseful ways, how he wished he had done things different, how he lived to be reunited with her. Very dull, indeed.

I accompanied her to the Solstice Kingdoms as her personal guard. What should have been an honor was more a headache. I was nothing more than a decoration, someone she could show off to Kings Hafgan and Arawn. Both are enchanted with her, as all men seem to be, but they see only her beautiful face and not her devious mind.

The dead dwell in the Solstice Kingdoms, though their forms are not as I expected. I expected to find gruesome darkness, decay, wreckage. I had given up my notions of brimstone and golden light as the afterlife waiting for us mortals, but still, what I found still has me marveling.

The dead know everything of their prior existence. Yet, they live in the Otherworld as if it is their only life, their one life, but knowing someday they will move on to new things. They come to it by way of the Summer Kingdom, given a place that reflects their worldly life. A baker is a baker. A noble a noble. They idle their time happily in a lush, prosperous reflection of life, falling in love, forming bonds. Eventually they become bored with the perfection of the Summer Kingdom, they wish for more, and they venture to the Ford. As the summer king gathered his army of adventurers, I followed at a safe distance and watched from afar as those people fought for a death that would lead them on.

In the Winter Kingdom, they begin anew, once more. They ally themselves with the winter king, Arawn, promising to fight with him once more in exchange for rich feasts and the grandest adventure they can imagine—a new life, beginning to end, on the other side of the veil. They fight against Spring's coming, all while hoping they will be released from the Otherworld. And as their Otherworld's lifeblood spills into the river, they slip back across the veil.

There are plenty of us who did not die to come here, but were brought to the land of the gods in our earthly bodies. I know, for she collects us. We are aware of the life we left behind, though many of us allow ourselves to forget it, allowing the Drink of Oblivion to truly cleanse our minds. We serve our patron or patroness, never expecting to leave this place.

But there must be some way to escape it. For, with every lock, there is a key. I will find it.

Flora sat back, her heart pounding. Owen gave no indication he knew anything of the life he had. If travelers like she and this Alexander Carlisle knew of their existences in the Otherworld and the dead know themselves to be dead. Why would he be here, otherwise? What was he?

She swallowed, her hope building. If he were not dead, and the woman had promised her he was not, then there was a way. For every lock has a key.

She flipped the page, searching voraciously for the answers she was now certain Carlisle would give her.

I think she's grown suspicious of my intentions. The tasks she has been giving me keep me isolated or by her side—never do I see any others except at the dining table, and even there, she keeps me close. She treats me as a prized lapdog, and I can see the others growing jealous and concerned for their own place in her household.

But I think she has a new favorite. They speak often, and she asks him questions, something she has never asked of me. I am merely here for her pleasure, of that I am sure. But there is respect for this other man. I'm going to keep my eye on him.

****

I think I was wrong. The new one is not new at all.

I overheard them talking in the shadows, and it seems he was one of the first. Perhaps even the first.

She praised him for his past efforts, told him she had much respect for him, but that she has grown disenchanted with the inability of her most-trusted followers to complete even the simplest of tasks.

She threatened him, telling him to come back with Ailsa. She went into great detail about how she would gut him and leave his corpse for the crows, his soul destined for death, his memory forgotten forever.

Yet I hope—nay, I pray—that means she is sending him to the other side of the veil. I have to assume she is suspicious of me and hopes to keep me here. She knows that to do so, she must find my wife. For, I will never be content until I have her sleeping in my arms once more. I will be staying vigilant, watching his movement. And I will follow him to my love.

****

I've been following him since before the first light.

He spent three sunrises in her court, keeping much to himself. He says little to the others, instead keeping to the shadows and himself. I've yet to see his face, for he keeps it hidden, even in her company. She has never asked him to do otherwise.

My perusal of his movements has yet gone unnoticed. She continues to keep me close, but I know she is restless and bored with my silence. She preferred me when I wanted nothing more than to please her, when she could lock me away in her bedchamber like a concubine. Elizabeth's fire is enough to keep me burning for eternity. Still, I pine for her, and it's been a thousand noons since we have last touched.

He's stopped to break his fast while watching the sun rise. I've been keeping my distance and I don't think he's any the wiser that he's being followed. Even now, I sit in the shadows of the wood. We've been traveling west, I believe, which will make my task more difficult. I can't throw a shadow and have him notice me. He'll tell her. Of that, I am certain. So, I must allow him space and hope not to lose him.

****

I know how to get through the veil. I followed the other man until he came to a circle of stones, high in the hills, but overlooking the sea. There, he stood outside the circle and dropped his pack. He rummaged through it and began to undress, replacing his black uniform with something that appeared far more familiar to me, for when he was finished, he was wearing the dress of my own time. One of the things I have come to understand is that we here in the Otherworld are outside the usual time constraints. Here is a place that exists outside of time, and thus, those of us who inhabit it come from all time, not a simple linear point.

As new men, new soldiers, filter into her keep, they come bearing all manner of clothing. Some I recognize from paintings. Others are foreign to me, looking nothing like the proper dress of a gentleman or an officer.

And so, I do find it curious what he wore. Yet after he donned breeches, shirt, vest, and coat, he walked into the circle and it was as if the wind broke him apart and whisked him away like he was made of no more than grains of sand.

I waited to be sure he was, in fact, gone before I revealed myself. I looked through his pack, but there was nothing in it but the leather armor in which he had traveled.

If I am right, all I need to do is find my old clothes. I pray I can remember where I discarded them. And that they are still there.

The following pages were blank. There wasn't any more of the looping scrawl. More than a quarter of the cream pages ruffled along the edges, but otherwise untouched. A sense of loneliness filled her. She had begun to feel a special connection to Alexander Carlisle, one that went deeper than their shared heritage.

Flora didn't know if he had found a way through the veil or not. She wasn't sure she wanted to go there. She imagined this man as someone she could see as a friend, a real friend despite his flowery, lovesick prose for his wife. And knowing he could have come to a bad end wrenched at her heart.

She was sure his benefactress was the same woman who had brought her here—a goddess he had called her—though she didn't know if that were truth or mere speculation. She wished he had named her—was she Arianrhod? Cerridwen? Or someone else?

In search of answers, she had only found more questions. So, she needed to focus. Find and solve one problem at a time.

And one thing was for certain. She needed to find a stone circle.

Chapter 13

It occurred to Flora that she didn't know what had happened to those who had died in the Otherworld, until she had been told a feast day would take place in their honor. The commander himself sent an invitation with one of his aides, asking her to join him. She hadn't been sure if she was supposed to respond, but she sent him a reply, anyway, thanking him for the invitation and assuring him she would be present.

The morning of the ceremony, she found Captain Evan Griffith waiting outside her door, ready to escort her to the general. He was garbed in ceremonial armor: a shining breastplate, gauntlets, boots, with chain mail and a red mantle. His head was still shaved smooth, and thick eyebrows stood out against his tanned flesh. Flora wondered how heavy the armor was but figured it was probably inappropriate to ask, even though the captain was often good-natured and willing to converse.

Eve and Iain dressed in remarkably similar ceremonial armor, polished and shining in the torchlight. Eve's, of course, had a more feminine cut to it, and Iain still wore a hood half over his face, though Flora supposed the blue velvet at least made it appear to be a formal hood. Delyth's own cloak covered her from head to toe in a rich green, but Flora never saw what she wore beneath.

Flora had agonized over what to wear to a funeral in the afterlife for far longer than she would care to admit to herself. She tried on nearly every item in her meager wardrobe twice, asking the opinions of her three companions each time. After the evening meal, and before she could force a third modeling session upon them once more, Iain shoved a bundle of folded clothes at her.

The gown was like nothing she had seen. The sleeves were long, the bodice tight, and the outer skirt had very little volume to it. A metallic waist cincher hit just below her breasts and ended just at the top of her hips. And from her hips hung a strange sash, almost like a belt, a sporran hanging from it. The sporran was fur, but silver ornaments decorated its underside, tinkling when she moved. Matching fur encircled her wrists and lined the outer skirt, the silver underskirt peeking through when she walked. In the low light of the castle, she had thought the gown to be gray, but as she walked out into the light, she could see it was a lovely shade of blue, like a thunderhead.

They were met in the main hall by the commander, who offered her his arm. He was also dressed in what she imagined was his finest armor, shining and silvery with a hound etched into the breastplate. A fur mantle covered his shoulders, and beneath it a cerulean cape fell to just below the knee. It was very formal, he was an escort, nothing more. Even still, her heart pounded against her breast, a quick tattoo that engulfed her.

The rush of her pulse reminded her she was as nervous as she was fascinated. The only funeral she had ever attended had been for her mother's great-aunt, and Flora had been very young at the time. She remembered nothing more than the long service, her impossibly uncomfortable black dress, socks with lace cuffs that stuck out from her ankles. She vaguely recalled sitting on the hard wooden pew, swinging her legs back and forth, her patent leather shoes flashing while light illuminated the stained glass windows of the chapel. Her mother had put a perfectly manicured hand over hers, squeezing in an effort to get Flora to stop fidgeting.

She looked up at Owen, but he was staring straight ahead, back ramrod stiff, gaze far away. Then he seemed to mentally shake himself awake and look down at her. “Ready?” His voice was almost a croak. He cleared his throat and looked away.

But she gave a small smile and a nod in answer, and then they were walking out the great doors and into the gray, wintery light. The soldiers lined up there, facing the entrance, their armor gleaming. Owen led her through the path they had created and out through the gate. Her companions and the officers were behind them. The soldiers fell into step next, and then the rest of the castle inhabitants. They pressed on through the brown grass to a rarely traveled path, its winding curves leading into the hills.

There, beneath the thick, gray-blue clouds were the wagons that had carried the soldiers of Annwn home. They were empty, however, and the bodies, wrapped in muslin, were carefully laid out across seven large pyres.

Owen led her to stand before the center pyre, the others fanning out around them. Behind the castle folk came what appeared to be villagers, for they didn’t wear the army’s colors nor the uniform of the castle servants. They waited a few moments, and then Arawn came riding up atop a magnificent white horse.

Arawn began his speech in a loud voice. She didn't understand the language, but the sentiment wasn't lost on her. He rode up and down the length of the seven pyres, his words becoming more animated, more fierce. She knew he was talking about their great sacrifice, how they had bravely fought against the enemy, conveniently leaving out the part where the men had been attacked by a pair of fire drakes. He rode to the far side of the field, taking up a torch one of the officers held out to him and galloped to the other end, lighting the pyres as he went. They burst into flames, licking at the white-covered bodies.

The smoke rose up in great columns, the curls joining in the sky, rising up over the crowd. Arawn tossed the torch into the middle fire and withdrew his decorative sword. He pointed it skyward and, as his horse danced in circles, cried something, a huge smile splitting his face.

She couldn't be sure, but something inside her knew he was wishing the dead a good voyage and a happy new life. The onlookers repeated his words, great cheers cutting through the air, the words chanted over and over. Arawn waved the sword in the air, and then urged his mount into a gallop, shooting back down the path and toward the fortress below. The people followed, falling away to dance down the hill in the wake of their king, some taking to song, voices joining in.

Flora's arm was still looped through Owen's. His arm no longer jutted out stiffly.

They were alone. The wind whipped at the flames, which still roared. Flecks of ash and ember flew into the air, dancing against the dark clouds as they soared towards the skies.

"I remember each of their names," Owen murmured gruffly.

She was almost afraid she hadn't heard him right, and looked up at him. She could see the pain in his eyes, the moisture he refused to let slip. It surprised her.

He blinked it away, but she knew to remain silent. "I think I will remember their names forever," he continued.

"There were so many," she murmured.

"Yes. And they were each my responsibility. I could have done better. I *should* have done better."

"There was no way you could have known a couple of mythical creatures would swoop down and burn your camp to the ground."

He gave her a confused look, and she realized she had slipped up a bit. Instead of pressing it further, he disentangled himself from her and took a few steps away, putting distance between them. "But I could have done more. I could have issued more training. Or better guidelines. I could have held a few more safety briefs."

Just when she was starting to forget he wasn't really the commander of some Otherworldly army, he reminded her he was very much from her side of the veil.

"I'm sorry," she called softly to him. "I wish I could have done more. For them. For you."

"Thank you. For staying with me, that is. I needed a moment before I could celebrate." He approached her once more, offering his arm.

She took it, and they began picking their way back down the mountainside.

****

The entire castle had transformed from somber silence to celebration. Flora could hear the music before they had even entered the great hall. It was fast, upbeat, and reminded her of the jigs played at Highland ceilidhs. Pipes, drums, and stringed instruments played as the people of Annwn swung and twirled one another. Laughs mingled with the tunes.

She understood why Iain had chosen the dress he had for her—it hadn't been for the ceremony on top of the ridge, but for the celebration here at the castle. The other ladies were also dressed similarly, many in bright, flamboyant colors. Hers was the most subdued, but she couldn't help but think it was the most beautiful in the room. It shimmered where the others were just bright.

Food was piled on one of the trestle tables that had been pushed against one of the stone walls. Large platters of expertly stacked rolls and breads stood at least three feet high. Bowls of root vegetables encircled the roasted meats, many of which were still on the bone, if not entirely intact, head and all. Flora was no stranger to large displays of animals or hunting.

Owen led her to a table and acquired a mug full of bragahd for both of them. He drank deeply while she took a tentative sip. It was more of the sweet ale she had come to understand was local, and while she liked it well enough, she also found herself wishing for a bit more variety.

Owen downed his first mug and then refilled. Flora watched him, wishing she knew what to say to him. Clearly, he did not share the others' joy at sending their fallen comrades off to new lives. "Do you…do you want to go somewhere to talk?"

He turned a startled gaze to her, his face going rigid. For a moment Flora thought he might take her up on her offer, but instead he said, "I need to stay here," as if he were talking to a child who had no idea what was going on.

"I know you need to be seen, but…you look as if you are taking this rather hard. Perhaps seeing their commanding officer so isn't what the other soldiers need?" She knew she should have kept her mouth shut the moment the words were out of her mouth.

He leaned over her, nearly growling. "What do you know of it?"

Flora swallowed and then opened her mouth to say something, but nothing came out.

"You have no idea what it's like," he told her.

"All I meant was maybe we should go somewhere for a few minutes. You could…you could tell me about it. I just thought that maybe talking about it could help you to put on a…more jovial face?"

His face softened a little. "I'm sorry," he apologized. "And you're right. I have to be the leader they need me to be."

Flora licked her lips apprehensively and placed her hand on his bicep. It was covered in whatever leather he wore, but she could feel the strength of him beneath it. "You are the leader they need," she tried to reassure him. "But that doesn't mean you have to keep everything you are feeling inside."

Here she was giving emotional advice to someone else. She, the one who was so wrapped up in appearances she smothered all of her own feelings to the point she usually forgot she even had any. She swallowed, turning her eyes down and away from him. And wasn't that exactly what she was doing now? Telling her to do exactly what she had done for years? She looked back up at him. "You know what?"

He frowned down at her.

"I'm wrong. Don't let anyone tell you how you should feel. And don't feel like you need to hide it from anyone. Your soldiers and officers… They need to know that emotion is all right as well."

"Are you telling me to brood in the corner and scowl at the happy party-goers?" he asked with amusement.

She sighed. "I think you should probably just ignore me entirely," she grumbled, more to herself than to him.

He reached up, sliding his fingertips across her cheeks. "I'm not sure I can do that," he murmured.

She gave him a tentative smile.

But he only frowned back at her, his forehead creasing into what she was learning was its natural pose; a scowl. "I have work I need to do," he said, and stepped away, threading his way through the crowd and away from her.

She tried to stamp down the disappointment she felt.

Chapter 14

Flora didn't know how many mornings she had stood at her window, looking down at the soldiers training below. Or their commander, which was probably a more accurate description of what she did every morning. It could have been days, or it could have been weeks. She didn't know. She probably should have been keeping track like Alexander Carlisle had because it all did seem to run together.

But that morning was different.

Her eyes opened a few minutes earlier than usual. Outside, the sky was as dark as midnight, the first glimmers of morning still held at bay. No sooner had the distinction in time been made than she was sitting up and swinging her feet to the floor. She quickly pulled on the leather leggings that laced up the sides, her boots, a white tunic, and the leather jacket that cinched at the waist and fell to her thighs. The air would be cold, that much she knew, and she wrapped a crimson cowl over her hair.

The others were still asleep on their pallets as she crept past them through the larger room, their breathing deep and long. The door quietly clicked shut behind her. She skipped down the stone stairs that would lead her to the courtyard. Her boots made only the quietest of taps, and then she was out the exterior door and hugging the shadows.

She listened as Owen spoke to the soldiers, not really paying attention to the words, for she knew they would be little more than daily instructions and the listing of patrols.

But as he turned from them, she moved away from the wall and quickly fell into step at his side.

"Good morning," she murmured, hoping she didn't sound too breathy. Her heart was in her throat.

He didn't even turn to acknowledge her, he just kept walking. She sped up to keep pace with him. Despite the night of dancing and laughing they had eventually been able to enjoy…however long ago it was, he had been avoiding her since. For a few hours, she had thought she caught a glimpse of the Owen she had known. But by the next morning, it had been as if the slate had been wiped clean and he was back to his usual stiff, brooding self. It was like a fist to the gut.

But she was determined to find the other man again. That night had only proved he was lurking inside somewhere; perhaps somewhere deep, some place where only drunkenness was the key.

That was a thought. Perhaps if this didn't work, she would resort to alcohol. In large quantities.

"I was hoping I could speak with you."

At the sound of her voice, he turned his head, lifted an eyebrow.

She was really starting to hate that look. "It's important."

"It must be to have gotten you down from your window," he said wryly.

He knew she watched him every morning. Of course he did. She didn't know why it surprised her.

"Can you just stop and talk to me?" she demanded.

He stopped and crossed his arms.

"I need you to take me to the stone circle to the west." There, she had said it.

"Me? No." He turned away.

"What do you mean 'no'?"

"I mean 'no,'" he threw over his shoulder as he strode down the practice field, Flora at his heels.

"But it's important I go, and I need protection."

"Why does your need for protection have to come from me?" he scoffed. "What's wrong with your own guards? How do you even know of the circle?"

"That's beside the point." She waved off his last question and rubbed her hands over her face. "I just… They can't know. And I couldn't defend myself against a training dummy. Please?"

He stopped, and she thought he was finally considering it, really and truly considering it.

"I'll assign you a few soldiers."

She was going to scream. Why did he have to make everything so difficult? "Why can't you come with me?"

"Because I have things to do. Speaking of which…" He turned away from her, heading in the direction of his own quarters.

"Damn it, Owen, you owe me!"

That had him stopping in his tracks. "Owe you?" he asked, drawing the words out as he turned to face her. Both eyebrows had gone up, a line crossed his forehead. It hinted at his age, whereas before he had seemed ageless.

She stood a little straighter. "Yes."

"How do you figure?"

"I saved your life." Or perhaps she had stopped him from progressing on to the next life. She didn't know for certain, and she didn't want to think about it. She thought back to the night they had spent dancing at the pub, the man who was so different from the man standing before her, and she held fast to the idea she had done him a favor. But if she didn't get him back through to the other side, if he stayed here, if he *died* here, he would never be Owen again. Never the laughing, joking, charming man he had been.

He shifted his weight into a more relaxed stance. "And in return you want me to escort you to some rocks up the side of a mountain?"

"Yes."

"In the cold. And snow?"

She nodded eagerly.

"No." He turned his back to her once more.

She groaned aloud. And no sooner had the sound emitted from her throat than she knew her next move.

"What do I have to do to get some time alone with you?" she demanded.

Her insinuation had him turning back and blinking in surprise. He stared at her for a moment, and then turned, heading back in the direction from which they had come, a third direction change in as many minutes. Feeling exasperated and not wanting to go back to her chambers to mull over the encounter, she continued on with a purpose she didn't actually feel.

So, she followed him.

****

Arawn stood by the archers. A large white hound sat docilely at his feet, not even picking up its head as Owen and Flora approached.

“Ah, a pleasant morning to you, General. And to you, Lady of the North.”

“Flora,” she corrected. And then amended with, “Your Excellency.”

He waved it off. “We’ll have none of that now, will we?”

“How would you have me address you?” she asked, playing the game.

He contemplated the question, briefly. “Simply Arawn. It sounds quite powerful all on its own, does it not?” One of the archers handed the king his bow, a large, intricately carved weapon, its shaft appearing to be made from the antlers of a stag. He let loose three arrows in quick succession, all well within the center mark of the target, and then turned back to her. “Come, dear Flora, join me.”

She knew better than to argue.

A bow was pressed into her hands. She had been forced into archery every year of secondary school as part of the physical education curriculum, but she’d never been a particularly good shot. She’d never taken out anyone’s eye or shot them in the leg, but she’d considered the arrow hitting the target at all a success.

She tried to remind herself no one here would expect her to be an expert. They knew, after all, she was an adequate healer at best, and her skills outside of that realm were not particularly suited to this world. But she took aim as best she could remember, pulled her arrow back, and let it loose. It buried itself in the ground a few inches too short of the target.

She let out a disappointed breath and pulled another arrow from the basket at their feet. This one made it to the target, but with not enough force to sink into the fabric and wood.

"Here."

She felt the heat of a body at her back, knew it was Owen, but turned her head to look up into his face, anyway. He was right there, his warmth seeping into her, his cheek inches from hers. Her heart sped up, her breathing became shallow. Her head swam and her cheeks reddened. She turned back so he wouldn't see her blush. His booted feet tapped at the sides of her feet, spreading them, his hands at her waist shifted her weight and repositioned her body.

"There. Relax. Keep your shoulders down. Now, pull back." She did as he instructed. "Breathe. Focus."

How the hell was she supposed to focus with him so close to her?

She let the arrow go, and it sailed just right of its mark.

"Better. Now, use the rhythm of your breathing." He took a step back, giving her space.

The arrow landed about two feet behind the target in the center of a tree stump.

Her next attempt was even worse.

"I apologize, this doesn't seem to be my sport." She smiled wanly at Arawn.

He didn't even look at her. "You probably have little need of it, anyway, with your magic."

"My magic?" she scoffed. "You mean a few well-mixed herbs?"

"Oh, no, my dear, I mean your energy. You have it in abundance. It fairly flickers off you."

"I'm not sure I know what you mean."

"Come now, you're a witch. And a very powerful one, I would gather. How Cerridwen was talked into letting you go from the Archives, I will never know. Why do you think I was so eager to have you at my court? We never did discuss that griffon of yours, did we?" he mused absently.

She didn't know what to say. Magic? Energy? *What?* She looked down at her hands as if she expected to see blue sparks burst from them.

Arawn laughed, and she looked up to see he had lowered the bow, balancing it on the ground as he looked at her lazily. She could feel Owen's presence behind her, could see the red of his mantle from the corner of her eye, but she didn't dare look at him.

"This is a place of great magic, Flora, Lady of the North. They may not be as in abundance as they once had been, but what still remains streams to you. I reckon that's why the great mother sent you from the Archives to me. When Beltane comes, you will protect my soldiers, and we shall be celebrating the harvest for all days to come."

I don't know what any of that means!

But he passed his bow off to one of the soldiers and walked away without another word.

Flora turned her attention to Owen. "Please take me to the circle," she begged. The sooner she got out of this place, the better.

His eyes looked right into hers. And he shook his head.

Chapter 15

She left under the cover of darkness, wrapped in a thick wool cloak the color of ash, lined in fur of the same color, with a hood protecting her head from the cold. She had left her hair down so it might help insulate her, creating a blanket of heat. The cloak skimmed the floors and wrapped her in much needed warmth.

The countryside was eerily quiet and still. There was a crispness to the air that gave her pause. It felt like snow—smelled like snow, even—and the thought of getting caught in a winter storm was not a pleasant one. But she knew if she didn't go, there might not be another chance before winter really set in. She slipped through the back entrance of the barracks, the one she knew she wasn't supposed to know about, and was gone, into the mountains to the west.

****

She had only the vaguest of ideas where she was going, and that might be a generous statement. She had learned of a village not far to the west of Caer Annwn, a True Believer village, as Delyth called it. Flora had spent a great many hours trying to muddle through the races of people who inhabited this world. The North, from which she supposedly hailed, was a great mystery. But here in the South, in the two kingdoms in which she had traveled, there were four groups: the dead from her own world, the Ellyllon who traveled in their caravans, a small population of Fae who lived in exile from the Fae lands somewhere to the west, and the True Believers. The True Believers were humans, like she, who had been brought cross the veil before the gods abandoned the mortal worlds, allowed to live out a life of immortality here as long as they so chose. And then there was whatever she was, but since she was fairly certain she was an anomaly, she wasn't going to count herself among the populations.

The Fae had been the original inhabitants of this side of the veil. She understood them to be the god-race, though not all were gods. They were the elite. The nobility. Their most powerful had sculpted the world, written the tale of man. They had crossed between the two worlds, living among humans, but also ruling over the forces of nature. When those most powerful were pushed aside for the single god of the Christians, they had abandoned the lands they had once ruled, retreating to the sanctity of a place no other religion could touch. They brought with them the Ellyllon, their first bastard-born children, and the humans who did not forsake the gods of their ancestors. The True Believers.

If Flora understood it correctly, the True Believers never left this side of the veil when death visited. They lived in blissful eternity, never forced to fight at the Battle of the Ford, to live in the land of the Fae forever. She didn't know if they lived through the cycle of life as the "dead" did. She didn't know if they grew from childhood into adulthood, if they lived long lives that eventually ended only to be reborn into another. She supposed she should have asked. She really needed to keep a list of questions to put to Delyth. But if they didn't—if they lived an immortal life—perhaps they could give her information about the circle. Perhaps they could tell her how to use it. And, if not, perhaps they could at least tell her where it was.

The first flurries began their descent as the sky lightened with the first gleam of morning. The sun never rose, not like it would on a clear day, but the clouds were illuminated from beyond, taking on a hue only a shade lighter than the cloak she wore. And as the clouds, heavy and thick, began to empty, she could just make out the slender streams of hearth smoke curling up toward them.

Quickening her steps, she fairly skipped down the merchant path and into the village. It was arranged in a circle, the center of which had an oddly stepped mound. The path encircled the mound, and outside the path were the stone cottages of the villagers. They were identical in no way, but were all about the same size and of the same general construction. High thatched roofs, square windows, some with wooden shutters, others with small glass panes. The outside circle was made up of stables, barns, and paddocks.

Few people were moving about the village. They were mostly men, tending to animals, but a few women bustled from one stone building to another carrying baskets of covered food or buckets of water. She noticed a pair of women looking in her direction and speaking in hushed tones to one another and figured now was as good a time as any to assert herself as the ignorant outsider.

She made her way to them, pulling the hood away from her face to greet them with a smile. "Hello," she murmured, "I'm—"

"The witch. From the North," one of them finished for her. She was a short, stout woman with a pillowy bosom and wide hips. She wore a plain brown dress, a white smock pinned to its front, and a chunky shawl wrapped around her shoulders. A kerchief was tied around her steel-gray hair, which fluttered in the chill breeze. Her nose was slightly hooked and her chin curled up to meet it. But she had kind, dark eyes and an accent that reminded her of Dame Maggie Smith.

"Well, I'm not sure—"

"Aye, the one at the castle. I heard talk the magic was strong with this one, but I never would have guessed if I hadn't felt it myself," the other one said, but to her companion, not to Flora. She was much taller, reed thin, and much the same age. Her hair was still dark, yet shot through with silver threads. Her gray dress hung off her, the plain white chemise she wore peeking over the neckline of the dress.

Flora frowned. "I promise you—"

"We are but dabblers. There is little need for us to practice here, on this side," the first was saying. To Flora? She couldn't really be sure. "Then we practiced much."

"Oh, aye, but I still perform little charms. You know, keep the men safe while they hunt or protect the wood from getting wet," the other was saying.

"Absolutely. But the involvement? Oh, so much less work without having to ride the hedge." The woman threw her head back, shoulders sagging in feigned relief.

"Ride the hedge?" Flora muttered to herself.

"Cross the barrier, dear."

Flora looked at her blankly.

"Pull the energies across the veil?"

"Oh, of course!" Flora pretended to know what the conversation was actually about.

The two women smiled, pleased.

"Back in the old world, it was such an ordeal, focusing all your energies to call up the magic. Some days I find myself missing it. The old world. But they keep us safe, here. They keep us happy." She smiled wistfully.

Flora packed those words away. She didn't want to prove her naïveté by asking if they had lived as immortals here, but if her assumptions were correct, that was exactly what they were saying. Another question for Delyth.

"What's brought you to the pentref?" asked the short woman.

"I'm actually hoping someone can tell me of the stone circle. The one in the hills."

"Which one, dear?"

"There's more than one?" Flora wasn't sure if she felt deflated or elated to hear she had options.

"Oh, there are many."

"Do they all do the same thing?"

"More or less."

"And, er, what…what is that?"

"What is what?"

"What is it that they *do*?" She sounded a little breathless even to her ears.

"Why, they are the gateways, dear. They channel energy between the Otherworld and the mortal lands. Do they not have them in the North?"

How was she supposed to know? She smiled wanly in response.

"It shouldn't be hard for one like you. It's no different than a casting circle. Well, except the barriers are thinner, there."

"And where is the closest?" Flora asked.

"Oh, just up the mountain path, there." One of the women pointed up into the snow-covered ridges. "If it weren't for the snow, you could reach it before midday."

"Thank you," Flora told them.

She turned and began walking in the direction of the circle.

"You're not going there now, are you?" One of the women called after her. But Flora pretended she didn't hear over the whipping wind and trudged up the steep incline into the mountains.

****

The circle was not what she was expecting. She had prepared herself to find giant monoliths casting shadows over the land like those at Stonehenge, or the Callanish stones in the Scottish Isles. But what she found were much less grand.

The stones were large, but the largest was no bigger than she. They rested upon the ground lengthwise, rather than standing straight. The circle itself was probably no more than ten meters in diameter and small stalks of holly cropping up along its edges. The berries were bright against the gray stones, the withered brown grasses, and the white snow beginning to accumulate.

As Flora approached, the wind howled harder, the gusts so powerful she had difficulty remaining upright. It pushed and pulled at her cloak, threatening to launch her into the air and send her flying into the valley below. And high up she was. The village appeared to be small enough she could fit it in her palm, and if she looked hard enough through the snowfall, she could make out the faint, dark outline of Caer Annwn.

The air around her seemed to hum, the humming becoming more fervent the closer she drew to the rocks. It was almost like an electric fence, a buzz just barely audible to the ear, but so soft it could easily be mistaken for an insect flying past.

Her skin prickled and she felt like she was being watched. She turned around. No one. The longer she remained there, the more uneasy she felt. Her pulse picked up; her hands became clammy inside her fur mittens.

Something about this place was terrifying.

Flora hugged herself, everything feeling wrong around her. She backed away quickly, stumbling and falling on the rocks. Scrambling up, she ran back in the direction of the path.

But it was buried under snow. Her footsteps had already been covered and snow was coming down so fast and furious, she could no longer see a foot in front of her, much less down to the village to orient herself.

She pulled the cloak tighter around herself, the hood down over her face, and trudged farther. But with each step, the snow felt deeper and deeper. Each step, her thoughts grew heavier, a fog settling in.

Was that the howl of a dog? Or the wind? She whipped around to look behind her. Nothing.

In which direction had she been traveling?

Down. She needed to walk down.

She shook uncontrollably now, her teeth chattering and her lips feeling cracked and sore. The cold seeped down into her bones, and they ached even as other parts of her were beginning to fade into a white-hot numbness.

She skidded on some loose rocks. Her arms went out to keep her balanced.

When she skidded again a few feet away, she fell on her bottom and didn't have the strength to pick herself back up again. The snow burned into her backside and she knew it was only a matter of time before her bum went numb, as well.

She was in a world of white. It swirled around her, white on white on white.

She didn't know what she had been thinking, coming here. She knew she would never leave without Owen, and he had made it clear he had no intention of traveling with her to the circle.

But she had needed to see it. Needed to know it was there, that there was a possibility. And perhaps a part of her had hoped that when she didn't appear at her window or down at the range, he would come chasing after her. He would find her at the circle and she would be able to convince him to return with her.

Knowing she needed to keep moving, she gathered the cloak tighter around herself and pushed herself back up onto tingling feet.

Down. She needed to keep going down.

When she slipped again, she tumbled several feet, sprawling in the knee-deep snow.

And she just didn't think she could keep going.

She wondered what would happen to her if she died in this place. Would she skip over this part of the reincarnation cycle? Would she wake and find it was all a dream? Would she cease to exist?

She looked out, hoping to catch a glimpse of the valley. All she saw was a soft glow. It was getting closer. That must be it. She would soon know her fate, she would have answers to her questions.

Chapter 16

Owen looked to the window again. Her chamber remained dark. He was moments away from dismissing the troops to the midday meal, and her chamber was still dark.

When she hadn't arrived for her morning archery lesson, hell, he needed to quit referring to it as such; he was delusional to think she was actually ever going to improve. Focus didn't seem to be one of the attributes she possessed, but he enjoyed the time with her, regardless—he had been disappointed. Mildly. Only mildly. She was probably avoiding him, after all. But even so, he still couldn't believe she was abed. And the clouds made it such that she would *have* to have a light of some sort for whatever sort of potion mixing she did up in the apartment of hers.

It was probably best if she was avoiding him, he thought to himself. He had work to do. Focus. One of them might as well focus on something, because by the looks of things, it certainly wasn't going to be her.

He looked to the lieutenant he had placed in charge of the morning's exercises and gave him the nod to ring the bell signaling the end of training. The snow was coming down with more intensity and the wind was starting to whip it up into their faces, the small flecks sharp with their chill. The troops would be useless to him with frost-bitten appendages and low morale.

The woman the ambassador traveled with, what was her name? Eve. She sheathed her sword and passed the back of a gloved hand over her forehead, pushing at the hair plastered to her face from sweat or snow, Owen didn't know which. She never missed an opportunity to train with his men. To hit something. Angrily. She was brutal in the most primal sense, and she perfectly channeled all of her passionate energy into her training; he almost admired it. A force to be reckoned with, that one was.

Eve was sauntering in his direction, her wooden practice shield swinging from her hand lazily. He put a hand out to stop her from brushing by.

"Your lady." He nodded to the dark window. "Is she unwell?"

Eve shrugged. "Seemed fine when she left this morning." She made to continue on her way, but Owen kept his hand firmly on her shoulder.

"Left?" He frowned.

"Yeah. I figured she was at the archery range, pretending to care about bows and arrows to impress you." She gave him a lazy, mildly amused smirk.

He narrowed his eyes at her, not amused. "No. She never showed up." And then he swore under his breath, the words coming out with a stream of steam in the cold. "She went to that damn circle," he told her companion with gritted teeth.

Eve didn't look at all perturbed by this. She regarded him with the same bored expression she usually wore. When it became evident he was waiting for her to say something, she shrugged. "She'll be back." And made like she was going to continue on her way.

He sidestepped her. “The blizzard blowing in doesn’t bother you in the least?”

Eve took a deep breath and rolled her eyes. “Fine. What do you want me to do about it?”

He threw up his hands. “Go after her, maybe?”

“Pfft,” she scoffed. “So that there are two of us lost out there in this? No, thanks.”

He glared at her. “Where’s the other one?”

She lifted a dark eyebrow.

“The one you work with.”

“Hell if I know,” she told him, almost as if she was enjoying stringing him along. He found that hard to believe the way the other one watched her, but he was willing to let it go.

“Fine. Go get warmer clothes. I’ll meet you back here before the midday meal bell rings.”

“You?” She looked entirely too amused.

“Yes. Me. Go.”

“I’m not yours to command, you know?” she shot over her shoulder as she sidled away.

****

Owen didn’t know why he was so scared of what he would find at the top of the ridge. The woman was a nuisance at best, crazy at worst, and he really should just be glad to get rid of her.

Except he couldn’t deny the fact that his pulse jumped every time he saw her. That every night, before going to sleep, he thought about seeing her at the archery range the next morning. That every afternoon, he rehearsed what he might say to her at the evening meal.

As much as he would like to deny it, she was a flame, and he a moth. No matter how hard her tried, he couldn't seem to keep his distance.

****

"I've got her!"

Flora knew that voice.

"I've got you," the voice crooned, warm and rich like dark chocolate.

She was shivering so uncontrollably, she was having a hard time forming a coherent thought in her head. Her limbs ached, the cold having burrowed into her very bones. Owen had her cradled against his chest. She wasn't by any means a large human being, but she never would have considered herself small, either. Definitely not light enough to be carried for any length of time. But he gave no objections to lugging her weight, and if she was honest with herself, she probably wouldn't be able to force herself to move if her feet were put back into the snow again.

"The stones," she murmured, begging. "Please. We're so close."

"Is that why you tried to kill yourself? To lure me up the side of this damn mountain?"

She knew he was angry. She probably would have been angry, too, had she been in his shoes. But what else was she supposed to do? "If you weren't half-delirious right now, I would just leave you here to find your own way back to the castle."

The wind was whipping up harder, sending him staggering.

"Please, Owen," she begged him. "They're just there. We could go there, and this could all be over. It could be done, I could go home, you could go home."

"I *am* home," he growled through gritted teeth.

"You wouldn't ever have to see me again. I-I know you don't like me much. I'm sorry about that, and I w-w-wish I could change it. And that's probably why you don't want to go to the circle with me. But what if I promised you I would never bother you again? I just have to get you back. Please."

He remained silent, continuing his descent.

Flora recognized her pleas were going to go unheeded, and she was too cold to really do anything about it. Knowing defeat at his taciturnity, she curled further into him, burying her nose in his cloak and pulling his scent in.

****

Flora heard voices around her. She urged her eyes open, but the lids were too heavy. Or stuck. Perhaps they were just frozen shut?

But she knew she was warm. Well, warmer. Her fingers no longer burned with cold, and her throat no longer felt scratchy from dryness.

She focused on the voices, willing the words to become clear so she could pull herself awake. She knew she was just on the cusp of consciousness but couldn't make out what was dream and what was reality. Did she hear her name? They were saying something about sheep. Had she forgotten to take an exam? Wait, no, she had graduated from university years ago. Where were her clothes?

"There she is," someone said.

Her eyes fluttered open and she saw Evan Griffith standing over her. He gave her a pleasant smile. She pushed herself up, the heavy blankets pooling around her waist, and took in the small crowd lining her chamber. Iain. Eve was scowling from a shadowed corner, and a pair of uniformed soldiers hovered before the door. Flora flicked her gaze around until she found Owen.

Well, Owen's back. He was gazing out the window, the one she often used to look down at the soldiers in training.

She immediately swung her legs over the side of the bed, throwing back the covers as she did so, and took to her feet.

"What are you doing here?" she demanded.

Owen turned and gave all of the others a rather hard look. Captain Griffith nodded to her, his smile adjusting a few watts, though he eyed his commanding officer with the barest hint of concern, his thick eyebrows coming together to form a line just over the bridge of his nose. Eve couldn't leave fast enough, and the stony set of Iain's mouth made it appear as though he might ignore the general's obvious order, but left, anyway, taking his time. Once the door was shut behind them, Owen turned his attention to her.

His arms were crossed over his leather jerkin, Arawn's double hound symbol etched into its center. He must have pulled it on quickly, because the white tails of his shirt were hanging out, trailing over his hips. It was very unlike him to look so un-put-together.

A series of belts crisscrossed his hips. The people here seemed to love their belts and buckles and brooches. It was a love she had yet to share, finding all of the sashes and cinchers and strange undergarments quite enough all on their own without having to add an assortment of accessories.

"What are you doing here?" she asked, again.

"Making sure you hadn't frozen to death. What were you thinking going out into a snowstorm? Much less climbing up a damn mountain in one?"

"I told you I needed to get to the stone circle," she told him. "I even begged you to take me yourself, but you refused!"

"And for good reason!" he yelled, pointing to the window where snow swirled.

"No, I had good reason to go. And now that I know where it is, I need you to go back with me."

He looked at her for a long moment. "I'm not having this conversation again." He turned away from her to the fireplace and the pitiful orange glow under the logs.

"I don't even know why I'm here trying to save you. I'm not even sure I like you."

He was kneeling before the fireplace, trying to coax a better fire out of the wood. At her words, he looked over his shoulder.

"That makes two of us."

Her eyes narrowed. "If I'm so objectionable, why did you come after me?"

"We'll call it a moment of weakness."

"Pfft." She collapsed back onto the goose down pillows. "You know, you don't have to stay. I'm all right. And I have people. People who do care." She pouted a little even knowing it wasn't exactly true.

"Is that so?" He was calling her out on her lie as he rose, silhouetted against the orange glow of the flames. He pretended to look around the room. "They left rather quickly. Looks like you're stuck with me."

"I'm not an invalid, Owen. I am cold, not dying."

"That's up for debate."

Flora started to open her mouth to say something else, but he held a hand up to stop her.

"You know you shouldn't have been out there alone and we both know it. I'm not sure what game you're playing, but it's over. Now."

"No, it's not," she said through gritted teeth. She rose from her lounging position. "You don't belong here. I don't belong here. If you want to keep living your life, you *must* come with me."

He threw up his hands. "I *have* a life. Here. A pretty good one, too. I command an army. The most powerful army in the land. I like what I do. Like where I live. The people I work with. Why would I want to leave it with some crazy witch from the North?"

"Because it isn't real!" she yelled. She felt her face go red. She had risen to her knees, the furs that had been heaped upon her falling down.

"Isn't real?" he asked. "Isn't *real?* Did you not witness the hundreds of soldiers dead in the valley camp? Or the rest who had to be carried back here, their injuries so bad? How was that not real?"

She had the feeling he didn't know he was in the afterlife. Or the before life? Well, whatever it was. Clearly, he didn't remember the life he had been living on the other side, but she had thought—no, assumed—he knew where he was.

Going around in circles about it in this way wasn't going to get her anywhere. What was the old saying? You catch more flies with honey? Did that apply to this situation?

"You're right."

His eyebrows shot up. He was clearly not expecting her to back down.

"But, I would appreciate it if you would hear me out."

His jaw twitched, and she knew he was preparing to give her what for again.

"Not now," she quickly added. "When…you are more open to it. But soon."

Chapter 17

The wind whipped at her hair, sending it flying around her head in a cloud of copper curls. She lifted her face to the cloud-heavy sky, her eyes closed, and she relived those moments with Owen in the snow.

She cherished those moments, him holding her close to him as he fought through the wind and the cold and the snow. He had held her so close, so tight, as if she might actually matter.

It gave her hope. Perhaps there was still a way. She knew she couldn't stay in the Otherworld much longer. She needed to return back to reality, back to her own life, if only so she could move on. She had been on the cusp of building a real life for herself, and this was nothing more than another derailment. But he had given her a glimmer of hope he might return with her. That she could still get him back to his own life. That they would be able to build a life together.

It was a pretty little fantasy she had construed for them. She would run the shop, and he would… Well, she didn't really know what he would do. If she was completely honest, she knew next to nothing about the military in her own country, much less the one she had recently adopted. Yet, in her fantasy, she knew he would be there. They would have the shop, they would have each other. They could go out to the pubs and restaurants, hold hands while they window-shopped, help each other decorate for the holidays. He would wrap his arm around her shoulders while they watched movies in her small flat, sharing a large bowl of popcorn and a pack of Smarties.

She would introduce him to her parents when they finally stopped acting like she had thrown her entire life down the loo. And they would have his sister over for dinner parties where Flora would serve fine European cheeses on those little toasted bread rounds. She would come to tolerate Flora, perhaps even like her someday.

She pulled in one more deep breath, the frigid air burning the back of her throat.

"You really shouldn't be out here. It's cold."

Flora turned at Owen's voice. He stood behind her on the ramparts, his golden hair ruffling in the wind, not wearing much more than she. The fur mantle was his staple accessory hung open, revealing what she had come to identify as his castle clothes: a dark doublet, suede breeches, tall leather boots, and of course, the ever-present sword. She often wondered if he expected a sword fight to break out around every corner.

"I hadn't noticed," she replied icily, turning back to the snow-covered landscape.

"Do you have some time to talk?"

The way he said it nervously, almost shyly, had Flora turning right back around. "You want to talk. To *me*." Her eyebrows drew together. "What about?" She felt a little nervous, herself. Surely if he wanted to talk to her, it was of something unpleasant. A good conversation between them was a few grunts and a glare.

"About us."

Flora's eyes widened, her brows shooting up. "There's an us?"

He let out a sigh, as if composing himself, ran his hand through his hair, then crossed both arms over his chest. "I've come to, that is I… I'm not very good at these things. Never have been." His gaze almost seemed to plead with her to put him out of his misery, but then it swung away. "I was wondering, no, hoping…" He paced, talking with his hands while Flora stood frozen.

She wondered what the *hell* was going on when he muttered, "Oh, sod it."

His left arm shot around her waist while his right hand slipped into her hair, his leather-encased thumb brushing against her cheek. She gasped in surprise, but it was smothered as he crushed his mouth to hers.

Her breath was gone. Lost. He had caught her off guard, and she went rigid. And just as quickly, she pressed back into him, wanting more of his heat and his taste.

He pulled back, and as her eyes opened, disappointed, his searched them, looking for some kind of answer.

"I'm sorry, I—"

Flora threw her arms around his neck, throwing herself into him, their mouths meeting as if drawn together.

The wind around them whipped harder, swirling around them, matching the intensity she felt. She wanted to melt into him, get so close there would be no way to tell where she ended and he began.

He caressed her mouth with his lips, but she demanded more. She pulled him closer, their lips warred until he pulled away, a wry half smile playing on his lips. He backed away, leaving her in the cold, her chest heaving against her tunic. He was leaving her? Her mind screamed as he backed away. "I thought you wanted to talk?" she accused angrily. She stood there, her body on fire, in *need*, and he was just going to leave her like that?

"Tonight. Give your servants somewhere else to be." And then he turned around and disappeared into the watchtower.

****

Flora burst into the anteroom. "Get out," she told her companions.

"Good to see you, too," Eve grumbled from the corner she had designated as her own. She never rolled up her sleeping pallet, and was laying on it, head propped atop one bent arm, the other raised above her head, spinning a silver chain with a ring—one that looked suspiciously like a diamond engagement ring—looped through it.

"It's important. Critical. I…I just need you all to leave."

"And where would you have us go?" Delyth asked serenely.

"I don't know. I don't care. You just can't be here."

Delyth's eyes went big, her translucent eyebrows turning up, and Flora felt like she had just kicked a puppy. Eve's frown had grown more pronounced and she looked like she had eaten something sour. But she stood up, nonetheless, slipping the necklace over her head and tucking the ring into her bodice. Flora had never seen it before, but then, she hadn't really been paying much attention to the way the other young woman spent her time. Flora wondered what the ring was and what sentimental meaning it carried.

She hadn't seen Iain in days when she actually thought of it, but she considered that more a blessing than something to mull over. She figured he was probably skulking around the shadows somewhere, waiting for an opportunity to inflict some sort of pain and suffering. She still hadn't figured out what his actual job description was, but she had to assume it fell along the lines of assassin or interrogator.

Delyth left, carrying a stack of books and a wad of parchment, an inkwell, and quills. Eve left with nothing at all save the expression on her face. And once the door to the apartments thudded shut, Flora hurried into her private chamber and began fussing over her appearance. She combed her fingers through her tangled hair, pinched her cheeks to give them some color and gnawed on her lips to plumpen them up. They were all tricks she had learned when her mother had deemed her too young to wear makeup, but she had desperately wanted the attention of their closest neighbor, Lewis Ferguson. She'd been twelve, and her mother had been right to deny her the makeup. Lewis Ferguson had been a wanker.

Flora opened the door at the quiet, yet strong knock. The door groaned open, a sound that had grown almost comforting to her in the days—weeks, months?—at the castle.

Owen stood, head down, in the shadows of the corridor.

She beckoned him in. He was uncomfortable, his brow slightly puckered and his shoulders tense. He strode into the room, his hand at the nape of his neck, fingers playing at the short golden hair there. He then paced back as she shut the door, leaning against it, keeping him from changing his mind and walking out.

"You wanted to talk?" She meant to sound seductive, but instead sounded desperately unsure, herself.

He came to a halt, looked at her for a long moment, and then continued his pacing.

"I—I haven't been honest with you. Entirely."

"What do you mean?" She leaned forward, away from the door, but was afraid to move any farther. She felt her heart skip and then race to catch up.

He squeezed his eyes shut, the space between his brows wrinkling. One hand was on his hip and the other squeezed the bridge of his nose as if to dispel a headache.

"I… When you showed up and saved the army…saved us. *Me*," he finally amended. "I…" He opened his eyes to look at her. "I recognized you."

Flora blinked. "What?" Well, that was surprising. "I mean… You did?"

"It's not what you think," he said matter-of-factly.

"Oh? And what do I think?"

Owen was glaring at her.

She decided to take a less threatening stance and moved to one of the simple wooden chairs slid under the large trestle table that had become her workspace. She often spread her notes and herbs upon it, for it was the only place everything actually fit. She sat, propped her elbows down, rested her chin on her folded hands.

"That this is some sort of twist of fate foretold by your benefactress."

Flora sighed, and then sat back, resting her palms flat on the wood. "Actually, no. But I do want to know more."

He pursed his lips as if he did not believe her. Perhaps he had been expecting a different answer and was unsure how to proceed. He began pacing, his presence taking up far too much space, filling the large room. "You. You've come to me in dreams," he finally confessed, eyes downcast. It ate at his pride to admit as much, as if it was reprehensible to dream.

"I have?" She perked up. Her heart took up its earlier pace.

He rolled his shoulders. "Not for some time. They began when I was first given the position here at Caer Annwn, but stopped not long before… Well, before the drakes."

Flora swallowed. They started when he went missing and ended when she arrived in Hafgan's kingdom. It had to be. She wanted to laugh and sing and dance. She didn't know what his confession meant, exactly, but it had to be good news.

"It's never anything noteworthy," he said softly, as if to himself.

"Oh." Well, that was less than flattering.

"That's not what I meant. Shit." He swore under his breath again, something she couldn't understand.

She almost smiled at it. He always acted so cool and collected. So stoic. And here he was acting like a stumbling boy talking to a girl for the first time.

"We mostly talked."

"About?"

Owen shrugged. "They were dreams. I don't know." He was pacing again, chin nearly to his chest.

His hand was back in his hair. "Once we just sat around a fire. You told me about being betrayed. But I can't remember the details. I remember just wanting to make you laugh. We danced. Badly. In another dream, we walked. There was a garden, I think. But, again, I don't remember what we talked about."

She watched as pink crept up into his cheeks.

"We… Never mind."

"I know," she said softly. "Owen," she began. "I need you to believe me, all right?"

His face was serious. He crossed his arms over his chest, almost as if to protect himself from what was to come. At her insistent look, he gave a single nod.

"Those weren't dreams. They really happened."

He remembered. Oh, thank all of the gods, he remembered! She wanted to scream it from the battlements, to do a dance right then and there. She couldn't help the smile that lit up her face. She stood, her feet feeling like they were floating just above the stone. She slid her arms around his waist and rested her head upon his chest. "You remember."

He held his arms out, afraid to touch her, perhaps, and then lowered them to wrap around her back and shoulders in an unsure hug. Flora tried to pretend it was good enough, but she couldn't. Something still wasn't right. She was so close, and yet, not close at all. She couldn't help the tears. She tried, but they came, anyway. She felt all of the frustration and fear and disappointment build up until she couldn't hold onto it anymore, and all of those emotions just spilled out of her. What had begun as a happy embrace quickly turned to her seeking comfort in any way she could get it.

He must have felt the change, for as the tears spilled down her cheeks, he tightened his hold on her. And then they were rocking, softly, from side to side like one might rock a child, his hand smoothing her hair as she fought to contain the sobs ripping through her. She managed to silence them, but they rocked her shoulders, reverberating through her chest.

And he continued to hold her. To run his hand over her hair. The man she had come to think disliked her and everything she stood for.

She calmed and pulled back, looking up into his face with watery eyes. "I'm sorry," she croaked, running the back of a hand under her eyes to smear away the dampness there.

He didn't say anything, just looked down into her eyes with his own green ones, lifting a hand to brush her hand away so he could be the one to rub the tears from her cheek. Flora could have counted the different flecks of green in his eyes for the rest of her life, getting lost in their beauty.

He broke the gaze first, his gaze dropping to her lips. She didn't even think, she just rose up to press her lips to his.

Hand in her hair, hand on her back, he tightened his grip on her as their lips explored. Softly. Unsure.

"Owen," she breathed, arching her back into him as she took a step back. Another one. The wood of the table pressed into her hip, and rose to her toes again to slide one hip onto the surface, bringing him with her.

He came to stand between her legs, and she leaned back until she lay on the table's surface, bringing the weight of him with her. He balanced himself over her, careful not to burden her with his weight.

His lips left hers, traveling to the place just below her ear, leaving a trail of light brushes there, down to where her neck met shoulder. She shuddered, arching into him, offering him more. His hands were no longer balancing himself over her, but were sweeping up her waist, holding her to him.

She felt protected. Safe. Cared for. Warm. Curling her arm between them, she palmed his cheek, the rough scratch of evening stubble rasping against her flesh. Insistently, she brought his mouth back to hers and when their lips met, again…

Fireworks.

It was perfect. Right. Fated.

All it took was a kiss to make her wild for him. Moaning with further passion, she pulled at the doublet, not actually knowing how it worked, but knowing it needed to go *away.*

Owen reared back, releasing himself from his clothing even as Flora struggled with hers.

He moved a stray strand of her hair behind her ear, exposing her neck once more. Another gentle kiss on her collarbone, one just above her heart, another between her breasts.

He worshipped her as she burned for him, begging for more and cursing him for not setting her free. The more she pleaded, the slower he teased.

And when she was sure she would die of wanting him, that she couldn't bear it any longer, he was kissing her again, hungrily, drinking her up and giving her control once more.

She knew why the French called it the little death.

****

"We never make it to the bed do we?" she said wryly, her mind on their first night together—the only night—she had spent with him. She swung her legs over the side of the table, sitting up so she could wrap his mantle around herself.

She looked at him coyly over her shoulder, but his expression had gone stony. "What's wrong?" she asked.

"You keep saying we know each other. That we've…got some sort of history. But I can assure you, this is the first time for me."

Flora frowned. "But you said—"

"That I had dreamed of you. That we had met as I slept. But that wasn't real."

"It *was* real!" she insisted, balling some of the fur and velvet in her hands.

"Not to me. To you, maybe. But not to me." He said this coldly, a stark contrast to the warm conversation they had shared not long before.

Flora knew there was no use arguing. She sighed, letting her shoulders sag and her posture deflate. "Owen, I'm sorry. I—I just don't understand. It's difficult for me to understand," she amended.

"Annwn is all I have ever known. I know you don't want to believe it, but it's true. I grew up here. I trained here. I became a soldier and an officer here. This is my home."

"Wait." It took a moment for his words to sink it. Flora allowed her mind to wrap around them, but pushed her emotions down. Something wasn't right here; she had to tread carefully. "Are you saying you actually grew up here? As a child?" Her thoughts were on what Delyth had told her. What Alexander Carlisle had written in his journal. *No one* was born in the

Otherworld but the Ellyll and the fairy folk. Not even the True Believers sired children. The other humans only passed through the veil in death and…well, whatever it was she was doing there.

Owen was looking at her like she had grown a second head. He had been laying back flat against the scarred wooden tabletop, his head resting atop his folded arms. But then he stood. "Yes." He drew the word out.

Did that mean they didn't know? The "dead"? Or was he not one of them?

Realizing she didn't have enough information—yet again—she skirted the table, staying his hands before they could pull his white shirt over his head. "I'm sorry," she murmured. She caressed his arm with her fingertips, playing over the soft blond hair. "I know this is a…" She searched for the right word. "Difficult subject."

"Can I just ask you one thing, Flora?" The way he asked it had her stomach knotting up in itself. He used her name so rarely. The sound of it on his lips was like a kiss. Not a heated, passionate one, but a loving, sincere brush of the lips. It didn't sound silly or wrong when he said it. It didn't seem like the punch-line to a joke or a funny story her parents told at social events.

"This." He held out his hands to indicate the two of them. "Is this about me? Or is this about this other Owen?"

There was the punch in the gut. She felt her mouth go dry and her chest ache. She swallowed past the lump in her throat. "I—I don't know."

He looked at her for a long moment. He pulled the shirt over his head and made for the door.

"Owen, wait," she called softly after him, almost afraid of who would hear. She would have followed him out into the hall, but all she wore was the mantle—his mantle.

He didn't stop, nor did he turn. Instead, he disappeared into the dark corridor.

"Shite. Bollocks. Piss." When she turned, Iain stood leaning in the doorjamb.

Flora pulled the fur more closely about her. "What do you want?" she snapped.

She could feel his gaze run down her from under the stupid hood he always wore.

"Tread carefully, Flora MacDonald," he murmured. "There is much at stake." And then he turned, quitting the room.

Chapter 18

Archery with Arawn in the mornings had become a habit. Flora woke with the dawn, dressed quickly, and arrived in the training yard with the soldiers.

When she awoke the next morning, it was to find the light streaming through her window brighter than usual and the other half of the bed cold. For a moment, she had allowed herself to forget he had left her hours before, and instead he had stayed with her.

It was a little fantasy of hers, one she had only realized after the morning she had woken in her little apartment above the shop, Owen gone. A little fantasy of waking up wrapped in his arms; someone who wanted to be there. Robert had always been an early riser, and he had definitely never allowed her to curl up into him in the night, much less wrap herself around him in the morning sunlight. She dreamed of those early morning cuddles, of lazing in bed, just…being.

But she was alone, just as she had been alone when she had climbed between the sheets. She swung out of bed, pulling on the leather leggings and matching jacket over her white tunic. A thick woolen cowl went over her hair and shoulder, and she pulled matching arm warmers up past her elbows. She hopped through the door on one foot as she pulled a boot onto the other and scurried down the stairs.

The snow had stopped falling and the ground was covered in a thick blanket of the stuff, but Annwn's forces were already training, swordsmen and swordswomen parrying, the sounds of steel and wood echoing against the stone walls. Her breath escaped into the frigid air in great puffs of steam that rose and mingled with the hundreds of others who worked the training grounds into a thick, icy sludge. Flora felt their eyes on her, heard their whispers.

"Witch" and "commander" seemed to fall off everyone's lips.

The night they had spent together was supposed to remain between the two of them, so naturally, the entire fortress knew.

She felt her cheeks grow warm. Ducking her head, she shielded her embarrassment from prying eyes.

"Ah, there you are, milady," Arawn greeted her as she drew near. "I was afraid my general had rendered you useless for the morning." He laughed heartily at his own joke as he pulled back his bow, aimed, and let the arrow fly. It hit the dead center of the target, as always.

Flora briefly considered telling him where he could shove it, but decided personal safety trumped wounded pride.

"Glad to see you're only walking sideways," he chirped gleefully as she took her place a few feet away from him.

Flora's eyes narrowed, and she bit the inside of her lip, but raised her bow and aimed her arrow. "How did you know?" she murmured before letting the arrow loose. It sailed toward the target but sank into the canvas's outer edge. She glared, took a deep breath, and pulled another arrow from the quiver at her feet.

“I know everything about my kingdom.” His next arrow hit the eye of the target squarely.

Flora lowered her bow, turned to him, and raised an eyebrow in question. Arawn might be the ruler, but she believed they had become fairly decent friends. She imagined if she had had a brother, he would be a lot like Arawn. Eternally laid-back, good-natured, and completely occupied with nothing of true importance. At least on the outside. She had a feeling he hid a darkness, however, something she hoped never to witness.

Despite that theory, their blooming friendship actually gave her anxiety over her deception. Part of her wanted to tell him his sworn enemy was essentially blackmailing her into removing the commander of his entire army. But she knew if he knew, he would eliminate Eve and Iain, and while she was definitely not their biggest fan, she didn’t want to see anything happen to them, either. And then she would have *no* help getting Owen back to the other side, because he certainly wasn’t a willing participant.

His grin returned. “It was only a matter of time. The glances you two throw at one another have had the whole castle wagering when it would finally happen.”

“That doesn’t exactly answer my question.”

He was shaking his head and tsking. “The general is a very busy man, my dear. It does not go unnoticed when he in unavailable.”

“In the middle of the night?”

“Especially in the middle of the night.”

She glowered and grabbed up another arrow. She started to take aim, but then fell slack. “We throw glances at one another?”

Arawn threw his head back and laughed, a great, hearty laugh. "You're jesting, are you not?"

Flora continued to frown.

Arawn sobered somewhat, though a smile still tugged at the corner of his lips, lifting his mustache into charming little curls. "The poor bastard can barely stand to have you out of his sights. Or did you not notice he went scaling up the side of a mountain when you failed to attend the morning meal but a few days past?"

"I thought he hated me," she murmured.

Arawn slid his gaze up and down her, and then gave her a look that told her she should be reexamining the thought.

She had spent more time than she wished to admit to pondering the question Owen had put to her the night before. Who had she so eagerly jumped into bed with? Had it been this Owen? Or the Owen she had spent three days with on the other side?

If she was honest with herself, she knew she desperately wanted this Owen to be *that* Owen. She wanted the happy-go-lucky Owen who was quick to smile and joke and tease. She wanted the tall, golden, beautiful, perfect man who helped her vacuum and encouraged her to dance.

This Owen only managed to infuriate her. He never seemed happy to see her. Hell, he never seemed happy at all. He was closed off, guarded, suspicious. He wouldn't listen to a damn thing, the stubborn arse.

But what she had to believe was that they were one in the same. And once they were gone from this place, the Owen she had been falling for would resurface so they could pick up where they left off.

****

The door to his chamber was ajar. Flora stood outside and found she was staring at the backs of several of the officers. They were all poring over a map while Owen murmured about troop numbers. She slipped inside, her back to the wall.

She could only see snippets of the map and only caught every third or so word. It wasn't anything that particularly interested her, and she found herself studying her boots. The toes were a little pointy for her liking, but they were comfortable enough. The soft brown suede came to the knee where it cuffed over. They were nearly identical to the other brown, knee-high boots in the room, but others had used long strips of rawhide to fasten lengths of fur to the boot between the ankle and knee for warmth. Inside her own boots, her toes curled in on themselves, cold from the subfreezing temperatures outside the castle.

It wasn't much warmer inside the castle, either, despite the roaring fires in every room. The one behind Owen was particularly fearsome, and yet she still felt like she was standing in an icebox. Clearly, she needed to become more creative with the clothing items at her disposal.

She wasn't sure how long she waited there, her mind wandering from shoes to fires to warm meat pies, but she was snapped back to the present when the officers began filing out of the room. One of the men smiled knowingly at her; she immediately sought out Owen.

He was staring right at her, his arms crossed over his chest and his expression one she couldn't read. He didn't say anything, just waited for her to speak.

When the door closed behind the officers, she pushed away from the wall.

"I'm sorry," she said.

His eyebrows shot up in shock. She felt rather satisfied at that. It was nice to give someone something they never expected.

"I thought about what you asked me, earlier. And even though I'm not entirely convinced you and the 'other Owen' aren't the same person, I haven't really allowed you to prove otherwise. Perhaps you can tell me more about you? Give me another chance?"

He didn't say anything. The pregnant pause between them was long enough she was seriously concerned he would turn her down, the thought of which had a lump growing in her throat. She was terrified he would refuse her, and not because it would endanger her mission, which would eventually endanger her life, but because it would break her heart if he did.

It was almost funny, if she really thought about it. Robert had strung her along, possibly for years. He had used her, allowed her to throw her life away on a lie. And yet, none of that had really affected her heart in any way. Not permanently, anyway. On days when she was particularly lonely, she had missed his friendship. And on those same days, she was often angry, so angry she almost felt blinded by it. But the anger was directed as much at herself as it had been at him.

But if Owen turned away from her—this Owen, the one who regarded her with suspicion, the one who never allowed himself to smile, the one who was perpetually angry at something, if not her—she thought all of the light and happiness would be sucked out of her world.

"All right."

Her heart slammed against her chest and she let out the breath she hadn't even realized she was holding.

"But I haven't eaten all day, so it'll have to be in the kitchens."

"Anywhere," she told him.

She'd never actually been to the kitchens. She didn't even know where they were. He led her down the back stairs of the army barracks, a narrow little passage with uneven, shallow steps. They must have gone down three flights before pushing out a small wooden door. Owen ducked down to keep himself from hitting the top of the doorjamb, and she did the same even though she wasn't entirely sure she needed to.

The training yard was a muddy mess, the snow having soaked up the mud to create a brown slush. It sank up to her ankles, sucking at the heels of her boots. His strides were much longer and faster than her own, and she leapt to keep up with him, mud splattering up high enough to land on the arms of her jacket. Opposite the door they had exited, not far from the door where she entered the training yard most mornings, was another small door set down a few stone steps. Owen sped down them to pull the door open for her, holding it as she passed through.

They were on another landing, and he gestured down the stairs. She took them carefully, for they were just as narrow and shallow and uneven as the one on the other side of the yard. At the bottom, she found herself in the vast kitchens. She stood over to the side, allowing Owen to take the lead once more. He made straight for a long trestle table, grabbing a round basket with a short handle before turning back to her.

He led her to the far corner, near one of the wide hearths, its fire low, a pair of wooden chairs to its side. He motioned for her to sit first, and then took the chair next to her.

"I miss the morning and afternoon meals fairly often," he explained as he rummaged through the basket. He pulled out a roll, tore it in half, and passed some to her. "The cook started packing me this rather than having to rummage something up when I finally made it in here. So…" He lifted a shoulder and took a bite of the roll.

She pulled at hers, popping a small piece into her mouth. Truth be told, she often missed meals as well, but had never thought to come asking after any leftovers. Instead, she usually hid bits of the meals she did make in a napkin, storing it away under her clothes to take back to her rooms with her.

"How long have you been here?"

His long pause had her wondering if perhaps he didn't know how to answer the question. "A while."

She frowned at her roll and tore off another piece.

"I grew up on the shore," he said. "I trained as a soldier there, at the castle. An…acquaintance of Arawn saw me fight at a tournament there and gave my recommendation. I was given the commissioning as commander shortly before the Battle of the Ford."

"Do you have any siblings?"

"A sister. She's a midwife."

"Did you leave behind anyone? A wife, perhaps?"

He smirked. "No, I've never been married. You?"

"Yes."

His eyebrows shot up. “You’ve been married? Are you a widow?”

She shook her head, but refused to meet his eyes. “No. We…we weren’t a good match.”

“I don’t understand.”

“He didn’t prefer my particular brand of…sexuality.”

She held her breath, waiting for him to reply. It seemed like forever, the seconds ticking by, strangling her.

“I find that hard to believe.”

She let the breath out. “Ask the man who shares his bed.”

“Oh.”

“Yes. Oh.”

“No, it’s just that… This sounds almost familiar.”

Flora felt a little smile creep up, but she forced it away by biting the inside of her cheeks. “Does it?” she murmured more to herself than to him, but she still couldn’t bring herself to look him in the eye.

He pulled out a wedge of cheese, breaking off a morsel and offering it to her. She shook her head and fidgeted with her roll.

“I feel there is something you’re not telling me,” he confessed between bites.

“What do you mean?”

“There’s something hanging between us. Something I think you’ve wanted to say from the beginning, but now you feel like you can’t.”

She felt the words boiling up, ready to spill over. Yes, she wanted to tell him. Yes, there is so much. But I am afraid that if I tell you everything, you will think I am mad because, well, I’m not entirely sure I’m not mad. And if you don't believe me, I will lose every chance to get you to leave with me, and if you don't leave with me, we're both dead. Well, I'm dead for sure, but I can imagine you will be dead as well. But I don't know what that means since this is the afterlife. And I haven't even finished my regular life.

Instead, she sniffed and said, "You're right."

"You can tell me. Whatever it is."

Flora smiled a sad smile. "I wish it were that easy."

"I should probably be getting back. There'll be more talk if I am gone too long." She could feel him closing himself off, but she desperately wanted him to open up more. If for no other reason than to trust her. Yet, she knew that for him to keep the lines of communication open, she would have to give him the answers he wanted, and she just wasn't ready to do that, yet.

"Thank you for…taking the time out of your day to talk to me," she murmured, reaching out to touch his arm. It was a gesture that was more for herself than for him. She had been fighting the urge to touch him all afternoon, and this was her last chance before he left her. Perhaps it would be her last chance ever. She could feel the muscle beneath and fought the urge to pull him close and refuse to let go.

When his gaze met hers, she swallowed, knowing he knew where her mind was. He leaned forward, gently brushing her lips with his. She caught her breath, waiting for him to deepen the kiss, but instead, he pulled back.

"Is that okay?" he murmured.

She leaned back into him with her answer, and he was kissing her again. He stole her breath and made her forget everything around them. All she could feel were his soft lips on hers, the fresh stubble on his chin, and the electricity that always ignited when she was around him.

"I promise," she whispered against his lips, "when the time is right, I will tell you. Everything."

And then she was the one who slipped away, leaving him before he could leave her.

Chapter 19

The type of magic Flora was asked to practice was nothing like she had expected. When her travel companions had begun to call her a witch, she had pictured something far more sinister in her head. Black cauldrons, warts, incantations, and devil worship. She imagined being forced to set curses and boil eye of newt with the tongue of a virgin and the blood of a bastard.

When Arawn called her to his study the first time, she had prepared herself for him to request some dark magic that would flow like a heavy mist across the lands and leave his enemies catatonic. Instead, he requested she place a spell of protection around him and the other hunters before they took to the wilds in search of boar.

She, of course, had no way to refuse, seeing as how she had been a willing participant in the lie. After promising she would do just that, she had disappeared into her workroom and pulled out the book of magic that had found its way into her store…however long ago it was.

Like the other texts, the strange language made more and more of itself known to her the longer she was in the Otherworld. When she had first opened the tome, it was to find long blocks of text—text she couldn't understand—a few English words written in the margins next to the odd sketch or doodle. But when she opened it to find a protection spell for Arawn, rather than a bunch of silly, rhyming incantations, she found instructions for basic rituals that would heal the sick, right wrongs, and bring peace.

Flipping through the pages, she quickly lost herself to the possibilities that lay before her—bringing forth rain and ensuring a bountiful harvest. Ending famine and calming a turgid sea. Helping a lover forget his jealousy and a soldier her fear. Flora almost forgot what she had been looking for in the first place until she came across a simple protection charm.

She rummaged through the bottles and jars she and Delyth had painstakingly organized on the shelves, pulling down what she needed and lining them up on the tables. In one of them, Delyth had cut small squares of red cloth. Flora sifted through them, finding a piece with a few frayed edges about the size of her palm. She laid it out flat, and then went in search of a few more items, a candle, some string, a knife.

It was then she realized she no longer had the little knife that had arrived at her shop. She rifled through her things, looking in drawers, under furniture, even under her pillow, but it was nowhere to be found. She reluctantly asked Eve if she could borrow one, and the other woman handed her one; a small blade she kept between her breasts. She didn't even look at Flora as she handed it over, just continued to lounge on her sleeping mat in the corner, her gaze on the wall. The blade couldn't have been more than three inches, its tiny hilt not even that. Flora thanked Eve, didn't get a response, and returned to the table.

She laid the knife down, uncorked one of the jars, dipped her fingers in, and removed a sprig of mistletoe. She dusted it from her fingers into a mortar, recorked the bottle, and repeated the action with some elderberries and rosemary. Once they were all in the mortar, she used the hilt of the small knife as a pestle, blending the herbs together, and then poured them into the center of the crimson fabric. Using the string, she tied everything into a simple little ball and whispered, so no one else could hear her, the incantation listed in the book. But no flash of light, no ring of truth burst out from the little sachet. Instead, it hung from her fingers, looking just as it had before.

Flora didn't know what to do, but she had completed all of the steps. Perhaps this was it? She hoped so.

Arawn seemed pleased enough with the little ball of herbs she passed to him, and promised he would return from the hunt with more work for her.

Arawn never told her whether her charm had worked, but she found herself decidedly more busy after the hunt. Every afternoon, between training sessions, they lined up in the dark corridor outside of her apartments, hoping to be seen before their duties called them back.

Most wanted time. They wanted to know that even though they had crossed the Ford, they would still have a chance to live a life in Annwn. Many, both men and women, would blush and confide in her when someone had caught his or her fancy. The first few times she heard the particular "secret" she had been surprised and a little sad, but as the afternoons passed, she found it was a common theme, and one that was innately human. A few did come asking for a charm for courage or peace. They, she learned when she questioned, had already lost someone who would have kept them in the Otherworld and wanted to move on and have another chance at a new life.

One afternoon, when the weather was particularly dreadful outside, the commander dismissed the soldiers from their afternoon maneuvers, and she found the line had grown into a rather large crowd. Feeling charitable, she remained through the evening meal, taking requests and hearing secrets. She found she was rather enjoying it until she realized the candles were near to snuffing themselves out and her stomach was twisting in hunger. She agreed to see the last three soldiers who waited, and then quickly left before any more found her door. Slipping away to the main hall, she was disappointed, though not surprised, to find it full of sleeping bodies, the tables cleared away.

She wanted to go to the kitchens, but she felt it wasn't her place to be rummaging around someone else's domain. She briefly thought about turning back to her own rooms and going to sleep, but she was actually starting to feel a bit faint. Instead, she made her way to the barracks.

The door was left ajar, as always, and Owen was at the desk, a single candle shining as he scribbled furiously. She gently pushed the door, knowing the creak of the hinges would be enough to announce her.

He turned and when he saw her, he instantly stood. "Flora," he said, almost breathlessly, nervously. A bashful look crossed his face, and he looked charmingly boyish in his delighted surprise to see her.

It was still a bit unexpected to hear her name on his lips. “Sorry,” she apologized. “I didn’t mean to disturb you.” Yes, I did.

He lifted one corner of his mouth in a half smile. He had reclaimed his confidence. “I think we both know that’s a lie.”

She slipped all of the way through the doorjamb, clicking the heavy portal shut behind her. “I missed the evening meal.”

“I know,” he said this almost lazily.

“There was nothing left.”

His expression remained placid.

“I was hoping you had one of your baskets”—she smiled awkwardly, refusing to look directly at him—“available.”

He gave her a withering look she knew held sarcasm and turned back to the desk. As he moved, she caught sight of the basket. He held it out to her by the handle and she took it, then leaned against the side of his desk. She lifted the cloth covering it and fished out a slender wedge of cheese. By the looks of it, he hadn’t ventured into the basket, yet. She offered the wedge to him first, but he shook his head at it and resumed his place at the desk.

Flora began nibbling on the thinnest edge, looking down at the pages scattered across his desk. “What are you working on?”

He pulled all of the loose pieces of paper together, into a stack. “Logistics,” was all he said.

“For the Ford?” she asked around the cheese. She already felt the wooziness that had plagued her retreat, but the hunger was still there.

He didn't reply, just slipped the pages under a heavy leather bound book in the corner farthest from her. He leaned back in the chair, stretching his legs out under the desk and looked at her, but said nothing.

"I half expected to find you outside my door, you know," she told him, wanting the conversation. "Your soldiers have been lining up all week. I think I've seen just about every last one of them. Even Captain Griffith came to see me this evening," she told him.

"Oh? And what did he want?"

She suddenly felt guilty for saying anything. She wasn't sure if they had all come to her in confidence. Well, it couldn't be too much of a secret since they had all been standing in the corridor together, but she wasn't about to say any more. "You know, this and that."

"This and that?" he questioned, eyebrows going up even though he wasn't looking at her.

"Most of your soldiers want more time."

"More time?"

"Is there an echo?" she teased. At his lifted eyebrow, she continued, choosing her words carefully. "They want to be sure they come back…from the Ford." She turned to rummage through the basket again, coming up with a leg of smoked poultry. She picked at it, peeling away a small piece and popping it in her mouth. She knew it was a sore subject for him. It was one of the few things that kept her certain she was right, and he really didn't belong on this side. Thinking back to the way he viewed death at the ceremony, how the others celebrated, but he couldn't let go of his guilt and his sadness. It was endearing he felt so much, even if he tried so hard not to let others see it.

"And the rest?" he asked.

"To…not."

Passing on was a much more difficult subject. She wondered if soldiers often went into battle hoping not to come out on the other side. She'd lived through years of her country being at war, but she knew it was different. That it wasn't the same as wars past, even so recently as World War II. Fighting and dying for cause and country had to be different than fighting and dying for an unknown ally at best, a reluctant partner at worst. At least, that would be her take on the subject, ignorant of what actually happens on a battlefield as she was.

"And you can facilitate that?"

Flora wasn't sure if his tone was accusing or curious. She swallowed. She really had no idea. She didn't know whether the recipes or spells she found in the book made a damn bit of difference or if they were just someone's imagination. Perhaps at one time the author had performed a charm or cast a spell and the fifty-fifty chance of the desired outcome came to be, and so it was decided the magic worked. There was no way for her to know, and perhaps she was doing the soldiers a disservice by going along with it all, but…they seemed to believe it, and who was she to cast doubt on their beliefs? Especially when she didn't know they *didn't* work.

Flora decided a nonanswer was better than a real one. She turned the subject back to him. "Do you not have a wish one way or the other?" she asked him.

He pursed his lips and shook his head. "No."

"You're not scared of what happens next?"

"Not as scared as I am about what happens now."

Her head snapped around to look at him just as he raised his hand to her visage. He drew his fingers along her face, just beside her hairline, tracing it down her cheek to her jawline. His touch was light, just barely skimming over the small hairs resting atop her flesh, sending every fiber of her being into hyperalertness.

She leaned into him. "What do you mean?" she murmured.

"We come from two different worlds." His fingers were now tracing the bodice she wore, traveling down the neckline to where it hooked together in the front, down the hooks. "And I imagine you'll be returning to yours someday." His fingers lingered right between her breasts. "Soon."

She leaned down, her lips next to his cheek. "Come with me," she requested.

"Stay with me," he countered.

And then their lips met and he was pulling her down onto his lap. She slid her hands around the back of his neck, her fingers pushing into the short golden hair there. He teased her, pulling away so she had to chase him, her mouth hovering just over his as he leaned back in the chair. When their lips met once more, she looked into his eyes, dark in the low light, though she could imagine their bright bottle-green color. She had never felt so connected to someone. Not when they had shared kisses before, not when they had met on the other side, not when she had spent years with Robert; married the man, even. Looking into Owen's eyes was like looking into his soul and seeing herself.

Her lips brushed his, but she refused to look away. His gaze matched hers, his hands resting on her hips, hers moving to cradle his jaw, fingertips scraping the strawberry-blond prickles of his beard.

His fingers plucked at the hooks, pinching them open like the hooks of a brassiere. The bodice popped apart, her tunic the only thing keeping her flesh from his fingertips. She instantly felt a little chilled and shivered against it.

His warm hand bunched up the muslin, pulling it up, slipping beneath the hem to cup her breast. She couldn't control the shiver that ran up her spine, and her eyes hooded, for she refused to look away from him. His thumb ran over her nipple. Once. Twice. Challenging her.

She gasped the third time, pressing herself to him, her eyes finally closing and her mouth hungrily seeking his. He covered another breast with his other hand, offering equal treatment.

Flora fairly hummed with desire, her mind losing focus until all she could think of was how amazing she felt and how much she wanted it to continue. How much she wanted him. Her skin felt as if it were on fire, burning in the sun. "Why are you wearing so many clothes?" she demanded, as she jerked away and tore at his leather doublet.

He chuckled deep in the back of his throat, husky amusement mixed with desire. He pushed her hands away and rid himself of his doublet and shirt, then pulled her tunic over her head. She pressed her naked chest to his, arching into him as she pulled his mouth back to hers, devouring his lips. The sensation of his hard, muscular chest, his chest hair against her smooth, soft skin was all the aphrodisiac she needed.

"Now," she said against his mouth.

His movements stilled, and he looked at her in surprise. “Not yet,” he told her.

She supposed she should be thankful she had worn skirts that day. He flipped them up, his fingers finding her center. Her breath caught in her throat, her eyes closing in ecstasy, her head falling back. Her fingernails dug into the arms of his chair, trying to maintain control, but failing miserably. He was working her up, all of the feeling in her body pooling between her legs, though what she wanted most he was refusing to give her.

“Please,” she begged on a whisper.

He dipped his head and laid a kiss on the curve of her neck, slowly, his lips barely brushing against her skin, attempting to slow the fast pace she was desperate to attain. She didn’t understand why. Or how. How could he want to go slow when all she wanted was *him.* All of him. At that moment. Hell, five minutes before.

“Please,” she demanded.

“I want to savor you,” was his response. He removed his hand from under her skirts, slipping it around the back of her waist, leaning her back so his lips could close around one of her breasts.

Savor you. The words were enough to sober her somewhat. No one had ever wanted to savor her before. Sex had always been quick. To get it over with, she supposed. But the thought of someone wanting to take his time with her. Wanting to know her, perhaps all of her… It made her heart skip.

His ministrations were light, soft. She took a deep breath, calming herself, focusing again on him and what he was doing to her. She felt like she should be reciprocating, but she didn’t know how. Despite being experienced, she was sadly inexperienced. That much she knew.

"Owen?" she murmured, surprised at how fragile her voice sounded.

"Mm?" he responded as he left one breast in favor for the other.

"I want to… Show me"—she gasped—"show me what you like."

He pulled away and kissed her lips, long and hard. "Not now."

"Wh-why?"

"Because I want to enjoy you."

Flora swallowed. Her lips parted, and she thought words would spill forth, but she had none. She tentatively leaned forward and kissed him again, but he pulled away and began kissing her breasts once more, his hand moving up her thigh to her very center. He knew exactly where he was aiming, and his thumb found her just as his fingers slipped into her. She fought to maintain control, but he continued to work her into a frenzy, slowly engaging and withdrawing, taunting her like he might taunt an enemy. She clung to him, her fingers digging into his muscle, her breath catching in her throat.

She was lost in a hazy cloud of her own senses as they built up into a fiery desire she could no longer resist. Every touch, every flick of a fingertip or tongue had her center begging for him.

Giving into her request, his mouth met hers once more. He kissed her long and hard, his hands leaving her momentarily, and then drawing her back to him, his warm skin against her own, guiding her hips down to his.

She sank down on him and nearly lost herself then and there. He groaned close to her ear, and she was reminded of all the wonderful things he had done to her body. She was determined to give him something in return.

Slowly, she rocked her hips, bringing him deeper into her. His hands pushed up, cupping her breasts once more, his fingers playing along her nipples. She moaned, rocked again, wanting more. She placed a hand on his shoulder to steady herself, rocking harder, loving the feel of him so deep inside her. She felt herself speeding up, but slowed once more, her body involuntarily clenching around him.

His hands fell to her hips, and he guided her, helping her move up the length of him and then sink back down. Her breath caught in her throat again, released in a hitching moan. Again and again and again. She sped up and this time he didn't protest, burying his face just above her collarbone, one hand leaving her hip to cross her back and rest upon the opposite shoulder.

She let go, and as the world spun around them, she knew he let go as well.

****

Flora wasn't sure how they made it to the bed. Or how she had come to be sprawled across him, one of his furs barely covering her hip, her legs entangled with his. It was like coming out of a dream how she found her head resting on his shoulder, her hair spread out across both of them, her hand resting upon his chest. His arm was wrapped around her back, his fingers idly caressing her shoulder.

She traced a finger across a smooth, faded white scar across his side, a straight line with virtually no jagging or puckering, no ridges or dimples. “How did you get it?” she murmured.

Her craned his neck awkwardly to assess the mark. “Training accident.”

She ran her finger down it, then back up. “That’s it?” She looked to his face, her chin shifting onto her opposite hand.

His eyes were closed once more, but a wisp of a crooked smile twitched across his lips. His fingers continued to play along her shoulder. “I was younger, just learning, really, and got a little overzealous in practicing without any armor. My partner’s dirk sliced right through my shirt.”

“And this one?” She moved her hand to another long scar running across the front of his shoulder, below his left clavicle and toward his bicep. It, too, was white and long healed.

His eyes opened to look at her fingers, but he frowned a bit. “I don’t remember.”

Flora passed her thumb over it, wondering if he had ever had a shoulder surgery. It was fairly substantial and not something she thought one would likely forget. She had a few minor scars, a hard-to-find gash on her outer ankle from a piece of glass on a loch beach, a thumbnail-sized slash across her smallest left finger from the lid of a cat food can. Even the smallest, most-obscure scar on her hip from having a mole removed when she was a teenager, she knew where it came from. Perhaps she didn’t remember a date or a time, perhaps she didn’t remember all of the circumstances surrounding the original wound, but she knew where they all came from.

But she didn't say anything. She was too happy and she knew if she brought up the "other" Owen, he would immediately pull away from her.

"And this one?" She pushed herself up to lay a soft kiss on the scar that ran from the corner of his mouth. It was her favorite, the most visible mark proving he *was* different than the Owen she had known on the other side of the veil. And though it was a blemish on his otherwise perfect face, it made him all the more attractive.

"I don't remember." This time, the words were a little less offhanded. A little more self-doubting. The line that appeared between his eyebrows when he frowned reappeared.

His hand fell away from her shoulder and he pushed up, dislodging her and standing. He pulled on his pants, allowing them to hang low on his hips.

Flora pushed herself up with one hand, the fur falling down over her hips. Instinctively, she used her other arm to cover her breasts, though she supposed the action was a little ridiculous considering he had explored every inch of her.

"I have work to do," he said, perhaps more to himself than to her, in a sort of low, churlish mutter. He didn't say any more, pulling out the chair at his desk and hunching back over the papers they had strewn across the surface earlier, in nothing more than the plain muslin shorts.

Flora swallowed, knowing she had been dismissed and feeling very alone in the soft light. She searched around for her own clothes, slipping out from under the fur when she spotted them, and quickly pulling them on.

She felt ridiculous, embarrassed. She didn't know what she had said to make him close up so completely, and tears stung the back of her eyes. She was afraid they would spill over, or that she would be unable to control the inevitable sob she could feel bubbling up in her throat.

Clothes on, but bodice only half-hooked, shoes in hand, she slipped through the door just as the first tear fell. Her breath caught and she hiccupped, nearly running into one of the soldiers who stood guard on the ramparts. She ducked her head and ran to the darkness of her own room.

Chapter 20

Flora entered the great hall to find everyone already sitting down to the evening meal. By the look of the candles, she could see she had skipped right over fashionably late and landed squarely in "Why even bother showing up?" She started toward her seat at the high table where she usually sat between Owen and Arawn, but stopped short when she saw her seat was already taken.

By the very woman who had sent her into this strange land.

Hers was the last face she would have expected to see here in Annwn. Of course, when she had first arrived she had hoped—maybe even prayed—her unnamed employer would reappear and give her some sort of guidance. Any sort of guidance. And seeing her now, in Flora's own place, made her feel a bit uneasy. The woman's beauty was definitely a sight to behold, and all of her attention appeared to be directed at Owen. Flora silently willed him to look away and see her standing there, but he couldn't seem to take his eyes off the raven-haired beauty.

Given that Owen hadn't spoken to her all day, the usurpation of her seat stung even further. She had continued on to her early-morning appointment with the king at the archery range as she did every morning, both hoping to see Owen and praying he would keep his distance. But he hadn't been in the training yard at all, instead one of his officers oversaw the maneuvers of the troops. Her disappointment affected her focus more than usual, and she didn't hit the target once.

But she did almost hit a stray cat. She could still recall the startled meow it let out.

She had mentally been preparing herself for the evening meal all day. Swallowing, she started to turn away and flee back to her apartments, but Captain Griffith had apparently seen her and stood, waving her over to come sit with him and some of the other officers. Smiling nervously, she scurried over, hugging the shadows so as not to draw attention to herself. She stepped over the bench to sit in the small gap left for her and took the pitcher passed her way, though her gaze was still on the woman.

"Do you know who that is?" she asked Griffith.

He leaned toward her. "No, I don't have a name. She comes and goes, though. And is always an honored guest of our lord."

"What does she do here?"

Griffith looked understandably uncomfortable. "I don't know that, either, but the rumors…" He trailed off.

"Rumors? What are the rumors?"

He shook his head and looked at her uneasily. "I can't repeat them."

Flora frowned. She knew she couldn't ask him to tell her anyway, but she was sure there would be someone somewhere who would have a looser tongue. She liked to think Griffith was one of the few people here she could count among her friends, and she certainly didn't want to jeopardize that.

Her neighbor to the left, a young woman she had seen working with the archers passed her a bowl of potatoes. Flora tried to concentrate on filling her plate and eating what she took, but she couldn't seem to keep her mind off the woman sitting in her chair at the high table. Or her eyes.

"I haven't seen your friend much," Griffith said, obviously trying to make conversation.

"Which one?" she asked absently.

When he hesitated, she turned her attention to him fully. He ducked his head a little, and in the dim light, she thought she could make out a bit of a blush.

"Your, um, the, um… Delyth, that is."

Delyth had never been one to stick around the apartments, not like Eve and Iain did. Eve was basically a permanent fixture there, and Flora was beginning to wonder if perhaps she was suffering from depression. It wasn't a subject she felt she could safely broach, however, considering their less-than-friendly existence since Eve discovered Owen was a general and not a prisoner.

But Delyth, despite being so friendly and forthcoming did seem to disappear rather frequently. Flora knew the quiet Ellyl woman had been around, her things never in exactly the same place about the work chamber, but Flora couldn't quite pinpoint when she had last seen her. Or where. Or if they had even talked to one another.

"No, I suppose she hasn't been around much, has she?" Flora mused. "I didn't realize the two of you were friendly."

"Oh, we're not. I mean, that is to say we are friendly, just not…friends."

"So, you…are fond of her?"

"I knew I shouldn't have asked," the captain grumbled.

Flora gave him a friendly, one-armed hug. "Sorry, love."

It was a momentary distraction, and with her companion no longer wanting to talk, Flora's attention was back on the high table.

The woman made her interest in Owen known, leaning toward him, smiling flirtatiously. Her black hair was worked into a long, thick braid that hung down one shoulder, and the same shoulder inched closer and closer to Owen as the meal went on. Flora could feel jealousy boiling up, but it was when she saw the other woman place her hand over Owen's that she decided she just couldn't sit around and watch the exchange any longer.

"Excuse me," she told Captain Griffith and left her seat, escaping out of the great hall through one of the side doors. She briefly considered going back to her apartments, but she had spent all day there and desperately needed a change of scenery. Instead, she climbed up the back stairs to the ramparts. It was the one place she could usually come to think. No one bothered her and it was always quiet.

She gnawed on her lip as she paced. Why was *she* here? Was it because Flora had failed to do the one task she had been given? What would be the consequences? What was she supposed to do, now? And why had she not come to Flora, first? Was this some sort of test?

Flora anxiously rubbed her hands together while she contemplated all manner of dismemberment. Her solitude didn't last long, however. Freezing rain began to pelt her and she was forced to quickly find shelter back inside the fortress.

When she returned to her apartments, she found Owen standing in the outer chamber, running his fingers over one of the pendants she had carried with her to the Otherworld in the leather pack, a silver tree. It lay amongst the others on the table. She had yet to figure out their purpose or even their meaning,

"Where did you get these?" he asked, a hint of gravity pulling at his voice.

"They were given to me by my benefactress," she answered. It was true, she supposed.

Owen eyed her as if he didn't believe her, and turned away, giving her only a view of his profile. He was acting aloof. Flora felt nerves begin to play in the pit of her stomach.

"Who is she?" she murmured.

His mouth was a grim line before, but it grew even grimmer. His lips flattened against themselves, pulling at the scar that jutted from between them. "*My* benefactress."

Flora's heart slammed into her ribs. She fought to maintain her composure, not allow him to see her surprise. She drew in a breath and moved to stand by the window, giving them each some breathing space. She forced her breathing to remain even and shallow.

He crossed his arms over his chest and made a show of avoiding her gaze just as much as she was avoiding his.

"How is that possible? I thought Arawn was your benefactor."

"It was she who acquired my position here with Annwn's army," Owen said, as if that explained everything.

"That's it? She found you a job? Did she not want anything in return?" She hoped she didn't sound too eager to know that last bit of information.

She knew she should probably tell him that they were employed by the same person. But she couldn't help but feel admitting it was the wrong move. After all, she had been led to believe Owen was held prisoner here, which was most definitely not true. And why would the woman send her here to rescue him if she not only knew he was here and free, but had been the one to send him here herself?

Flora's unease was growing by leaps and bounds; she could feel herself becoming suspicious of Owen. Pulling back from him. The thought he might be untrustworthy was like a knife in her gut, leaving her feeling as if she were being backed into a corner, for she hadn't felt she could trust many people in this world to begin with. Without him, she was left with only Delyth and perhaps Evan Griffith, and she was frequently absent at best, he subordinate to his commanding officer.

A muscle in Owen's jaw ticked. "She saved me, once, and I owe her."

"Owe her? Owe her what?" Flora wanted to know, wanting something, anything that would restore her faith that they were on the same team, if unwittingly.

"My life." He ran his hand through his hair and finally looked at her, actually looked at her.

Flora felt her insides melt a little of the fear that had churned inside her. "Were the two of you… Are the two of you…" She didn't know how to ask him if they were or had been lovers. It was something she wanted—no needed—to know, but she couldn't make herself say the words. It was in that moment, that she knew, despite telling herself it wasn't possible, she was in love with him.

Seeing Robert with another man had given her life. It had pushed her to wake up, to experience, to live. But if she found out Owen had another, she was almost sure something inside her would die.

"No. I think she would have liked us to be, once. But no, I never could."

"Why?" she whispered.

He gave her a soft look, one that told her he desperately wanted to tell her, but couldn't.

It was enough, though. She felt all of her pent-up nervous energy deflate, and her strength with it. She reached for the back of the nearest chair, pulling it to her and falling ungracefully into it.

"Why did you come?" she finally asked.

"I knew you'd have questions. That you were upset about last night."

"Oh, did you now?" She immediately regretted her sarcasm. "Sorry. I didn't mean that." She rubbed her palms down her face. "So, how did you come to benefit from her patronage?"

Owen raised an eyebrow at her question, and then pulled up the chair opposite the table from her. He sat down, folding his hands on top, his thumbs forming an X. "I don't remember." His hands were suddenly no longer clasped, his right hand going to the back of his neck where he rubbed, as if he were trying to banish sore muscles or the beginning of a headache. "I mean, I do. There was a lot of water. She pulled me to shore. I just don't remember how I came to be there."

Flora's heart quickened. The helicopter Major Drummond had been piloting had gone down over the sea. She was so close to fitting all of the pieces into the puzzle. She could feel it.

"What do you know of Pwyll Pendefeg Dyfed?" he asked.

Flora remembered the name from the book—oh, what was it called? It had been too large for her to fit in the pack, so she had left it and another one, Canu Taliesin, behind. The *Mabinogion*! That was it! But what of Pwyll? She couldn't remember.

"I know the name is all," she told him.

He gave her a look of disbelief. "Pwyll Pendefeg Dyfed? Who ruled for Arawn for a year and fought and won against Hafgan?" She shook her head and lifted her shoulders.

Owen continued to eye her but went over the most basic of the events. Of how Pwyll had come across Arawn's hounds as they hunted but took the kill for his own. And when Arawn confronted him, he apologized rather than making excuses. Instead of demanding justice, Arawn awarded Pwyll by allowing him to rule over Annwn in his place, Arawn taking Pwyll's own likeness to rule over Dyfed. And under Pwyll's guidance, Arawn fought Hafgan into submission for the first time. Arawn even rewarded Pwyll further at the end of the year when he learned Pwyll had not once lain with his wife.

"Wait, Arawn has a wife?"

Owen lifted a golden eyebrow. “Yes. She sits on his other side. Small blond woman? Pretty eyes, big teeth.”

Flora frowned. “I guess I never noticed her. Hmm. But what does this have to do with you?”

“After Pwyll returned to Dyfed, Arawn took up the running of his own army again. His campaigns never matched that of Pwyll. At first it bored him, and then it angered him. For every battle he won, Hafgan won another. Only Pwyll had been victorious one hundred percent of the time.”

“Until you,” Flora said. This was why Hafgan wanted Owen gone. Why he had sent Eve and Iain with her. Hafgan wanted Owen gone out of the way so the playing field would once again be level.

“She secured me the position as general so Arawn could go back to hunting, but his forces could also go back to winning battles.”

“And what does she get out of this?” Flora wanted to know.

His stony gaze told her he had been wondering the same thing.

He broke eye contact first and reached up to rub the back of his neck, as if to subdue some of the tension. “I think it would be best if we…ended this.”

Flora’s stomach dropped. “End this?”

“I can’t afford the distractions,” he mumbled.

Flora was still blinking. “I’m sorry, you want to *end* this?”

She could see his Adam’s apple bob as he swallowed, but he still looked her in the eye and said, “Yes.”

"But…why?" she choked. Obviously, she wouldn't be controlling her emotions as well as he.

"I need to focus. I have a battle to win, and I can't do it if all I am thinking about is you."

Flora's brow knit. "So, you want to end it."

His control broke and he slammed his fist on the table, and she jumped. "Yes! She was right. I'm not as good when you're around. I can't focus on anything else because all I can think about is you. I let my troops down every time I seek you out rather than plan movements or check over inventories. I spent a whole damn day hunting you down in the snow rather than doing my job, Flora!"

Flora didn't say anything. Her mind was too busy trying to work through the bizarre puzzle he was laying out before her.

"I'm needed to ensure Annwn's forces succeed," he told her with an almost deadly calm.

"Why does she need you to make sure Arawn wins?" she asked quietly.

"It doesn't matter, Flora. I owe her this. That's all that does matter."

She shook her head in disbelief. Maybe it was a mechanism to hide the hurt she felt. The shattering of her heart. "Why do I always feel like I've been run through the emotional ringer after I've spent an hour with you?" she mused, then turned on her heel and stormed out of her own apartments.

Chapter 21

Flora thought she would go crazy if she had to continue listening to Eve sharpen the blade of her sword for another moment. The sound of the steel hitting whetstone over and over was worse than nails on a chalkboard, and she was almost sure it had been going on for hours. The pounding in her temples had been steadily increasing, and she could no longer concentrate on anything but the metallic ring.

She felt her irritation bubbling up, and she was just about to scream for Eve to cease when the door opened. Delyth passed through the portal, Iain on her heels.

Flora had sent her bodyguard-slash-servant to find Delyth some time ago, the questions finally rising to the surface. She had to have answers, and she would drive herself mad if she didn't have them soon.

Delyth gave her a wisp of a smile and moved to take the seat next to Flora. "You requested my presence?"

Flora bent her head close to the Ellyll's and spoke in hushed tones. Iain was leaning against the stone wall next to the door, his razor-sharp gaze trained right on them, and the scraping of Eve's blade had become less vigorous.

"I have some questions. Questions I think only you can answer," Flora murmured.

Delyth looked straight into her eyes and nodded once, slowly.

"Do they know they're dead?" Flora continued.

Delyth's lips lifted, as if she had a secret she was trying to keep, but desperately wanted to let it spill. "Who?"

"The people who are not…Ellyll. Or Fae. The rest."

The smile deepened and Delyth's gaze cut to where Iain stood. "Oh, yes. From your world, at least. This is their reward. A chance to live without fear or starvation or illness."

Flora frowned. "But that doesn't make any sense. What about all of the soldiers I treated for injuries? All of the burns?"

Delyth let out a sigh and Flora knew the Ellyll thought she was no better than a small child asking ridiculous questions like "Why does it rain?" and "Where does the sun go at night?"

"You can't think of the Otherworld as one place," she scolded Flora kindly, shaking her head from side to side a little as she said it.

"That makes no sense."

"The river we crossed? It separates Hafgan's kingdom from the Kingdom of Annwn. Here, give me a bit of parchment." Delyth indicated a stack Flora always kept out on the table for charms and spells. The small woman reached for a quill, dipped it into the inkwell and started drawing a squiggly line down the center. She indicated one side. "This is the Summer Kingdom. And this is the Winter Kingdom."

"Hafgan and Arawn," Flora murmured, showing the other woman she understood.

"Yes, exactly." She continued to draw. "When your people cross the veil, they go to the Summer Kingdom. They live simple, happy, lives. And when the time comes and they dream of more, they move on."

"How? They just leave?"

"Most join the army. They fight at the Ford. And those who fall move on to fight for Arawn."

"And if Arawn's soldiers fall?"

"They go back to your world. They get a new life. A new chance. The cycle begins anew."

"And what happens if no one falls? If no one dies?"

"There is always someone. That is the way of things," Delyth told her simply.

"I'm just confused. Why would people knowingly go into battle to be maimed and hurt?"

"It's an honor."

"Why did we try to save them, then? Why not just let them all die in the mouths of those dragons?"

"Because if no one fights for summer, it will never come. And there will be no forces to ensure winter arrives."

"So, they all know this?"

"Yes."

"So, the dead know they are dead. The Fae know they are Fae. The Ellyll know they are Ellyll. The True Believers remember crossing through the veil. What of the ones who think they have lived here their whole lives? The ones who think they have a story here, but aren't Fae or Ellyll or True Believers? What happens to them when they fight at the Ford?"

Delyth's forehead creased in thought. It was a look that spoke her words even before she did. "I don't know."

****

Flora was still angry with Owen. Which was probably an understatement, but the anger festered every time she walked into the great hall to see him sitting next to the other woman. Ugh. She still didn't even know her name.

Most nights, he ignored Flora. His blatant disregard for her was probably the most infuriating part. Other than the whole "breaking things off" thing. She shot daggers at him as she entered the hall, but this night was different. This night his gaze was on her. His face was an unreadable mask, as it often was. He was probably good at cards. The bastard. She narrowed her eyes at him, letting him know she saw him. His expression didn't change.

Banishing him from her mind—or telling herself she was banishing him from her mind—she sauntered over to the table where Captain Griffith and the other officers sat, a space left for her. They had been kind enough to welcome her to eat with them, and at best she had been a quiet spectator. She decided right then and there she would rectify her lack of participation. If nothing else, it would keep her mind off the fact that Owen hadn't said a single, bloody word to her in days.

She took the pitcher offered by the female officer sitting opposite her and filled her mug with the bragawd before passing it on to Griffith, who did the same. She pulled the flagon to her, cradling it and leaning forward a little. "I, uh, I've realized I haven't exactly been the best company the last few days. I do apologize. And I was hoping, well, I was hoping perhaps I could get to know you all a little better."

Flora was met with blank stares. She looked around, and then came back to Griffith. "Where do you come from? I mean…" She searched for the words. "Before?"

"I was a flapper."

Flora turned back to the woman who had passed her the pitcher.

"I would sneak out to go dancing and flirt and drink. It was after the war, and we thought we were young and invincible. Car crash snapped my neck." Flora remembered her, now. She was one of the few who didn't want more time. She was ready to move on, or was done, at least, with this place. She had wanted a charm that would assure her bravery in her pursuit for the next life.

Flora hadn't expected such a candid response.

Evan spoke next to her. "Insurgents in Syria."

The man across from Griffith drank heartily and slammed his mug down. He had wanted more time. As much time as he could get, he had told her. There were battles to be won. And he wanted to be sure he was a part of them all. "Marched with Llwelyn ap Gruffud."

Flora hoped she looked suitably impressed because she really had no idea who Llwelyn ap Gruffud was.

They looked at her expectantly.

"Oh, me. Sorry." She said the first thing that came to mind. "Heart attack."

Griffith looked her up and down. "But you were so young."

Flora shrugged. "I had a bad heart as it was. And then when I found my husband in bed with another…"

She dropped her hand to the table to indicate falling over. "Poof."

They all nodded, and she was saved from having to explain more as the servants brought out the trays of food. Arawn stood to give his usual speech about a plentiful harvest and bountiful hunt, to which the entire hall toasted him before going on with the meal. Flora took the opportunity to refill her mug, which, somehow, she had managed to drain.

They all served themselves from platters of parsnips, turnips, and mushrooms; potatoes, carrots, and cabbage; duck, goose, and partridge. Large slabs of hearty bread were passed around, and Flora immediately tore off a bit of hers, popping it into her mouth.

"What do you all do for fun around here? Other than train troops, obviously."

They all looked at each other. "Cards," they answered in unison.

"Maybe I could join you?"

"Of course." This from the woman. What was her name? Margaret? Mildred? Millicent!

"I've never played, though, so you'll have to teach me."

****

They huddled over the table, their cards held abreast, their voices low.

Many of those who unrolled their sleeping pallets in the great hall were beginning to do so, the meal having long been over.

The three officers had taught her an Otherworld game, something they called "fording." It wasn't much different than poker, she supposed. But also a bit like blackjack, as well. It had taken her a few minutes to get used to, but she thought she had done a decent job of getting the hang of it.

The dealer dealt out three cards to each, the black cards representing positive numbers, the red negative. Jacks, kings, and queens were all worth ten, and the ace just one. The object was to get as close to thirteen as possible, but also convince the other players you either held thirteen in your hand or didn't, based on the amounts you bet into the pot. He or she who had thirteen won. If there was no thirteen, the next closest took the pot. There was no passing or folding, one just simply bet less or more each round until there were no cards left to deal.

Flora was losing horribly, yet having a fabulous time. They played for military coins, little brightly painted mementos given to each of them for their service, for battles, jobs well done, and the like. Because she had none, Flora had confiscated the forks from the tables as the servants cleaned up and used them, instead. None of them had use for currency, and so there simply wasn't any. This land simply operated on a barter and trade system, something Flora found equally fascinating and confounding.

She had probably consumed her weight in bragawd, the effects leaving her mind a little fuzzy, her mouth upturned in a goofy grin, and her spirits exorbitantly lifted.

Hugh, one of the other officers who had joined their little party, was regaling them with tales of his fellow officers and their bad decisions. He had, it seemed, been in Annwn the longest of any of the officers, though she got the impression he hadn't been in the Otherworld as long as Arnall who had fought with Llewelyn ap…someone or other.

Hugh waved his hands about as he retold the tale of their commander's first encounter with what she was led to believe was a particularly buxom sergeant by the name of Beathag. The general was by far Flora's favorite subject of the night, especially the more and more she drank, and hearing stories of his misfortune, was putting her in a much better mood.

"He walks in and sees them large teets." Hugh held out his arms in a wide circle in front of him to indicate how big Beathag's bust supposedly was. "Just hanging out. His eyes nearly popped, but he did, he looked her straight in the eyes and he said, I jest not, 'You look very intelligent.' And then he turned on his heel and walked straight back to his office." Hugh threw back his head and roared with laughter, the others joining in.

Even Flora couldn't hold back her giggle.

Unfortunately, there was a loud chorus of "shhhs" that came from those who were trying to sleep, and the card players sobered enough to realize they, too, needed to find their beds.

They all stood, clearing away their coins and forks—Flora only had two left, so it was a good thing the night's festivities were over—and saying their good nights.

Evan offered to see Flora back to her apartment, but she waved him off. "You'd be going out of your way, and it isn't like I don't know where I'm going," she told him.

He eyed her suspiciously. "I'm just afraid you'll tumble down the stairs."

She gave him a bleary smile as she clutched her remaining flatware. "I'll be fine. Promise. I'll crawl up them if it makes you feel better. All fours. Promise."

He gave her a resolute nod. "Done." And then he turned and went to the officers' quarters after the others.

She started to turn toward her own apartments, but the stairs were rather daunting. And while the game had provided her with an opportunity to forget about Owen—for a minute—she suddenly knew she needed to give him a piece of her mind.

A big one.

She marched back through the great hall, grabbing one of the half-empty pitchers as she went, feeling she needed the liquid courage.

Better to get some of that in, she thought, and gulped some of it down straight from the earthen vessel. The bragawd had gone warm, but it still went down fairly easily, warming her well enough she didn't even notice the icy air when it hit her.

There was no candlelight coming from his window. That meant either he was asleep, or he was elsewhere.

The guards who were posted outside made no move to stop her, and she pushed the door open into the chamber. It was quiet, but for the soft sounds of his breathing, long and even and deep. He was asleep.

Suddenly unsure of what she was supposed to do, and perhaps a little bit dizzy, she hastily turned to exit, but fell over her own feet. She threw her weight to one side to save the bragawd, and fell hard on her arse. She let out a yelp of pain, then instantly quieted, for she didn't want to wake him up. Glad none of the bragawd had spilled, she took another sip, and then giggled at the ridiculousness of it all. She had come to yell at him, but instead she was cowering in the shadows drinking ale.

Shite. Where were her forks?

She sat up and began patting the floor for them. Had they fallen? She couldn't remember hearing them drop on the floor. She stretched out her hands, farther and farther, looking for what was left of her winnings—losings?—and then her hand came in contact with warm flesh. She patted it a few times to make sure that was, in fact, what she was feeling, and then looked up.

Owen was standing over her. He was dressed in nothing but his braies and his arms were crossed over his chest while he looked down at her.

She bit her lip and then giggled. "This isn't what it looks like."

"And what does it look like?" he asked, his voice husky from sleep.

"I'm just trying to find my forks."

There was a pause. "Your forks?"

"Yes. And now if you don't mind"—she took a sip of her bragawd—"I will just be finding them and then leaving."

Another pause. "But why are you here in the first place?"

Flora sat back to think about it. "Hmmmm," she mused aloud. "I think I was going to come and yell at you. But then I saw there was no light, so I was making sure you weren't sleeping with her."

"Her?"

She nodded sagely and drank more. It was nearly all gone. "The woman. I still don't know her name. The one who made me come here for you but is making it nearly impossible for me to get you to leave with me."

She tipped back the pitcher, swallowing the last of the ale. "Oops. I think I've said too much. Oh, look, there's one!" She caught the glitter of light on a tine and reached out for the fork, nestling it to her bosom.

Bosom. Such an odd word. She giggled and sank back against the stone wall next to the door. "Mmm." She sighed. "When you find the other one, could you…" She trailed off. The words were thick in her mouth. "I need it for…"

Her eyelids were so heavy. And her mouth was dry. She wished she had some water. Or more bragawd.

"Flora." There was a hint of annoyance in the way Owen said her name.

She snapped her eyes open. "Hello," she said happily. He had knelt down in front of her so their faces were only a few inches apart. She reached up and ran the pad of her thumb across the scar at the corner of her mouth. "I came here to yell at you."

"I figured as much. Here, let's get you up," he said, taking her empty hand in his and wrapping an arm around her back to help her stand.

"You're not done with me," she told him.

"Is that so?"

"Exactly so," she answered.

He let out a heavy sigh. "It isn't something I wanted, Flora. It's just something that…had to happen. It's for the best."

Flora shook her head like a small child. "No." She stopped because it was making her dizzy. She swayed a little on her feet. "No, you're just scared. Because I love you and you're just scared you love me, too."

Her words were met with silence.

"It's okay to be scared, you know," she told him seriously. "Because being scared means you're invested. You're paying attention. Taking risks. Being scared means you're alive." And then to herself, she said, "Alive. *Alive*."

Flora reached up, pulling his head down to hers so she could give him a big, smacking kiss. "You *are* alive!"

She couldn't seem to wipe the huge smile off her face. It was making her cheeks ache and her head hurt. Owen might not be here in the Otherworld the same way she was, but she was sure he was alive.

For a moment, she thought he would say something. But he didn't. Instead, he scooped her up and tossed her down on his bed. "Go to sleep," he told her. "Tomorrow isn't going to be a pleasant day for you."

She frowned at him, but snuggled into his pillow. It smelled of him, a woodsy scent. She was asleep in moments.

Chapter 22

Flora had been awake for some time, but kept her eyes tightly shut. She felt like she was spinning at a rapid rate, her insides knotting and her head threatening to explode. But her arm, which was caught underneath the rest of her body was starting to ache and tingle from falling asleep, and if she didn't move soon, she was going to rip it off.

On the count of three, she pushed herself up and opened her eyes.

She wasn't in her own room. But she instantly recognized where she was. How had she ended up in Owen's room? She vaguely remembered telling Griffith she didn't need help going to her own apartments. And she did recollect having a conversation with Owen, but none of the particulars. She didn't know what she had said. Or what he had said. Only that she now felt rather embarrassed.

The first rays of morning light were beginning to stream over the mountains, casting the room in an odd, grayish light. At the foot of the bed, Owen was hunched over in a chair, his legs crossed at the ankles and stretched out before him. A blanket had slid down to reveal the scar on his shoulder. His head lolled down and to the right in what had to be an incredibly uncomfortable position and his face was scruffy from overnight beard growth.

Wanting to avoid the awkward conversation that would have to take place if she was still there when he awoke, she gritted her teeth against the pounding in her head and swung her feet over the side of the bed. If she hurried, she could probably make it back to her own rooms before the soldiers trickled into the training yards.

The moment her feet hit the stone floor, something sharp made contact with the ball of her foot and she sucked in a pained breath, falling back down onto the mattress and cradling the offended foot. The pain quickly subsided, and she looked down before leaping, this time, to see a fork on the floor, its tines sticking straight up.

"I'm surprised you let go of it."

She whipped around to see Owen getting up, the blanket falling down around his waist. He winced and rolled his head around his neck, then rubbed at the back of it.

"Sorry, I didn't mean to wake you," she apologized sheepishly.

"No, I—"

"And whatever it is I said last night. I apologize for that, too," she interrupted him quickly in a flurry of words.

"You don't remember?" He frowned.

She narrowed her eyes at him. "That sounds bad. Very bad. What did I say?"

He shook his head. "Nothing. You didn't say anything."

She knew he was lying. He was horrible at it, his eyes refusing to meet hers and his voice going a little high.

“Oh, well, what a relief,” was her sarcastic retort.

Sighing with disgust, she stood up, avoided stepping on the fork, then reached down to claim it. Her shoes had been placed at the foot of the bed, and she slipped her feet into them. “I’m sorry to have disturbed you,” she mumbled as she made for the door.

“Wait.” Owen tossed the blanket onto the bed. He was still wearing only his braies, but reached for the breeches that were tossed haphazardly over a trunk. He stepped into them, pulling them up over his hips but leaving them untied.

“Is she really your benefactress?”

****

He didn’t know why he asked. He had promised himself he wouldn’t ask, and because she hadn’t really meant to say what she had to him last night, he would forget it, all of it. But it didn’t matter because he hadn’t been able to keep his damn mouth shut.

She looked at him with surprise, her blue-gray eyes wide as the implications of releasing her secret sank in. She rubbed at her temples with the tips of her fingers, her eyes closed. If he had to guess, she was trying to conjure up just what had been said the night before.

“What did I say?” she demanded.

“You said she made you come here for me, but she’s making it impossible for me to leave with you.”

She closed her eyes and her shoulders sank, her demeanor visibly deflating.

“You never trained at the Archives, did you?”

“The Archives?” she questioned. She had never heard of such a place, even if the name had come up a time or two in conversation.

"You're not really one of Cerridwen's witches. Nor are you the ambassador of Arianrhod. Are you?"

She looked at him with large, unsure eyes. "I don't know."

He turned to one of his trunks, rummaging through it and coming up with a small knife. Its blade flashed as he laid it down atop his desk, letting her see it, but not giving it back to her. He ran his fingers over the symbol of lightning over the anvil on the handle. "I am guessing you are not the speaker of Govannan, either?

She fell back against the door, leaning on it as if she couldn't bear her own weight anymore.

"I don't know what to tell you because I don't have the answers, myself." The words seemed to pain her. Her lips trembled and her eyes became haunted. Her skin, always as pale as fresh milk, lost the last of its color, highlighting only the little brown freckles speckling her nose and cheeks.

"Then tell me what you do know."

She pulled her lips between her teeth, biting down on them. It was a move he had seen before, one she used when she needed time to think, to sort things.

"No lies, Flora."

"I wouldn't lie to you," she told him softly, her voice small and higher than normal.

"Oh?" he bit out sarcastically. "Then please, tell me, why are we having this conversation?" he demanded.

"I didn't lie. I'm only working with partial truths myself."

He folded his arms across his chest and gave her a look he hoped would encourage her to just get on with it.

"I'm not dead."

He lifted an eyebrow. "I'm not dead, either."

"No, you're not. At least I don't think you are. But the people here…most of the people? They are dead."

Oh, he thought to himself. Oh, she really *was* crazy.

"Let me start over," she begged. "This…this is the Otherworld. It's where people from my world go when they die."

Yup. She was crazy.

She rolled her eyes at him. "Just go with it for argument's sake," she said.

He waved her on.

"I met you on the other side of the veil. Your sister owns the shop next to mine, and you and I… Well, we became close. And then you disappeared. I went to your sister, but she insisted you had been missing for some time and were presumed dead, all during the time that I knew you. You were like a ghost, but one that only I could see. All of those conversations you remember from your dreams? That's when they took place. I was as confused as you are. Hell, I probably still am, so don't give me that look." She glowered at him, but then continued. "The woman who you've been flirting with every evening? She came to me. She told me if you were to have your life back, I would have to come here and 'rescue' you. I thought I would be sneaking into a dungeon and picking a lock, dragging my grateful lover out and returning home. Instead, I was dumped in the middle of a forest. I found my way to Hafgan's castle, met Eve—"

His dropped his arms from his chest and took a step toward her, his brows furrowing. "You were in Hafgan's kingdom?" he demanded.

"Do you want me to tell you what happened or not?"

He gritted his teeth and nodded for her to continue.

"Eve saw my pendant and assumed I was sent by Arianrhod—is that who *she* is? Is she Arianrhod?" She waited for him to nod or shake his head in the negative, but Owen did neither. "Fine. Anyway, Eve told Hafgan I was an ambassador of Arianrhod. He treated me as a guest, but when I mentioned I was looking for you, he threatened me. Kind of. If I don't 'rescue' you before the next Battle at the Ford, Iain and Eve are supposed to kill me. The trouble is, I don't know what death means here. He thinks I am one of them, one of the dead. Perhaps a True Believer at best. But if he does as he promised here, and I die—I don't know what happens to me. And I don't know what happens to you." She choked a little on the last bit.

He was surprised by her matter-of-fact manner. She barely seemed fazed at all about one of them taking a knife to her throat or shooting an arrow to her heart. The prospect angered him and he had a mind to storm out of his chambers and snap both of them in half.

"I've found how to get back, Owen," she told him softly. She moved closer, reaching out to lay her hand on his arm, but drawing back and dropping it to her side, instead. "Please. We can go now, and this will all be over."

"I don't think you understand. This *is* my life," he told her through gritted teeth. "I don't know about this other life you keep telling me about. I had a few dreams, that was it. And you want me to just give up everything I am, everything I've built, just because you say so?"

"No, because *she* said so. Why would she send me here to take you back to the other side of the veil if that isn't what she wanted?"

"That's odd. When was the last time you spoke to her? Because I talked to her last night, and she seemed pretty sure she wanted me to command the forces at the Ford. Not once did she mention gallivanting off with some crazy woman into the great unknown. In fact, she even suggested maybe I needed to spend a little less time with you and a little more time doing my job." He saw the hurt in her eyes. For a second he felt triumphant, but it quickly dissipated and he only felt ashamed for having tried to hurt her on purpose. "Flora, I—"

"I don't know what her game is," she said quietly. "I don't care anymore. I just want to go home, Owen. I'm tired and I want to go home."

She sounded so small, so young. All of a sudden, the façade of confidence she carried had disappeared, leaving her looking vulnerable and afraid.

And it was his fault.

"Let me help you get back, then," he offered, even though he didn't want to. The thought of her leaving him forever caused a lump in his throat, an ache in his heart. But he couldn't ask her to remain here and be miserable. To remain here and risk her life.

She turned her pleading gaze on him. "Don't you see? I don't *want* to leave without you, Owen. I should, but I don't want to. For the first time in my life, I am doing what I want to do instead of doing what I should do. And I'm not leaving here without you, even if you refuse to have anything to do with me anymore." She choked up a little on the last bit, and in the soft light, he could see a small tear trail down her cheek.

"Flora—"

"No, it's okay, you don't have to say anything. I know you don't believe me. I don't think even *I* believe me." She was hugging herself as if she were cold coldness. "I'm not a witch. I'm not an ambassador. I'm just…me. I'm just a woman who's scared. Scared that I've made all of the wrong choices my entire life and that I'm destined to make all of the wrong choices. I'll just be sad and alone and *wrong.* But Owen, I wanted to do the right thing. I just…" She sighed. "I just wanted to do the right thing."

She didn't even look at him when she left.

****

Owen liked lists. He liked charts. And organization. He liked lining up all of his options into columns, checking them off, cross-checking them, adding up the possibilities and seeing what course of action yielded the best possible outcome.

Alone, he sat down at the desk in his chambers, spreading rolls of vellum out and inking a quill. And he began to list everything he didn't know about himself. It was a surprisingly long list.

It might have been easier to write down what he *did* know.

That was a good plan. He shoved the original sheet away and pulled a fresh one before him.

He commanded an army. Annwn's army. He was well trained in melee attacks, and he had an aptitude for ranged defenses. He had been recruited to the position by a woman he knew nothing about; he didn't even know how she was connected to Annwn or its king. And he had fallen in love with another woman he had met in his dreams.

The more he tried to remember—where he grew up, what his parents were like, if he had siblings, how he had gotten some of his more significant scars—the more Owen knew there was some truth to the story Flora had told him.

The longer he had been around her, the more suspicious he had become of his own story. He, the only one who feared death. The only one who was saddened by it. He, the one with scars crisscrossing his body, but no recollection of where some of them had even come from. He, who had been given the greatest commission he could ever imagine, but as what?

He knew there were others who had seen far more battles than he, men and women who had fought at Arawn's side at least a dozen times, who had seen more victories than he could imagine, and just as many defeats. He didn't know why he was special, what having him at the forefront gained anyone.

He ran his hands down his face and absently chastised himself for not having shaved.

The problem was he still had a job to do. A responsibility. And if he had loyalty to anyone, it was Arawn. Flora would have him leave it all for the unknown. She would have him betray his friend—dare he call Arawn a friend?—and leave everything he had come to know, to work for.

No, what he did know had to be enough. It had to be.

****

Flora fell back onto her bed, the covers fluffing up around her. She was tired. So, very tired. Whatever optimism she possessed had fled. Whatever hope stamped out. She was lost, hollow, a husk.

She was done. There was nothing left for her to do here but wait. Wait for her friends to charge into a battle they would continue to fight for all of eternity. To die or not. It didn't matter, for they would be back here someday. Just as she would be back here someday.

If she ever left.

She waited for her own end, a terrifying mystery of an end, one no one could predict for her. If she died on this side, the side that *was* death would she stay here? Would she return to her own time? She had no way of knowing. She wondered if anyone knew; if they ever would. All she knew was the awful ache of failure. And the hurt of heartbreak.

She kicked off her boots, curling her legs up so she could pull her blankets up over her. She turned to her side, knees to chest, as small as she could be. It was then, curled up, eyes dry but stinging with tears, she saw it.

It wouldn't have given her pause before, the skein of ugly yarn sitting in the corner. But it looked exactly the same as the one she had had on her bedside table right before… It was something that doesn't belong. It must work the same way here. She knew she could reach out and touch it. She could go back to her shop and pretend that none of this had happened.

Pretend Owen had never happened.

Pretend she had never learned to take a risk.

Pretend the unexpected could be so beautiful.

Pretend she had never learned what it really was to fall in love.

Her fingers almost itched to reach out, glide over the coarse woolen strands. But she couldn't do it. She still had time, didn't she? She still had time in a world without time.

Chapter 23

The forces of Annwn made the march back to the Ford as the sun rose over the mountain ridges. The snow had given way to slightly warmer temperatures, melting under the wheels of the wagons and boots of the soldiers, sloshing up the hooves of the horses. Owen rode in the middle of the group, battle armor glinting as the sun caught it, fur mantle ruffling in the breeze. His horse, a massive white destrier, was outfitted in the red colors of Annwn, its gait smooth. He wore no helm upon his head, instead resting it at his hip, his left hand cradling it nonchalantly. His golden hair had been recently clipped, and the longer strands at his crown caught the light, glinting like polished, precious metal.

Flora rode not far behind on her own similarly fitted mare, Eve and Iain flanking her, Delyth at her back. She felt trapped there, like a prisoner being escorted to the gallows. She found herself wondering what they would do if she spurred the little mount forward, if she took off, dodging the general and his officers, shooting off into the distance. Not that there was anywhere to go but back to the man who promised her death should she fail to do his bidding.

Owen had come to her the evening before to request her presence on the journey. In fact, his exact words had been "Arawn wants you to accompany me." He had not met her gaze as he informed her, his focus pinned on something just north of her head. She hadn't even realized the army was to march out so soon, and to find out the battle was a handful of days away, that she had so little time left…

A perpetual lump seemed to live in her throat, and she knew she was an anxiety-ridden mess. Her mind was swimming in every direction possible, playing out every scenario she could think of, how she could possibly get him to leave with her—some involved tears, some yelling. In one she threatened him with a knife, but it always ended with him laughing as he knocked it out of her hand. Most of the scenarios she played through her mind involved her dying at the hands of Iain and Eve, Owen watching and not caring. And that stung.

She watched him as they rode. The wind played in his short blond hair. Though many of his soldiers wore helms, he did not, and though she wondered why he held it to his side, she was oddly glad he didn't, for it allowed her the chance to catch sight of him every once in a while when he would turn his head and scan the landscape around them.

Flora resisted the urge to nudge her horse up beside him. Not that she had anything to say to him. He had made it clear he wanted nothing to do with her, and she was consumed by wanting to talk about the one thing he had made clear he didn't want to talk about it. It was gnawing her up inside.

The march took them long into the afternoon, and then they came to a stop, the troops bunching together like an accordion being pressed in on itself. The horses needed to be watered, fed, and rested, the people needing much the same. She followed the direction of the others, dismounting and stretching her legs. No one said anything to her, not even Delyth, and she felt more alone than she had since arriving in the Otherworld.

Flora wandered away, off toward a rock overlooking the creek they had followed. Soldiers were filling buckets of water for the horses and oxen that pulled the carts, and she curled atop the warm surface to stay out of their way.

The warmth of the rock reminded her the snow was long behind them, for here the brown grasses were merely damp, the paths wet and muddy. The few clumps that had edged the roads were either far behind them or had melted in the warmth of the sun. The white horses were brown up to their knees, splattered with flecks of dirt even higher. It was as if they had trudged toward the first signs of spring.

She turned her back to the army behind her and looked out over the valley. It spread out before her, a plain between the great, snowcapped mountain ridges. They were surrounded on all sides by the mountains, but the ones to the north, the ones she had supposedly come from were larger, more looming and whiter than all of the rest. She wondered if it was anything like home.

Flora closed her eyes and imagined home, not the little shop she had made her own, but the place she had come from. The places with the rolling mountains thick with heather, the streams that cut through rock, gouging the earth. The cold lochs, the sky that seemed never to end. Her mother's garden with the manicured lawn and the pretty flowers that swayed in the summer wind. Her father's study with the antique deer heads lining the wood-paneled walls.

She wondered if she would ever see home again. Or if she would cease to exist in this place, this other world so like her own, but yet so incredibly different.

Off in the distance, hovering just above the ridge, she could make out the faint outline of a fire drake soaring in the air. It was so far away she could barely make out its shape. A reminder, nonetheless. Flora turned back to the army and saw they were beginning to saddle up once more. She uncurled herself from the warm rock, adjusted the strap of her pack, and made her way back to the group.

None of them said anything, and she climbed back into the saddle, her legs and backside already aching. She didn't remember being uncomfortable when she dismounted, but she suddenly wished she had so she could have done more walking or stretching.

Flora shifted, rolled her head on her shoulders to see Owen glancing back at her. Then he quickly turned away.

****

They stopped to make camp before dusk while the sun was still in the sky, offering its light to the soldiers as they erected their tents and built their cooking fires.

Owen instructed that Flora's tent be set up near to his own, though he made the request out of her earshot. Despite wanting to keep her at a distance, the closer to the battlefield they marched, the closer to her he wanted to be. He no longer felt the confidence he had felt before, and she comforted him.

He'd long been drawn to her, feeling there was a connection that far surpassed his conscious being. When first he had seen her hurl herself in front of him, he'd been in awe of her courage, if a bit surprised at her stupidity. She was a fascinating contradiction—self-assured and confident one moment, quiet and meek the next. At first he had been sure she would fling herself at him—and hadn't she, a little?—but then she pulled back, only to plow forward again, like a young girl who had no idea what she was doing.

And yet she had been exactly what he needed when he needed it. Even knowing she was a distraction from his mission and his duty, she had been the only one who seemed to understand the emotions only he felt. He should have suspected something was different about him; looking back it seemed so obvious he didn't fit in, yet it had taken a nervous redhead to force him to confront it.

"You asked to see me, sir?"

Owen looked up from his hunched-over position. He had been perched atop his trunk, his elbow resting on his knee. "Captain Griffith," he said in greeting as he rose. They both still wore their armor; Owen thought he might never be without it while on the road after their last encounter with the dragons. He wondered if Griffith felt the same. Owen cleared his throat. "You, uh, you're rather close to the witch."

Griffith looked amused. "I would have to say I am not nearly as close to her as you," he said with a twinkle in his eye and a twitch of his lips. He suddenly remembered himself and straightened. "Sir."

Owen grunted and rubbed at the back of his neck absently. "What do you…think of her?"

Griffith's eyebrow's shot up. "I, ah, she's very pretty. But not obviously so; it just sort of grows on you. And she's…nice?"

It was Owen's turn to raise his eyebrows. "The two of you look like gossiping schoolgirls and your assessment is 'she's nice and pretty'?"

Griffith shifted nervously. "Forgive me, sir, I'd just, um, like to keep my position, if it's all the same."

Owen went back to rubbing his neck. He hoped the tension would just drain down his spine. It didn't. "Your job is safe, Captain."

"She doesn't seem to belong here," fell out of his mouth as if he couldn't keep it inside anymore. He hurriedly added, "But I have never known anyone from the North, either. Maybe…maybe they are a different sort than us down here."

Owen knew nothing of the North. Everyone offered at least some sort of preconceived notions about what "The North" was. It was mentioned a handful of times in the book his benefactress had given him before his arrival at Caer Annwn. The tome had included the backgrounds of those who ruled the land, but no more. It was like a playbill, but with charts and pictures. He had studied it, memorized it, and could likely recite any part of it, yet it still told him so little.

He couldn't help but feel anxious at his lack of knowledge. He was the commander. If anyone should have all of the information, it was he. Why had Arawn even entrusted so much to him? Because she had asked him to? And why did she want him here? That was the question, wasn't it?

Unfortunately, he doubted he would ever get answers, much less have them before the next Battle at the Ford. Which meant he had a choice.

Owen crossed his arms over his breastplate, and readjusted his stance, his feet shoulder width apart, jaw set. "And me? Do I seem to belong here?"

The other man blinked in surprise and his mouth worked for a moment before he snapped it shut. Owen could tell he was trying to gather his thoughts without completely insulting his commanding officer. But he needed to know what his subordinates thought, even if it wasn't what he wanted to hear.

"You have been the best commander I have ever known—this side of the veil or otherwise." He swallowed audibly, his Adam's apple bobbing in his strong, thick neck.

"That doesn't really answer my question." Owen sighed wryly.

"I just… I don't know, sir. Your presence here is exactly what we have needed, and you do seem to belong…."

"But?" Owen interjected when the captain trailed off.

"But your arrival is rather odd. And you seem unaccustomed to….everything here."

Owen ran his hand over his face, the stubble on his chin catching against the skin of his palm. Did doing his job well count for anything? he wondered. Or should he believe Flora was right and he belonged elsewhere?

"I've known so few True Believers, however," Griffith admitted. "And while it's odd that the king would appoint one of you as the commander of his armies, stranger things have happened. I mean, he gave the control of his whole kingdom to someone from the other side." He looked at the floor. "It isn't really my place to speculate on the decisions of our liege, however, is it?"

No, it wasn't his, either, Owen thought to himself. Even though he couldn't seem to help himself.

"Thank you, Captain," he said in dismissal.

The officer left the tent and Owen sat down by his desk.

Chapter 24

Flora had slept little. Every time she thought she was slipping into sleep, she would be jerked awake by the thought of Eve or Iain standing over her, ready to end her life, or Owen falling in a battle she couldn't imagine, or waking up in a mental institution, her arms bound to her torso by a thick, canvas straight jacket.

When she heard stirrings outside of her tent, she finally unfurled herself from her bedroll, stood, and unenthusiastically dressed. She ran her fingers over the things she carried with her. The bowl, the jewelry, the books. She felt no real attachment to any of it but Alexander Carlisle's little journal. For some reason, she felt a connection to Alexander Carlisle, whomever he was. She took the journal and shoved it into a pocket and then tossed the rest of the items into the satchel.

The morning dawned gray and hazy, the clouds hanging low over the rolling hills, their reflections darkening the shallow waters of the Ford. The wind had picked up. Soldiers rushed about, their chain mail and armor clanging and tinkling. The acrid stink of campfires rose up all around, the hammers of the blacksmiths a distant clink. Some had looks of pure terror written across their faces, others excitement. A sense of urgency thrummed through the camp like an electric current. Even the horses were restless, stomping and snorting, ready to run.

She wondered if anyone else would be eating this dawn. She didn't think she could have suffered even the plainest of toast, her stomach churned. Flora scanned the camp. She couldn't seem to make her feet move forward, though she knew this was her last opportunity to persuade Owen to leave before the battle began. But what did she say that she hadn't already said? She had exhausted her repertoire, and it had all fallen on deaf ears. Her stomach rolled again, and she took a cleansing breath before going in search of Owen.

****

"Please, Owen," she begged, her voice cracking. "Please, there's still time. We could go now, we could climb on the horses and ride back to the circle and be done with it. *Please.*"

He hated the desperation in her voice almost as much as he hated that she was begging. Not because it didn't pull at him but because it did. She had always been persistent, but this was even out of character for her.

She had just pushed her way past his guards and into his tent. She was disheveled, her copper hair falling out of the braid, curling around her face in a wild halo. Her eyes had big, dark circles under them, attesting to the lack of sleep she had gotten since the march began. The freckles on her face stood out in stark contrast of her pale skin. She wore an odd combination of leather leggings, long-sleeved tunic, and bodice from one of her gowns, as if she couldn't decide what she wanted to wear, so she just threw on the first things she pulled from her satchel. She must have known she looked a fright, but he got the feeling she also didn't care. If she cared, she wouldn't be one step from flinging herself onto the ground at his boots.

He, on the other hand, was pulling on his armor, freshly polished and well-oiled, Arawn's hound on the breastplate. He was almost afraid to look at her, afraid she would be able to talk him into leaving with her, abandoning the army and all of the promises he had made. He knew if he did, it would be all over, and he would do anything she asked of him. So, he didn't. "We'll talk about this after the battle," he told her.

"Have you not listened to me?" She almost sobbed. "There won't be an 'after the battle' for me. And maybe not for you, either! I don't know what happens to you if you die in this world, Owen. Or me. Either of us. Please."

He shook his head, eyes still refusing to take in her pleading face. "Scare tactics won't work, Flora. I made a promise, not only to Arawn, but to every single soldier out there. I can't abandon them." His tone was even, calm.

"Do you not understand that this is the way of it? That they know what the stakes are? That if they die here, they get another chance at life? They are already dead, Owen! They are moving through their afterlife, preparing for a new and wonderful existence. They are meant to be in this world, you and I? We're not."

Owen stood up, adjusting his gauntlets before reaching for his sword and shield, which had the same hound etched into it. They were heavy, but it was a weight he welcomed. A weight of courage, command, responsibility. Duty and honor meant much to him, and he would see them through.

"The only reason you are here is to cast a protection spell over the forces," he reminded her. "whether you believe yourself to be a witch or not, you are here only to invoke the Goddess of War before we go into battle. Let's go."

He finally did look at her, just in time to see her face turn red and her eyes tear up. Owen admired her ability to stamp down on her emotions, for that was as far as she went. No tear trickled down her cheek, no sob escaped her throat. It almost tore through him, seeing her struggle with it, jaw clenched, throat working to swallow it all away.

He turned on his booted heel and marched out into the sunlight, chain mail and armor clinking, ready to mount his steed. The great beast had already been brushed and saddled by one of the soldiers, a young boy probably only a handful of years into his teens. Owen looked at the boy, his pock-scarred visage, the way he looked so at peace with the battle ahead of him, the battle that could rip him apart.

He stood to the side of the horse, while the boy positioned the mounting block and wondered if what she had told him was true. Had the boy…had he died at such a young age? He thought of the girls who were at the far edge of the field, their drums and fifes at the ready. The children who worked the forge next to the blacksmiths. Had they, too, been just small children when their lives were taken from them?

He swallowed the thoughts down and hauled himself up and into the saddle, adjusting his equipment around him, and looked to the witch.

Flora was helped onto her own mare by Captain Griffith. She smiled down at the other man, reached for his hand and gave it a long squeeze. The captain always had a smile and a twinkle in his eye, and this day was no different. She looked at him as if she were saying her goodbyes, though she said nothing. The other man gave her a wink, patted her leg, and turned away to his own mount, his step jaunty.

Owen nudged his horse forward, and Flora did the same, following him obediently until they faced Annwn's troops. Across the shallow river, Hafgan's forces were lining up much the same, their colors streaming against the green grass background.

****

Flora had never invoked a god before, but at Owen's urging, she closed her eyes, held up her hands, and just…spoke. The words that fell out of her mouth were foreign to her, lilting and of a language long dead, at least in her own world. She didn't know how they came to her, and when she opened her eyes, a crow circled above. She watched as it hovered just below the gray clouds, cawing furiously, much to the delight of the troops before her.

Their cheers rose up over her, deafening even her own inner thoughts, and she backed away, giving the field to Owen who called on them to fight for Arawn, for Annwn.

She felt a little rush of pride at how he riled them up, but it quickly gave way to her own waning spirits. She had run out of time. She had failed. She had seen neither Iain nor Eve all morning, but she knew they were somewhere. Would they bleed out of the rocks as the troops rushed into battle and slit her throat quietly? Would an arrow soar through the sky and pierce her chest? Would they feed her poison so her agony would be long and slow? And then, what would they do to Owen when they were done with her?

She shook with the fear of it.

****

"To Vic—"

Owen stopped short as he turned his steed toward the Ford, ready to signal the charge, to see Eve pressing the tip of a dagger to Flora's throat. The blade was an ugly, jagged one, the steel flashing in the dim light. The tip dug a dimple into the witch's soft flesh, and with any more pressure, bright red blood would bead there.

Flora, pale and terrified, stood against the other woman, her neck stretching away from the blade, her chest rising and falling, eyes wide with fear. Eve had the other arm wrapped around Flora's waist, holding her captive.

Owen lowered his sword and the whole world ground to a halt around him. "What are you doing?" he croaked in a voice he almost didn't recognize.

"You quit the field, commander, or I slit her throat," Eve said. Her legs were splayed and she shifted on the balls of her feet.

Owen couldn't tear his gaze from Flora

"Eve." Iain stepped into Owen's line of vision, his hand outstretched in the same way the stable master soothed the horses. "Careful."

Eve narrowed her eyes at Iain. "You know what he commanded," the dark-haired woman said to her companion.

"We don't answer to him, Eve. There is more than you know. You don't—"

Flora let out a gasp, the tip of the blade finally pricking her skin, a bright red bead of blood appearing.

"No!" Owen held his hand out to stop her. "No. Don't hurt her."

"Quit the field," Eve demanded.

He was so focused on the knife to Flora's throat, he was caught unawares when Iain grasped the baldric holding Owen's scabbard, and yanked him to the ground. Pain shot through his shoulder as it collided with hard earth, his sword knocked from his hand.

There was no greater humiliation. Not for any soldier. He could feel a thousand eyes on him, a thousand eyes accusing him, questioning him. A thousand eyes confused, disappointed. They had looked to him for his leadership. He was above reproach. And he had dropped his sword. They had not even ridden into battle and he had already failed the entire army he commanded. He had failed Arawn. Annwn. Himself.

Iain had the sword in a second, then pointed it to Owen's throat. "Get up," he said.

Owen pushed himself to his feet, the heavy armor making his movements sluggish. The sword's tip followed him.

Iain nodded and Eve pushed Flora into the throng of soldiers. Iain ordered Owen after them. As they approached the camp, Owen heard the call of one of his officers followed by the battle cries of the force as they rushed into battle.

He had been replaced.

He hoped it had been Captain Griffith, despite others outranking the young man. But the captain deserved it more than any of the others, and the soldiers respected him. He would lead them well.

Owen briefly closed his eyes, the disappointment, the shame washing over him, but it was quickly gone. "Flora," he called.

"I'm…I'm all right," she called back softly.

"What the hell are you doing?" Eve ground through clenched teeth.

"Fixing your screw up," Iain growled.

Eve blinked. "What?"

"Fixing. Your. Screw. Up," he hissed.

"My screw up?" she railed. "Her screw up!" She shoved Flora, sheathing her dagger in the same motion. Flora stumbled and fell hands out, keeping herself from falling flat on her face. She pressed fingers to the spot where Eve's dagger had nicked her skin, and then pulled them away to assess the blood on her fingers. It was bright, but there was little of it.

"If she had done her part to begin with, I wouldn't have had to take matters into my own hands!" Eve shouted.

"There are things brewing far beyond your knowledge," Iain bit out. "You think he wouldn't have continued the battle if you split her throat then and there?"

"He never would have let it get that far," Eve said confidently, her eyes blazing.

"Are you so sure about that?" Iain's voice was deadly. "It doesn't matter, now. She's fine. Let's move."

Flora swallowed and shifted to push herself fully to her feet. Arms were around her, helping her and she was pressed into his warmth, engulfed in it. She rested her face on Owen's chest, her cheek against the cold metal of his armor, the fur of his mantle tickling her nose, and she sighed. One of his hands cupped the back of her head, pressing her to him, and he placed a soft, light kiss to her hair.

They were both safe. They were both okay.

"I'm sorry," he murmured, barely audible over Eve's yells about duty and sacrifice. "I made a promise, it was the only reason… I… If I had realized. I never would have let anything happen to you. I do…love you."

He pulled her away and looked down into her face. "Do you love me?"

She looked back into his eyes and lifted a hand to his face, her fingers brushing against his cheek. "I do. But I am also not sorry that Iain took the decision from you."

Iain pushed them toward the mountain ridge. "Let's go."

"Where are we going?" Owen asked. He and Flora had parted, but he still clung to her hand, as if she was his lifeline.

"We need to get you to a circle," Iain said and sighed, as if he would have chosen a much different outcome.

Chapter 25

The crow followed them. It circled lazily in the air. Flora kept her own gaze on it as it soared in and out of her line of sight. It played in the clouds, disappearing into the low-hanging clouds only to reemerge.

Iain knew exactly where he was going as he led them. Something told her he had climbed these mountain paths before, the little slivers of bare earth barely visible between the scraggly branches and leaves of the heather.

The crow swooped down as they crested the ridge and came to rest on a crooked, jagged stone. As they drew nearer, Flora could make out the fallen stones of the circle, the one upon which the crow danced, the only one upright.

As they drew nearer, Delyth skirted the standing stone, her flaxen hair whipping in the wind, mimicking the movements of her green cape.

"So, this is the way of things?" she mused on a sigh, her face betraying her disappointment. "All right. Give me the satchel." She held her hand out to Flora.

Flora frowned and gathered the small leather pack in her arms, holding it close. "What? Why?" She didn't want to let it go. Its contents had seen her through her time here, had kept her alive, had ensured she had the knowledge she needed. She felt no great attachment to any of it, but she also didn't want to see it leave her possession. It had been given to her for a reason.

"Insurance," she said, simply, as if that was all they needed to know.

"But I need it for—" Flora protested.

"You don't need it at all," Delyth interrupted with more anger than Flora had ever heard from the small woman, her voice growing to a crescendo. "Give it to me, *now*, and you and your man will be allowed to return to your world." Her eyes were wild, her mouth drawn down in a frown, her chest expanding and contracting rapidly.

When Flora made no move to hand over the satchel, Delyth turned her gaze to Iain and gave him a small nod.

Iain reached out with a knife, cutting the straps of the satchel and pulling it from Flora's fingers. He flipped it open, reached in, and pulled out the T-shirt Flora had stuffed in there and tossed it to her. It was the only thing she had that could bring her back if she followed Alexander Carlisle's instructions. Iain must have known it. He then turned and handed the satchel to Delyth.

The elven woman pawed through the items, and then looked up. "Where is the knife?"

"I don't have it anymore," Flora told her.

She rolled her eyes, as if Flora were an idiot. The expression tugged at Flora, wrenching at her heart. She had thought this woman was her friend—perhaps her first friend. "I know you don't. Him," Delyth bit out and looked at Owen. "Where is it?"

"In my trunk. At the fortress."

She sighed. "That'll have to do, I suppose." She executed a mock bow with a flourish. "It's been a pleasure," she said. She pushed past the small group, heading down the path, but when Flora turned to watch her descent, the small woman was gone.

"What just happened?" Owen asked.

But neither Eve nor Iain answered. Eve was too busy staring slack-jawed at Iain. "You—"

"I'll explain once we have them safely back to the other side of the veil," he said.

Her face reflected the betrayal that Flora felt at Delyth's actions just moments before. Here they were, two women who thought they knew their companions so well, only to find out things were not what they had seemed.

"The veil?" Eve demanded, her voice rising in pitch. "What the hell is this veil that you all keep talking about? We were supposed to help her take him back to Arianrhod, weren't we? To the North? This isn't the North, Iain!" she exploded

"I told you I would explain—" he began, his voice even and calm.

"Explain now!" Eve screeched, her hands fisting at her sides, her face going red.

Iain ignored her and turned his attention to Flora. "Both of you, hold tight to that." He nodded to Flora's old T-shirt. "You'll know what to say," he told her. "The magic will come to you."

She nodded, remembering the words in the diary, and looked to Owen. He took the opposite end of her shirt in his hand. She could make out the uncertainty and fear in his eyes. It hadn't been there as he had stood, ready to lead an army out into a brutal battle, but here, now, with her and the unknown, he let her see his vulnerability. "Whatever…whatever happens, know that I love you," he murmured low, so only she could hear his words.

"It will be fine," she told him in her best crooning voice. She knew it would be. It had to be.

He nodded once, and she led him into the center of the circle. They held the shirt between them, her end on her left hand, his in his right. She scrambled to take his other hand in her empty one, wanting to feel him, hold on to him, as they plunged into the unknown. She needed to grasp onto something solid Flora took a shaky breath.

And just as Iain had said, the circle told her the words. They were whispered in the wind, echoing against the stones. She repeated them. They came out like a song, soft and lilting, and she looked up into Owen's eyes, hoping to reassure him. It was her turn to be calm in the face of battle. They didn't blink, didn't move as their bodies seemed to be lifted like sand, breaking into infinite grains as the wind carried them off.

And just as she felt herself go weightless and free completely, she saw Eve jump into the circle as well, her fingers twined around the necklace that held her ring, her hand outstretched for the T-shirt, Iain's "No!" cutting through the air.

****

Flora woke with a start, her breath whooshing into her, as if she had been holding her breath for far too long. Her neck was killing her, feeling as if she had been stuck in an odd position for hours, and her shoulder was tingling with the loss of feeling. She shifted into a sitting position, rolling her shoulder to loosen. As the awkward feeling finally melted away, she took in her surroundings.

She was in her bedroom, the one above her shop. It was sparsely decorated and small, but hers. The little clock on the bedside table ticked charmingly, and the shadows cast by the streetlights came through the blinds. The *Mabinogion* was spread out across her yoga pants, and her T-shirt was bunched into one of her hands.

She rolled her neck and searched the room for Owen.

But she was alone. Flora reached for her mobile, swiping it awake. Three in the morning. November.

She must have fallen asleep while reading.

Her heart shattered.

Chapter 26

Flora looked up as the bells tinkled on her door. They carried out the Christmas theme that was worked into every nook and cranny of the shop, from the branches of fake fir to the plaid ribbon bows. In the center of the store stood a ten-foot Christmas tree she had erected earlier that morning, draped in twinkling white lights and ironic red telephone booth and police box ornaments.

It had been a slow morning, and she was exhausted, nodding off into her coffee more than once. Only a handful of customers had come through, each wanting nothing more than to poke around and then leave empty-handed. She didn't blame them—she would have escaped if she saw her blank expression as well.

The hours ticked by painfully, the hands moving at a glacial pace. She couldn't keep her gaze from straying to them, watching as each passing minute grew longer and longer. All she could do was replay the events of her dream through her mind, trying to relive every moment, to capture each look, each feeling, and brand them into her being forever. She was afraid she would lose them, all of the people who had begun to matter to her, as she went about her life.

Her eyes were drifting closed, and she was losing the battle she wasn't exactly sure she wanted to fight.

Perhaps she could sink back into the Otherworld if only she let herself go.

She looked up to see the black-haired woman standing in the doorway, light streaming around her. Flora jolted awake.

"It appears you were successful in your endeavor," the woman said as she stepped in front of the counter. She was once again in all black, the perfect cut of a black dress under an expertly tailored black jacket. She stood tall and willowy on spiked heels and the only slash of color against her pale skin and black attire was the rich red of her lipstick.

Flora couldn't form words. They stuck to the back of her throat, jumbled and not making sense. All she could do was blink. "Wh-what?" finally slipped out, a stutter of all the feelings swirling inside of her.

"You rescued your commander."

Flora felt like the great weight that had been pulling her under was lifted and she could finally kick her way to the surface. Her breath stuttered out through her slightly parted lips. Did this mean it wasn't a dream? Or was she still crazy? She had so many questions, all of them breaking to the surface with her, rising up like bubbles. "You told me he was a prisoner." The dark-haired woman gave a sweet smile, but it didn't reach her eyes. "He was. I was the one who imprisoned him."

The ticking of the antique clock slowed. The room seemed to spin around her, and she felt weightless, lost, desperate to be grounded once more. Was this some sort of trick? What reason, what possible explanation could there be, for this? Why had she been put through such torture? Was it a game? A trick of the gods? Was she being punished for altering her fate from the plans of her parents? Her ex-husband? Hell, even herself?

The questions were coming harder, faster, rising up more quickly than she could take stock of them all. She grew panicked as she tried to pick the next one, the most important one, but they all swam out of reach too quickly. They were pulling her back under, again, dragging her away from the surface.

"I see you are still confused." The woman cut in, easing some of the tension that wouldn't release Flora from its hold. "Know that I don't usually feel the need to explain myself to anyone. But..." She let that one syllable word sink in for a moment, eyes glittering. "You are not just anyone. And since our relationship goes far deeper than a single mortal man, I feel it only fair I give you proper warning of our arrangement. You've completed the test and now that I am sure I have found you, it is time we track down the others."

Arrangement? What arrangement? Flora wanted to rant and rage at the woman. Did she have to force her through this unexplainable madness once more? Who would she have to dive into the Otherworld for next? Would she be forced to love another only to have him ripped away forever? She wasn't sure she could handle the feelings of loss she already felt. More would surely break her.

"Yes, I imprisoned Owen in the Otherworld. I saw an opportunity floating on a piece of debris, and I took it. He was exactly what I needed—someone well versed in combat, in many different kinds of combat, with new and fresh ideas. He was perfect. He would set things in motion. And the best part of all was that he had a rather strong bond with his sister. Twins, apparently. Who knew? Did you know?" She asked this, not really wanting an answer, and Flora knew it. But no, she hadn't known they were twins. She never would have suspected, either, but why would she?

The woman continued, not even noticing Flora hadn't bothered to respond. "I couldn't fully sever his grip on this world, for he came to it in dreams, dragged here by that connection to his twin. And then he met you, and the ties grew stronger. Soon, he was going to figure it out. The battle was good for him; he was so worried he couldn't sleep, and that gave me the time I needed to recruit you. I knew my grasp on your soldier was shaky at best, but he offered me a chance at a little insurance while the other pieces fell into place. If you couldn't send the worlds into chaos by messing with the order of things, he, planted there, could accomplish much the same thing. But, oh, what a treasure I found when I discovered him floating in the middle of the sea, Flora MacDonald. He was a nice bit of bait, and one that reeled you right in, mmm? A love that transcends time, worlds. Two people who find each other despite all the odds. Some might even say it was fate."

"I… You duped me. I was just some sort of…pawn." Flora didn't know why it hurt so much, why it felt like such a betrayal. She had been used before. Robert had used her in the worst possible way—letting her believe her life was something it was not. Letting her believe he was something he was not. And yet, this seemed even more personal. It hurt more, anyway. "I don't understand," Flora sputtered. She wanted to be done with this, now. She was alone, had nothing to show for it but a broken heart and a couple of old books.

"I'm not done with you, Flora MacDonald." The woman laughed to herself. "Such irony. Your family wished to remember your ancestor Flora MacDonald, savior of a Bonnie Prince. I should have seen it from the beginning—I have no idea how I even missed it."

Flora said nothing. Pointing out her name had always been a favorite pastime of her classmates when she had been growing up. How could it not? Flora MacDonald, the young woman who smuggled the upstart Jacobite prince out of Scotland as her lady's maid, was the poster child for the Scottish resistance's last hurrah. She had never felt she lived up to the other woman's legacy.

"I will call on you, again, my flower," the woman crooned smoothly. "You have proven yourself quite useful, seventh daughter. Quite full of magic. Far more than I expected. We will meet again."

"And if I refuse?"

"You won't. This is only the beginning. Fate is in your hands, as it has always been. You'll be quite busy, I am sure. In the meantime, I suggest you find a daughter of Ann McKinnon and prepare. I'll be sure to send along instructions. Eventually." She turned to leave.

"Prepare for what?"

"A great many things. We're going to change the world, my girl."

"What about Owen?" Flora called after her, needing to know before she disappeared forever. Please, she begged to herself, let him be all right. Let him remember me, she pleaded selfishly, hope flickering in her heart for the first time since she found herself alone in her bed.

The woman paused, then turned. The little bells jangled prettily. "He's alive."

"But will he—"

"No. He was given the Drink of Oblivion. Just as he remembered nothing of this world in the Otherworld, he will remember nothing of that one. But take heart, girl. You can always try to win his affections again." And with nary a flourish, she quit the small shop.

****

News of the lost captain spread like wildfire. It was on all major news sources, a miracle of which everyone wanted a piece. Everyone wanted to talk of the man who was back from the gates of death. The small town exploded with reporters when he was found, alive, floating on an emergency raft just off the coast of Wales. They camped out on the square, their cameras pointing in every direction. In the evenings, she would watch TV, and catch sight of her little shop in the background.

Flora kept abreast with the news, wanting to soak up every minute detail on which the news anchors reported, but she kept her distance. She did not walk to the baby shop to offer his sister—his twin—the hug she so desperately wanted to give. But, she supposed, the other woman had likely closed up shop, anyway. At least for the time being. Why wouldn't she? It wasn't every day one's brother returned from the dead.

And when the reporters gave word he was recovering from the ordeal in his hometown, staying with his sister and her family, Flora turned off the news and promised herself she wouldn't turn it on again. At least not until the media had moved on and she was no longer at risk of seeing his face splash across her screen, a reminder of her part.

And as much as she hoped to bump into him on her way to the pizza shop or see him sitting across from the fire that burns in the back of McGregor's, Flora wasn't sure she could suffer through seeing him again, and him not knowing who she was. The prospect was far too painful.

****

It was a Saturday afternoon, and like all Saturdays, the square buzzed with activity. Even as the days grew colder, tents were erected and trucks pulled up for the weekly farmer's market. Many offered seasonal produce, some had baked goods, and a few had locally made jams and jellies. Crafts and even a cart of locally roasted coffee were shoved in between stalls. She had come to learn the outdoor market meant more foot traffic for her, and so, instead of waking late or strolling through the stalls, she had her door unlocked and a fresh cup of tea ready as soon as the first customers arrived at the stalls outside.

That morning, heavy gray winter clouds did little to detract from the holiday shopping frenzy and she had quite a few customers through her shop. They picked through her odd assortment of knickknacks and grocery goods, many of the other expats purchasing their favorite canned puddings and sauces. It made her happy to make them happy, and she smiled as she readied each of their purchases.

But a lull had settled, and the shop was quiet but for the soft sounds of the traditional Highland music she had playing over the speakers.

She was in the back storeroom, rummaging through boxes for a few more stuffed hairy cows, which were a favorite amongst her youngest customers, to put on display when the little clump of bright holiday bells rang. “Just a moment,” she called, hauling a handful of the fuzzy plushes into her arms and returning to the shop.

She immediately dropped them all onto the floor. They scattered around her feet.

It was Owen.

He was browsing, looking at the collection of books on one of the antique barrister cabinets. He was just as tall as she remembered, yet maybe not quite as broad. His shoulders stretched the fabric of his gray-blue sweater, and his jeans were a bit loose about his waist. His hair was clipped short, but still golden even in the gray light.

“M-may I help you?” she asked tentatively.

He turned and she could see the faint scar at the corner of his mouth as he smiled.

“I was hoping you had a copy of the *Mabinogion*.”

Her heart leapt. It beat wildly beneath her ribs and she was afraid she had stopped breathing. Taking a long breath to calm herself, she gave her most polite, professional smile.

“As a matter of fact, I do,” she told him. She pressed her sweating palms against her thighs. “But it’s an antique and I’m not sure I am ready to part with it.”

He nodded sagely. “I understand. Any chance you can order one? I’m particularly interested in the stories of Annwn.”

She didn't say anything for a long moment. She looked up into his face, into the eyes she knew so well. And he looked right back.

"Owen?" she said.

And with a faint smile, he answered her. "Hello, Flora."

A word about the author…

Kyra earned a Bachelor of Science degree in History, Technology, and Society from the Georgia Institute of Technology and a Master of Arts degree in American Studies from Kennesaw State University.

Before turning to writing full-time, she worked in higher education and was a contributing author for college-level textbooks.

She lives with her husband and four children wherever the U.S. Army sends them.